# VOLUPTUA

# VOLUPTUA

Jason Martin

AN IMPRINT OF LUNA STATION PRESS

Cover design - Tara Quinn Lindsey
Layout - Jennifer Lyn Parsons
Author photo - Jyoti Chrystal

*Chacruna*

AN IMPRINT OF LUNA STATION PRESS

www.lunastationpress.com

To Jyoti

A story is like the wind.

It comes from a far-o place and we feel it.

*– The !kabbo (San) People of the Kalahari*

# Chapter One

Okay, you've really done it this time, Ellen muttered to herself, leaning against the ancient trunk of a gnarled tree dominating a small clearing.

For too long she had followed a serpentine path through the jungle and the time had come to admit it— she was in a bad way, hopelessly lost with no food, a half-filled water bottle, and the sky darkening to nightfall.

Allowing a moment's rest, she pressed her head into the trunk and looked up to follow the flight of yellow and black birds nesting high in the branches of the tree. They sang her favorite birdsong, unique and memorable, like an underwater gurgling coming from a deep Amazonian lagoon. But they would soon fall silent, replaced by the nocturnal din of cicadas and the persistent croaking of male frogs luring the stubborn females.

Damn! She knew exactly where she screwed up. "If only I'd gone right at the last T," she thought. She had hesitated between the two choices, looking left and right puffing on a *mapacho*, the acrid cigarette of the jungle. She chose left and now it was too late to turn around. Even if she did, it was unlikely she could navigate her way back to camp. She had made several other turns and was deeply imbedded in the rainforest, where so many paths, all looking alike, crisscrossed and twisted. The jungle easily swallowed gringos in its labyrinth.

Her options dwindled to spending the night under the tree, which, despite its plume of leafy branches, afforded scant protection. She thought of the encounters that might easily materialize before dawn—a hungry jaguar pouncing on her weary bones, a boa wrapping itself around her like a lover, or the thin, venomous viper, the velvet death, flinging itself at her like an arrow. And these were just a few possibilities. There were many more.

As daylight faded, the mosquitoes swarmed. From her shirt pocket she pulled another *mapacho*, slightly damp with sweat, and lit it, allowing the harsh taste of tobacco to fill her mouth. Deploying the smoke around her, she forced the insects into a tactical retreat. They circled, regrouping for a fresh assault.

A twig snapped. In the gray, fading light, her eyes surveyed the brush in front of her. Something moved. With a sharp intake of breath, she saw a form taking shape. She was not alone. A man, a native, with straight black hair covering his forehead, stood very still, watching her from the underbrush. Her body froze, her fingers stiffened and she dropped the cigarette. He blended so well with the leaves that she blinked thinking maybe he was an illusion. When he didn't disappear, she stooped to retrieve the cigarette, and gather her thoughts. Upon straightening, she realized he was not alone either. Holding her breath and moving only her eyes, she scanned the foliage. A number of tribesmen, equally motionless, surrounded her, staring with expressions so deadpan, they appeared threatening. All at once, they started toward her.

Heart pounding, her eyes popped open and she saw a familiar wall. Blinking, she knew it wasn't her apartment—but where was she? Shifting, paper crinkled as she pulled her head up and realized she had been slumped over the desk in her library carrel with her face pressed against the open pages of *Amazonia*. Off to the side, her laptop had also fallen asleep. Other books, some opened, lay scattered around her. No one was near, as her workspace in the library was secluded among the shelves housing books from 18th Century France.

Frowning, she combed fingers through her hair and recalled the dream, the jungle, the tribesmen, the feeling of being lost and vulnerable.

Smoothing the pages of the book she'd read so many times, she questioned how well she knew the jungle and wondered what it would be like when she actually got to the rainforest.

Glancing at her watch, she remembered the lecture. Knowing she had plenty of time to bring her laptop to her office beforehand, she sat back in her chair, undecided whether or not to go. In her hideaway on the 9th floor of the stacks, it was quiet and she was seldom bothered. Sometimes a graduate student stopped by for a chat, rarely a colleague, but for the most part, she was left alone.

Maybe she could get a little more work done converting her dissertation on *Amazonia* into a book. It was her favorite novel, the story of a middle-aged Frenchman, Yves, who, after a difficult divorce, traveled to Peru, fell in love with the jungle and spent several years in a remote native village. She had read it at least five times now, and she never read anything twice. Yves was not only the hero of the novel but her hero, as well.

Sitting there, she noticed fine particles of dust hanging in the parched, still air, as if they were suspended undisturbed for days, weeks, months, years, decades, centuries, millennia, illuminated by shafts of sunlight coming through the slim, leaded glass windows, without even the suggestion of a breeze to set them dancing.

She liked being surrounded by the aisles filled with books on one side and the thick fortress-like walls on the other. It gave her the feeling of being cocooned and she realized that the familiar surroundings made her feel safer, dispersing the fear left over from the dream.

What the hell, she thought, and closed the book, shut down the computer and gathered her things. The subject being presented at the lecture was one that interested her—Lorca and Dalí, though she liked Lorca's poetry more than Dalí's paintings. "Verde, te quiero verde," reminded her of the first time, as an undergraduate, she had fallen in love, when her boyfriend at the time recited the poem and turned her heart to mush.

Standing, she took one last look around, leaving the books as they were and walked away.

Leaving the library, she knew attending the lecture meant dealing with Roy, her department chairman whose eyes devoured her every time he saw her. But she was intrigued by what she heard about the guy giving the talk, Steadman, a Rhodes scholar now teaching at Princeton. She had it on good authority (from Val, who somehow always knew such things) that he was brilliant and easy on the eyes, a combination almost unknown in academia. It was also rumored that he had something new to say about the relationship between the poet and the painter, in particular how they influenced each other's artistic trajectory.

Lifting her chin to the breezy air, Ellen enjoyed the walk on this soft, lazy September afternoon. She liked this time of day, this time of year. The campus, with its green lawns and ivy-covered buildings was at its most charming. Day classes were over, evening classes had yet to begin, and few people were around. Off in the distance students tossed a Frisbee. To the left under a tree, a couple snuggled, lounging on the grass. Ellen smiled wondering what they were talking about. Politics, literature, classes? Probably sex.

***

Quite an impressive number had shown up for the lecture. Most of the Spanish faculty and graduate students, whose attendance was mandatory, sat in front. Ellen saw a few of her French Lit. students scattered about. Several professors and graduate students from Art History and the Theater Department had also turned up, together with a satisfactory sprinkling of undergraduates. Ellen was happy to see that interest in Dalí and Lorca transcended the borders of the departmental fiefdoms.

She took a seat beside Stelios and Val, the quintessential attractive couple, or so Ellen, with a tinge of envy, had always thought. But today, something was amiss. Val's back was turned to Stelios, who sat with his arms crossed, staring straight ahead. Neither greeted Ellen. She spotted Carl, from the Music Department, a few rows down. Wanting to change seats, she got up but then sat down again as Chairman Roy strode onto the stage with the speaker close behind.

Steadman, the lecturer, wearing standard WASP attire, stood well over six feet tall. Lithe and graceful, Ellen liked the way he walked. She also noticed his good hair—straight, light brown, parted on the side, long but neat.

"Pretty preppy," Stelios said.

"But it looks good on him," Ellen said.

"He's the closest thing to an academic hunk I've ever seen," Val said.

Beside him, Roy, in brown polyester, looked tacky. Mercifully, his intro was brief.

"As part of The Foreign Language Department's ongoing lecture series emphasizing the importance of interdisciplinary studies, it gives me great pleasure to introduce Professor James Steadman, of Princeton University, who will be speaking to us on 'Dalí and Lorca, the Forging of Two Aesthetics.' Professor Steadman."

Though there was nothing wrong with what Roy said, his tone made Ellen cringe. Roy's voice always had a whiny edge, and today an irritating smugness crept in because he was able to lure someone of Stedman's caliber to Wellington.

Steadman fished his paper out of his briefcase and stepped up to the podium. He made an arresting figure, perfectly at ease with his audience, although he must have known that a few were academic heavies. Ellen admired his poise. At once serious yet relaxed, he launched into a summary of the dynamic artistic scene in Madrid at the time when Lorca and Dalí, still students and at the beginning of their careers, came together. He spoke with a resonant voice that effortlessly filled the auditorium. It was clear that he found his subject intriguing and was actually excited (so rare in academia) to be speaking about it. Ellen was impressed that he read his paper as if he wasn't reading at all, making frequent eye contact with his audience, as if he knew the entire paper by heart. By the time he began to lay out his theory on what surrealism meant to each of the two men, he had everybody's attention.

Well, not everybody's attention. Stelios nudged Ellen's elbow and nodded to the left. "Check it out."

And there was Foxwhistle. The fact that he had decided to come, was in itself noteworthy, especially since his specialty was 17th century French lit. Perhaps that was why he seemed not to share the audience's interest in the presentation, because before long, first his head, then his entire upper body, began a slow descent toward the desk in front of him. Over and over he caught himself, gave a little start and shook his head to sit up, only to slowly sink down again. Ellen wished she hadn't been made aware this little sideshow which she couldn't help seeing out of the corner of her eye. Nevertheless, she found the lecture riveting and made a special effort not to be distracted.

By now Steadman, all warmed up, was hard into illustrating how surrealism both shaped and was reflected in their works, examining in detail their respective use of color, primarily greens and reds in the case of Lorca, blues and very light browns for Dalí. Ellen had attended all the previous lectures in the series and had noted one particular flaw shared by the presenters. They were all much more at home in their own area than in the second discipline. Strong on literature, light on philosophy; strong on literature, light on music. Yet Steadman seemed equally at home in both Spanish Literature (his field) and Art History.

"Has this guy got *duende* or what?" Val whispered.

By this time, mercifully, Foxwhistle's head had finally come to rest on his desk in a state of complete immobility.

"Think he's drunk?" Ellen asked.

"Isn't he always?" Val answered.

"At least he's not snoring," Stelios said.

"Not yet," said Val.

Steadman, now in a zone, was cruising, carrying his audience along with him into a speculative and intriguing discussion of what would have happened if Lorca and Dalí had never found each other.

"What indeed," Val whispered.

Then, he turned a page in his paper and, just like that, in a split-second, everything changed. Stedman's jaw dropped and his eyes bugged out. For a moment, he didn't lift his head.

Then he looked up, a little sheepishly. "Sorry, page 17 seems to be missing."

He rifled through the remaining pages, checked his inside coat pocket, all around the podium, in his brief-case. It could have been anywhere. Back at the hotel room, in the airplane, on his office desk, lodged in a copy machine somewhere. Or perhaps it had simply disap-peared into a parallel universe.

Although ruffled, he kept his cool. Looking out over

his audience he said, "I hate it when this happens." People chuckled and he smiled.

Wasting no time, he launched into a summary of the errant page, getting himself back on track. His voice, at first tentative, regained its richness and he delivered the rest of the paper flawlessly, even finishing with a flourish: "If anybody finds page 17 floating around somewhere, please let me know." He was applauded warmly.

***

People were already attacking the hors d'oeuvres when Ellen, who had meandered over, entered the reception hall filled with the din of conversation. It was easy to tell the faculty from the students, not just by age but also by dress. The students wore mostly jeans, with the occasional grad student in a jacket or dress. The professors wore inexpensive suits that no longer fit, looking out of style with material grown shiny from excessive wear. Many of them looked dehydrated. No doubt from inhaling too much chalk dust, Ellen thought.

She lingered a moment too long in the doorway before setting off toward Carl. She was only halfway there before Roy intercepted her.

"Hello Ellen, so glad you could attend. I thought it was a marvelous lecture, despite the little glitch, which I thought he handled very well."

"Yes, I'm not sure how well I would have done."

"Oh, I'm sure you would have acquitted

yourself admirably," replied Roy, as his eyes dropped to Ellen's breasts.

"Maybe."

He took hold of her upper arm. "Speaking of lectures, will you be attending the Modern Language Association convention in New York this year?"

She knew this was coming, having received a memo a few days ago urging conference attendance and reminding everyone that the MLA was our professional organization and its convention was the most important one of the year, and blah, blah, blah. Although it was directed to all department members, suggesting that, if at all possible, they present papers, he had already made it clear that he had a particular interest in her attending.

"Well, I'm not sure. You know, my mother..." "Of course. How is she?"

"For the moment she's okay, but you know, at any time..."

The pressure of his fingers increased. "I understand. At the same time, it would be a very good idea, especially since it's three years now and your contract is coming up for renewal. And you know how keen the Dean is to see the department well represented among the presenters there."

Ellen was aware of a stranger over by the hors d'oeuvres table, watching her obvious discomfort with some amusement. In his mid-to-late fifties, he was dressed in khaki pants and shirt and looked as if he were about to embark on a safari to some remote destination. Deeply tanned, with reddish-blond hair, he appeared fit and robust, which made him stand out, especially in this assembly. She watched him pop an olive in his mouth and wondered what on earth he was doing there.

Ellen shook her arm free. "I'll think about it."

Mercifully, Beveridge, the Chair of the Music Department, joined them and she was able to move away gracefully.

Ellen spotted Carl again across the room, drinking red wine, looking lonely. She headed over to him, taking in bits of chatter along the way.

"He was hitting it out of the park."

"That guy is smooth. He could make it anywhere, even on Wall Street." "So why is he a teacher?"

"Maybe he loves literature." Guffaws and howls of laughter…"Something like that happened a couple of years ago at the MLA convention."

"Oh, yeah?"

"Some guy brought the wrong paper."

"How could he do that?"

"Who knows? Maybe he was late for his plane, maybe his wife was hassling him."

"What did he do?"

"He gave the one he had."

Carl, never comfortable inserting himself into conversations with people he didn't know, looked relieved when Ellen finally reached him.

"Nice to see you here supporting foreign languages," Ellen said.

"Well, you come to lots of musical events."

"True. Hey, Steadman's by himself. Let's go talk to him."

Ellen realized that Steadman looked even better close up than he did from a distance. Moreover, he was easy to talk with.

"Carl's a composer, an exceptionally good one," she said.

"Oh, should I know you?" Steadman asked.

"Not yet," Carl commented.

"Soon," Ellen added.

"I'm flattered you came to my talk."

"Well, Lorca's poetry is so musical," Carl replied.

"You read it in the original?"

"My Spanish is okay. I can muddle through with a facing translation. After the symphony I'm working on, my next project is an opera on his death."

"Now that would be really interesting," Steadman said.

Carl took a sip of wine. "I'm a big fan of Spanish music, which I think is much underrated. I actually got into Lorca through de Falla."

"Ah, de Falla. He was like an artistic father to Lorca. He tried to get him released, after he was arrested. Put all his prestige on the line," Steadman said.

"Yes, they say he was timid, like me." He smiled at Ellen. "Lived all his life with his sister who took care of him," said Carl.

"Are you Carl's sister?" Steadman asked Ellen.

"Oh no," Ellen laughed and Carl joined her. "Just friends. I'm a French prof., so I'm interested in the Paul Eluard connection to Dalí. I like his poetry."

"Yes. Eluard's wife, Gala, hooked up with Dalí and the poet of liberty was set free, although that probably wasn't what he had in mind. Now I feel remiss that I failed to mention either de Falla or Eluard in my talk."

"Maybe you did. On page 17," Carl said. Steadman laughed. "I can't believe that happened."

Ellen's head turned hearing Foxwhistle and Oswaldo Cocayne, engaged in a heated discussion. It struck her how much they looked like Mutt and Jeff. Ellen glanced over at them and thought of her father sitting in his favorite armchair, reading the Sunday comics, and laughing out loud. Mutt and Jeff was his favorite.

Foxwhistle was tall and lanky, with leathery skin that had acquired a weather-beaten look from overexposure to the elements or to alcohol or both. Cocayne was short, bald and overweight

"The little one's Oswaldo, the other one is Foxwhistle," Ellen said.

"That's Foxwhistle?" Stedman stared in disbelief.

"In the flesh. You've heard of him?"

"Hasn't everybody? He slept through my lecture. I took offense." "It's nothing personal. He does it all the time, even during departmental meetings," Ellen said.

"Why does he come?" Steadman asked.

"Who knows? I was a little surprised to see him there, since he claims never to read anything written after the 17th century."

"I've read his article on Molière," Steadman noted.

"And?" Ellen asked.

"Brilliant!" He looked Foxwhistle up and down. "So what's with the rugged getup?"

"He always dresses that way," she said. Foxwhistle was wearing a red and black checkered lumber jacket, a pair of jeans and cowboy boots, to which he added the perfect touch of a buzz cut. Foxwhistle boomed out, "Well, I don't know if Dalí was a fascist or

not but he sure as hell was bisexual."

Heads turned.

Cocayne, in sheer frustration, answered with a barrage of Spanish.

"Speak English, Oswaldo. You're in America now and goddamned lucky to be here."

"Please. I am trying to have a nuanced discussion." Oswaldo said. "Nuanced, eh? Get real, my friend. When you're talking about Lorca and Dalí, all people really want to know is who was fucking who."

More heads turned.

"Interesting department you have here," Steadman said.

Some other people came over and buttonholed the speaker. Ellen wanted to have dinner with Carl but he was determined to go home and work on his symphony. His department commissioned him and the premier was scheduled for March, so he was facing a deadline. He told Ellen the first two movements were done but he couldn't figure out how to finish it.

After Carl left, Ellen saw Stelios talking to the safari guy. Val was talking to a young gun from the Theater Department who was putting on a production of Lorca's *Blood Wedding*. Ellen was about to make her getaway when Roy reappeared, moving as close to her as his large belly would allow.

"Hmmm…do you have dinner plans?"

Ellen's jaw tightened. She wanted to say, "Will your wife be coming?" And before she knew it, she had.

Unfazed, Roy answered, "It would just be us. Erica is not well. A headache…or something." He finished his wine. "We could go to Sunil's Palace. You like Indian food, don't you?"

"Yes, but…"

Then, out of nowhere, the safari guy appeared at Ellen's side. One minute he was across the room and the next he was here. He touched her elbow lightly and said, "Are you ready for that beer now?"

Startled, she almost blurted out, "What beer?" but caught herself.

She took a moment to size him up. Somehow he knew to rescue her. Interesting. He flashed a pleasant grin. She thought why not and said, "Yeah. Okay, I'm ready."

Roy, obviously put out, got redder in the face than

usual. Motioning with his glass he said, "Aren't you going to introduce me to your friend?"

"Oh, yes, I'm sorry, this is…"

"Hugo Coffey," he announced, as he seized Roy's hand and shook it with a vigor that startled the chairman.

"Hugo, this is my department chairman, Prof. Roy Matts-Haas." "Delighted, Professor, delighted."

Roy was not. " Hmmm…are you in some way connected to the University?"

"No. I just live in town. I read in the paper how President Dillworth wants more interaction with the community. So here I am, just doing my part. Wonderful lecture, enjoyed it thoroughly. So nice to meet you."

And with that, he whisked Ellen out the door, leaving a scowling Roy in his wake.

Outside, it was warm and balmy.

"Do you always do things like that?"

"You looked like you needed rescuing."

Perhaps he sensed that Ellen was about to say thanks and goodnight.

"Shall we go and have that beer?" he asked.

Ellen hesitated.

"Come on, it's okay. I may look well-preserved but I'm plenty old enough to be your father."

She saw a kindness in his eyes and said, "Okay."

And there she was, strolling across the darkened, silent campus under a sky filled with stars toward the local watering hole, The Wild Bore, squired by a sort of good-looking, sort of distinguished (if you liked the outdoors type), sort of intelligent, sort of gentleman who had already demonstrated he knew how to make things happen.

As usual, The Wild Bore was noisy and crowded, but they managed to grab one of the few remaining tables.

"So how do you happen to be in town? You're obviously not from here. I've never seen you before. You look like you just got back from a safari."

"I don't go on safaris. Actually, I just got back from Peru. Spent the better part of a year in the rainforest."

Ellen couldn't believe her ears.

"Did I say something wrong?"

"No, no. I did my dissertation on *Amazonia*. You know, by Hubert Gervin. It's all about the rainforest, shamanism."

"Yes, I've read it."

Ellen felt herself warming up. "I've read every book on shamanism I can get my hands on, and researched the sad history of Peru." She stopped abruptly. "I…I suppose someone with your experience finds that a bit, I don't know, pathetic. You've probably spent time with real shamans, worked with them."

"One or two."

"So here I am writing about the rainforest and shamanism, as if I'm some kind of expert, which is what scholars do. But you've done a total immersion in everything I've only read about. You've actually been to the rainforest, spent a lot of time there. You don't need to write about it. You haven't, have you? Why should you? You've lived it."

"No, no. I'm not a writer. Books are fine but they only let you know things from the outside."

The waitress came over. Hugo ordered a pitcher.

"Oh, my."

"You never know who else might come along." "So you like it?" Ellen asked. "What, beer?"

She laughed. "No, *Amazonia*."

"Yves is a great character."

"I've probably read it six times. Sometimes I sort of dream of doing what he did."

"Getting divorced and going to live with a tribe in the rainforest?" "I'm not married."

He took a big swig of beer. "So why don't you?" "Well, I have my job."

"So did Yves. He was a...a..."

"He did publicity."

All at once, a large shadow cast itself across the table. A student, not especially tall but decidedly overweight, greeted Ellen.

"Hi, Professor Metran."

"Hello Albert."

"You remember my name? Already?"

"I try to remember as many of my students' names as I can."

"A monumental task in such an enormous class." He

scrutinized Hugo for a moment. "Don't get to see you too often in this den of iniquity," he said to Ellen.

"Blame him," she said, motioning to Hugo.

"Albert, this is my friend, Hugo."

They shook hands.

"I'm looking forward to class next week," Albert said, "we'll be discussing...umm..."

"Gothic cathedrals."

He rubbed his hands together. "That's sacred geometry. Juicy. Well, I must be off to my study," he said, indicating a booth back in a corner his friends had already laid claim to.

"Your students seem to like you. You enjoy teaching, don't you?" "My class in 20th century French Lit is great and I'm giving a graduate seminar in existentialism."

"Ah, Sartre and Camus."

"It's going like gangbusters. At least I think it is. I hope the students do."

"They do, I'm sure." He finished his glass, topped hers off and gave himself a refill. "And you like the research part, writing articles?"

"I love it. I love books."

"Do they love you back?"

"Some do."

"Enough of them?"

She laughed. "Maybe. I'll tell you something I've never admitted to anyone else. Every once in a while, I go to the French Lit section in the stacks, and starting with the Middle Ages, I read all the titles of the books, taking down the interesting ones, skimming through the chapters and the bibliographies. Sometimes I make it all the way through to the end of the 20th century. And I imagine that someday maybe books by me will be there, too. Pretty pitiful, huh?"

She took a gulp of beer, amazed she was opening up like this to someone she didn't even know. "But something's changing. Today, I fell asleep up in my carrel, something that, not so long ago would've been, well, unthinkable. I used to love doing my research. It made up for all the papers I had to grade, the committee meetings, the departmental meetings. Actually, I dreamt I was in the Amazon," she held his eyes. "It's as if I were there."

"Is that the first time you've had a dream like that?"

"No, I've had a few others. I suppose it's normal," she shrugged. "I mean I do so much research on the place. Why are you smiling?"

"The rainforest is calling you."

She looked at him, startled. "I...I never thought of that." "You should."

Ellen leaned back, nodded and said, "Maybe."

"Well, I can see how you might be getting restless; you have a truly appalling chairman. What does he teach?"

"German. You know, it's so ironic. When I was applying for the job, I came here to give a paper and he seemed genuinely interested in my research."

"Maybe he was."

"I was really flattered. Felt appreciated. It turns out he just wanted to hire someone who'd gone to Yale."

"Is that a terrible thing?"

"No. That was fine, until he started hitting on me. And he hasn't stopped. Actually, he's getting worse." She took a hefty swig of beer.

"Much worse."

"I suppose he could like your work and like you, too."

"I always imagined that once I had a job in a university, things would be okay. I put so much time and money into getting my PhD."

"No matter what you do, that won't have been wasted."

"If I didn't teach, I wouldn't know what else to do."

Anyway, she didn't want to talk about herself, she wanted him to talk about his experiences in Peru and was about to say that, when Chad, one of her grad students, appeared.

"I can only stay a minute," he said.

Ellen was about to introduce them when she realized they already knew each other from the yoga class Stelios taught at the local studio, Blue Dharma.

"Chad is a very good yogi," Hugo said.

"You're not so bad yourself."

"I'm just trying to stay active."

Chad turned to Ellen. "You used to come all the time last year. How come you stopped? You're flexible and you were improving."

"I don't know. I was thinking of starting up again. Now I will." "By the way, I really enjoyed re-reading *L'Etranger.*"

"One of my favorite novels. I like Camus, even if he's fallen out of favor these days," Hugo said.

"Me, too," Ellen agreed.

"I'm getting so much more out of it this time around," said Chad. "By the way, I got your article on it."

"And?"

"I thought it was brilliant." He finished his beer and got up. "I have to go. I've got a soccer game tomorrow."

"You play soccer?" asked Ellen.

"Yeah. I'm on the same team as Stelios. The Wellington Tigers. He's an amazing goalie. Jorge plays, too. It's a very international team. Some Africans, some Indonesians, a few Latinos. I'm the token gringo. Do you like soccer?"

"Yes, as a matter of fact, in high school, I had a boyfriend who played center forward," Ellen said.

"Like me," Chad said.

"He was good. Plenty good enough to get a scholarship to college. He could score, but then he got into partying. Drugs."

"Like me."

"Stop it! Not like you."

"Where is he now?" Hugo asked.

"He's an undergraduate somewhere, trying to get his life back together. He lost about ten years."

"Too bad. Come to the game. The weather's supposed to be beautiful." He looked at Hugo. "You, too."

"I might drop by."

"Two o'clock. You know the field, over by the river," he said as he left.

Ellen was glad to have Hugo all to herself again.

"So you're recently back from Peru?"

"I'm often recently back from Peru."

"Where do you go?"

"Iquitos is my jumping off point. In Loreto Province. In the northeast."

"I know where it is."

"Of course. Yves spends some time there, doesn't he?"

"Yes, in Iquitos, getting up the nerve to take the plunge into the rainforest."

"From there I go a few miles upriver by launch and disappear into the jungle to work with Don Pablo."

Val came over and joined them. Hugo knew Val. He seemed to know everyone.

"Where's Stelios?" Ellen asked, as Val settled into a chair.

Val shrugged. "Otherwise engaged. We don't spend much time together these days."

Ellen let that one alone and glanced at Hugo, who pushed back his chair and said, "I should be going."

"Oh, no! I have a million questions."

"I'm going to yoga in the morning. If I'm to be any good at all, I'd better get some sleep." He stood. "We'll be seeing each other again." He disappeared into the crowd of students standing five-deep at the bar, somehow parting them like Moses before the Red Sea.

"Did I interrupt something?"

"No, no, that's all right," Ellen said, thinking, damn! She motioned to the pitcher of beer, to which considerable damage had already been done. "Have some."

"I will." She grabbed Hugo's empty glass.

"You know what was written in big letters on my blackboard this morning when I got to class?"

"No."

"101 ways to wok your dog."

Ellen made a face. "Is that supposed to be funny?"

"Don't worry, I didn't let it set the tone for the class. Second-year Spanish."

"So tell me what you thought about Steadman," Ellen said.

"A breath of fresh air. He knows his stuff and, let's face it, he's hot. We could use a few like him around here. Roy was bemoaning the fact that he could never attract a guy like him here."

"I don't know. He managed to get Foxwhistle."

"That's a special case."

"Uh oh," Val said.

"What?"

"There's Masasato."

"Where?"

"Over by the bar."

"Who's he?"

"A student of mine in Spanish."

"He'll come over as soon as he catches sight of me. I already know what he's going to say. Yup, he's looking over. Get ready. Here he comes."

Masasato bowed formally. "Good evening, Profesora."

"Hi, Sato. How you doin'?"

"Uh, all right, thank you." Suddenly, his voice rose, as if he were in an argument that was getting out of hand. Each sentence was now preceded by a deep, audible intake of breath through the nose, so that the words could be expelled forcefully back out through the nose, some given special emphasis.

"Uh...I must APOLOGIZE."

"What for, Sato?"

"For lately having missed many classes."

"Whether you come or not, that's your call, Sato, my man." He brushed her comment aside, as if he hadn't heard it.

"I had very...uh...IMPOHTANT work to do in..." he took a quick breath, "COMPUTER SCIENCE!"

"We're cool, Sato. You comin' tomorrow?"

His voice returned to its normal level. "Yes. I will come more regularly now."

"Good." With another bow, Masasato took his leave.

"I've had him in class for two years now and that little scene has been repeated quite a few times. It's become almost like a ritual. It's okay. It seems to have a certain importance for him. And he always makes up all the work he's missed."

"At least he's polite."

"Yeah, sort of, but you get the drift. Computer science is much, much, much more important than Spanish could ever be. It's a little insulting, but what the hell, I don't think he's even aware of it. Besides, in case you didn't notice, he's got a dreamboat ass."

"I didn't."

"Well, check it out. Come on, El. Don't tell me you've never thought about sleeping with any of your students?"

"I've never done it."

"You should try it some time."

Ellen looked at Masasato's ass as he marched toward the bar. She had to admit it was cute. "Have you?"

"Done it with Masasato?" Val drank some beer. "Well, let's just say I'm not opposed to a good old-fashioned Samurai fuck, but the occasion has yet to arise."

# Chapter Two

Maybe it was the beer, but Ellen found it difficult to get out of bed the next day. She slept late, laid around for a while and instead of jumping up and running off to the library, sat on the window seat of her apartment with a cup of coffee, taking in the beautiful September afternoon, Hugo's words about the rainforest calling her and still rattling around in her mind.

When she finally roused herself, she still didn't feel like going to the library to grind out a few more pages on the book project, so she gave herself permission to take a little walk around campus. Without actually deciding to, she wandered over to the soccer field where the game was already in progress.

She sat on the grass by the side of the field, not far from a small group of women whom she took to be the Indonesian contingent, and started picking out the players she knew: Chad, who played forward like her old boyfriend, Jorge, famous for his homegrown grass, and Stelios in goal. It looked like the two teams were evenly matched and it might be a good game. Whatever charms her carrel might have provided couldn't compete with the warm sun and the gentle breeze on her skin. She asked someone who was walking by what the score was. He thought it was 0-0.

"How long have they been playing?"

"Ten, fifteen minutes."

Stelios was quick and agile as a cat in goal. He made a couple of incredible saves, once diving to his right, stretching to the max in mid-air, barely getting his fingers on the ball, deflecting it just outside the post. On the corner kick, although not tall, he leapt high in the air, pulling in the cross, getting the ball quickly out to Jorge who launched a lightning counterattack.

Jorge was fast, with prodigious ball control and deceptive moves. Darting by a few defenders, he delivered a brilliant pass to Chad, who got off a hard shot. He had the goalie beat but it was deflected at the last minute by a desperate stretch of a defender's foot.

A young boy with black hair and dark eyes came over to her. "My mother wants you to come and sit with us." He motioned

toward where the Indonesian women were sitting.

Ellen looked and a woman smiled and waved for her to come over. When she got there she realized she had actually been invited to an exotic picnic, all laid out on a wide tablecloth. Her protests that she had already eaten were brushed aside. When she said she had to watch her figure, the women looked at her as if they didn't know what she was talking about.

"There's plenty of food. Don't let it go to waste."

There was, indeed. A big bowl of fried rice and another of fried noodles. Ellen relented and took a little of everything. As she was eating, the little boy sat beside her, telling her the Indonesian name for the dishes. The fired rice was *nasi goring*, the noodles *bami goring*. As a language teacher, she found this culinary introduction to a language spoken in a far-away land—one that conjured up Kipling and sailing ships—lots of fun, although she assumed she wouldn't remember many, if any, of the names of the dishes. The boy laughed when she mispronounced something, looking at her with sparkling eyes beneath his thick, black lashes.

"What's your name?"

"Oetomo."

The food was even more delicious than it looked. She found the *sambal* a delicious mix of chicken and tomato chutney. And she repeated the name for sweet soy sauce, *ketjap manis*, and salty soy sauce, *ketjap asin*.

"Probably where we got the word for ketchup."

"Maybe," said Gema, Oetomo's mother. She pointed toward the four Indonesians in the backfield. "The tall man, that's Laxman, my husband," she said proudly. "My father," said Oetomo, with even more pride.

Ellen had noticed Laxman before; he was an attractive guy and a commanding presence on the field. She looked back at Gema with a tinge of envy.

Toward the end of the first half, the tempo of the game picked up. One of the better forwards on the other team scored a phenomenal goal on a scissor kick. Chad had one more chance but was brought down by a hard tackle just outside the penalty area. Not long after, the whistle blew for halftime.

Ellen was munching on some tasty chicken *satay* on a stick with peanut sauce, when Chad came over.

"Glad you could come."

"Too bad they scored but it was an amazing goal."

"Yeah, well, that guy is really good. It was just a matter of time before he put one in the net." He wiped his face with his shirtfront. "Stelios is incredible, isn't he? So is Jorge."

"What about you?"

"Oh, I can shoot. I can usually get the ball in the goal, if I get the chance. But I'm not much good for anything else."

Laxman, who had been talking to his little boy, came over and put his arm around Chad. "Every team needs a good striker. If you don't have one, you don't win."

Ellen noticed Hugo out on the field, kicking the ball around with a couple of other onlookers and Oetomo.

"You like our Indonesian food?"

"It's delicious," she said, finishing her satay. "You guys sure know how to put on a nasty offside trap. It's as if you give some secret sign, everybody moves up at once and you've got 'em."

If he was surprised she knew what an offside trap was, he didn't show it. "That's our specialty. You put it together with a good finisher like Chad and you can win some games."

He wore a red bandana around his forehead, which added to a kind of maritime air he had about him. He had a scar on his right cheekbone that made him, if not exactly handsome, interesting. She thought perhaps he had been in a knife fight, perhaps he had been onboard a ship that was attacked by pirates, or perhaps he had been a pirate attacking a ship. Lots of pirates in the Java Sea, all very intriguing. Although his English was pretty good, his voice still had a trace of an accent, just enough to make it sexy. No doubt about it, he was what Val would call a hunk.

After the game got going again, Hugo came over.

"Hi. You looked like you knew what you were doing out there." "Oh, when I was younger, I played in leagues like this. In San

Diego, upstate New York, and a little in Greece." "Peru?"

"Just with some kids in a tiny village. I was never particularly good. Not like these guys. A hacker, good enough to lose with."

"Sometime I want to talk more about what you did, what you do in Peru."

"That's a long story."

"Do you have a card?"

"Me? A card? Certainly not. Don't worry. Stelios knows how to reach me."

They were watching the game and before she knew it

he had drifted away. She saw him standing over by the goal. Then, when she looked over again, he was gone.

The second half was pretty much a standoff, until Jorge suddenly accelerated, dribbling the ball up the field, passing it to Chad, who moved swiftly to his right and took a long shot on goal, which hit the crossbar. The rebound came darting toward him and he swooped down on it and fired a second shot off his first touch. The ball knifed between two defenders and exploded out on the startled goalie, drilling him straight in the chest with its sheer force knocking him back into the goal and down. He lay on his back without moving. The ball trickled over to the side of the net.

Ellen and the ladies jumped up, cheering. Chad's teammates mobbed him, forcing him to the ground in what looked like a rugby scrum. Even before the celebration began to wind down, one of the opposing backs, who had gone into the net to retrieve the ball, realized that something was wrong. The goalie hadn't gotten up. In fact, he wasn't even moving. Players from both teams gathered around him.

At first everyone thought he had just gotten the wind knocked out of him. He had, but it soon became clear something else was wrong. It really hurt him to move, so much so that someone went for a cell phone to call an ambulance.

The paramedics who took him away thought he might have one, maybe two, broken ribs.

Nobody blamed Chad—all part of the game. Since there were less than ten minutes left to play, under the circumstances, both teams agreed to call it a 1-1 draw.

"Not the way I would have liked the game to end," Chad said. As the Indonesian women picked up the food, Oetomo stood in

front of Ellen and looked up. "Are you coming again?"

"I don't know, maybe, I guess so."

"Promise?"

Gema took his hand and the Indonesian women left without their men.

Jorge sat down, crossed his legs, pulled some of his own homegrown grass out of his athletic bag and, separating the good stuff out, sprinkled it onto a cigarette paper. "Best grass this side of heaven." Stelios and then Laxman came and sat down with them.

"Do you mind if I join you?" Laxman asked.

"No, not at all." Jorge said, pleasantly surprised. No one was more generous with his stash. Ellen got the impression that the Indonesians pretty much kept to themselves.

Jorge took a long toke and passed it to Ellen. "You know what they say about grass, don't you?"

"What?"

"Marijuana is the opiate of the masses."

She took a toke. "So long library."

The guys talked about the game, razzing each other about bad passes and assorted other miscues. She didn't mind just sitting there listening, getting high and playing hooky. Now and then Laxman would toss a soft smile her way. Well, well, fancy that, she thought. When they had finished the joint, Chad stood up. "I'm going over

to the hospital to see how the goalie is."

Laxman got up to leave as well. "I have to grab a shower and get to work."

"Come on. I'll give you a lift," Chad said.

She wondered vaguely what he did to be going to work at such an odd time. Some kind of graveyard shift— something you could do stoned, something which might prove much less onerous if one was stoned—but he was gone before she got around to asking.

"I'm glad I don't have to go to work."

"I hope I never have to go to work," Jorge said.

As they watched them walk to Chad's beat-up old car, Jorge shook his head. "Fuckin' Chad. He really kicks the shit out of the ball."

# Chapter Three

Close to the end of the month, Ellen got the phone call she had been dreading. Her mother, Beverly, was having another crisis. Beverly had a system with her next-door neighbor Judy who kept an eye on her. Every morning, Bev would raise the shade on her bedroom window to signal she was okay.

This morning, the shade had not gone up. Worried, Judy grabbed the key Beverly gave her many years ago and rushed over to find her on the floor, weak and pale, breathing with difficulty. It was hard to tell how long she had been there.

These crises were all too predictable. The arteries leading to her heart were blocked. For years her doctors had been trying to convince her to have an operation but, too terrified to have the surgery, she always refused.

Ellen's mom lived only a few hours drive from Wellington. She got there as fast as she could.

She found her in the hospital in Intensive Care. Seeing her hooked up to an intravenous drip, with more tubes in her nose giving her oxygen, Ellen stopped in her tracks, overwhelmed with sadness and helplessness.

One of her mother's doctors drew her aside.

"We've tried to convince her she must have the operation. Hard to say if we've made any headway. Perhaps she'll listen to you."

"I don't know."

"Do your best." He stopped at the door. "She's run out of time." Her mom stirred and opened her eyes. "Oh, you're here."

"Hello, Mom. I came as soon as I could. I can't stay long. I have to get back for classes tomorrow."

She took her mother's hand, which was cold, and explained as best she could the necessity of the operation. By the time she left, she felt that her mother had finally come to understand that she didn't have much choice.

Beverly picked at her evening meal. "Perhaps you should have it, dear."

"That's okay, I'm not hungry."

"It will just go to waste."

When they said their goodbyes, Beverly watched her go, her eyes filled with fear. She clutched her daughter's hand.

"Ellen, I don't want to die."

When her father died, her mother had been stoic; it was hard to see her so scared.

"You're out of options, Mom. You have to have the operation." By the time Ellen called the cardiologist the next morning, her mother had finally given in. When Ellen spoke to her mom briefly,

Beverly's voice was very shaky.

***

A few hours later, Ellen went to see Stelios in his office. He was sitting at his desk, staring out the window, something he seemed to be doing more and more lately, listening to some music on a little shelf stereo system that put out great sound considering its size. She was about to tap on the door and walk in but something about the piece was so arresting that she stopped and waited until it had ended.

"What was that?"

When he turned around, she saw there were tears in his eyes. "The adagio from Mahler's Ninth. Some people believe he knew he was dying and that was his farewell to the world."

"What do you think?"

"Well, his life was going south. His beautiful young daughter had died; his wife had had an affair. He was sick."

"Is that what you were looking so pensive about?"

"Not exactly."

"Well...?"

"You don't want to know."

"Try me."

"I was thinking that, all things considered, I would have preferred not to have been born. Of course, no one asked me."

Ellen had no idea what to say. To her, Stelios had so much going for him.

"But you didn't come here to listen to me being gloomy."

"It's about my mother." She explained the situation. "I'm so worried. I don't know what to do. I feel like she's too panic-stricken to make it through."

He looked out the window. "You have to involve the shaman." "What?"

"You have to involve the shaman."

"You mean Hugo?"

"Yes. Do you have his number?"

She shook her head. He scribbled it down and handed her the phone. She dialed the number and there he was.

"I have to see you."

"There's a coffee shop near my place, the Java Hut." "I know it."

"I'll be there in ten minutes."

***

Hugo was sitting at a window table sipping herb tea. She told him what was going on. "Can you help me...her?"

"Maybe, if she's open to it."

"At this point, I think she's so scared she'll try anything."

"We can do it by phone. She has to be relaxed and quiet. No one must interrupt."

"I can arrange that."

"I'll record the session on a cassette. Does she have a cassette player?"

"I'll get her one."

"After the phone session, you have to pick up the cassette and run it over to her, so she can listen to it again. When's the operation scheduled for?"

The day after tomorrow. They have to get her blood pressure down."

"Good. We can do two sessions before and one after, to help her recover."

"Okay."

"That's a lot of driving."

"I don't care."

"She should listen to the cassette as often as she can. Get her some headphones, too."

"Okay."

"What do I owe you?"

"Three hundred dollars."

She wrote him a check. "When will you be free?" "Whatever time is best for her, I'll be available."

Ellen made the arrangements, bought a cassette player, headphones and collected the recording of the first session from Hugo. She managed somehow to teach her 20th century French Lit. class in between, although after, she didn't remember much, except that the hour seemed endless.

Out on the highway about halfway there, she glanced at the speedometer, realized she was going eighty five miles an hour and slowed down to around the speed limit.

Like most cities, Brentwood had grown much larger than when she was young. Most of the stores she remembered had disappeared, replaced by boutiques selling expensive Italian shoes and trendy clothes. As she drove, she noticed new restaurants of various ethnicities—French, Mexican, Indian, Thai, Peruvian, even Ethiopian. One little section of a few streets was filled with coffee and teashops, even a few wine bars, one of which served *tapas*.

Some things, of course, had not changed. Brentwood Hospital stood where it had been when Ellen was born and later had her tonsils out. Although quite young at the time, she still remembered waking up in the room after the operation with her parents there, looking anxious. She kept throwing up blood and the nurse, who had to keep changing the sheets, became quite put out. She remembered telling her mom, "I can't help it."

The area around the hospital had not participated in the yuppification of the city, but the hospital maintained its excellent reputation. As she waited at a red light, she saw a lot of empty storefronts. The little hot dog stand where her father had taken her once for lunch was gone.

By the time she got to the hospital, it was long since dark and her mother was already asleep. That was a good sign. She tiptoed into the room, left the cassette and the player with a note of instructions and she was back on the road. She liked driving to and from the city where she grew up. It gave her something useful to do. It was late at night, traffic had thinned and there were fewer commercials on the radio. It was 2 AM when she parked in front of her apartment.

The next day, except for a quick call to the hospital to make sure her mother was okay, she was busy preparing her lecture on one of her favorite plays, Sartre's *Huis clos*, for the existentialism seminar that afternoon. As soon as it was over, she swung by for the second tape. She was on the road again, picking her way through rush hour traffic, not so bad in a small college town like Wellington, and then onto the thruway.

It was about eight o'clock when she parked in the visitor' s section, tired, but nonetheless still keyed up, completely unprepared for what awaited her.

Beverly was sitting in bed, propped up by pillows listening to her cassette. Her eyes were closed but she wasn't sleeping. Ellen took a chair and sat quietly watching her mother as her chest rose and fell gently. From time to time, her left hand moved. Ellen's mind wandered back to her Amazon dream. The vividness of being there had not diminished—the scary feeling of being lost, the mosquitoes, the fading light, the natives. She wondered what would have happened if she hadn't awakened. She was aware that cannibalism was not unknown among certain tribes and didn't want to think about it.

She looked around the Intensive Care Unit, wondering what the other patients, all who looked pretty wrecked, were there for.

Presently, her mother opened her eyes and slipped off the headphones. Ellen jumped up to take them and put them on the night table but what she saw stopped her in mid-motion.

"Oh, there you are. Hello, Ellen."

Her mother's voice was soft and calm. The expression on her face, which, since the death of her husband, had taken on a look of permanent dissatisfaction, was serene. Her eyes were radiating, if not happiness, contentment. She seemed at ease and well rested.

"You look tired," Beverly said.

Ellen slumped back down again. "I'm okay." She paused, aware that she was staring. "But you look…" She searched for the right words and finally came out with "pretty chipper."

Beverly laughed, something she seldom did.

"You sound just like the doctor. That's what he said, too, something like that. He wanted to know how I slept and when I told him I slept like a baby, that I had the best sleep I had in years, his eyes bugged out. I guess nobody but me sleeps well in Intensive Care."

"Probably not, what with all the nurses bustling about and all these monitoring machines pinging and bleeping, and how worried you've been about having an operation."

Beverly leaned forward conspiratorially toward her daughter. "That's just it. What I didn't tell him, because he…well, he wouldn't understand and I didn't want to end up in the psycho ward, but during the night, I had this incredible dream."

Ellen's eyebrows raised. Now mom's dreaming too?

"I'm here in the hospital, right here in ICU, but the unit doesn't look like it does now. It's more like an exhibition hall, owned by one of the nurses. She's a painter, very artistic, by day, and a nurse by night. The hall was beautifully decorated with ribbons and other stuff from the unit. I don't know how to explain it."

"There were found objects."

"That's right, found objects. And the nurses were all dressed in my favorite color. You know what that is."

"Lilac."

"Yes, even the head nurse was wearing a deep lilac uniform. Very striking. I was so surprised, maybe even shocked, to see it." She took a sip of water. "You know, during the session, Hugo asked me what my favorite color was. He told me to see it in my mind's eye, which was easy, and to let myself be enveloped in it and to let it come in and go all through my body, right into my cells. But I never expected to see it in a dream being worn by all the nurses." She paused for a moment, savoring the memory.

"These monitors, they weren't making all the ugly, electronic noises they're making now. Oh, no, last night, I'm here to tell you, they made music. Not like they were playing instruments but the most enchanting sounds were flowing out of them. It was as if they were serenading me, singing me a lullaby. I listened to them for what seemed like a long time until I dropped off into the deepest sleep imaginable. No more dreams that I remember. But you know how restless I always am in bed, tossing and turning all night. Well, I don't think I moved a bit. Now, of course, when I woke up, the unit looked like it always does, the nurses were wearing their usual boring green uniforms and the music had become all this electronic beeping again."

Ellen settled back into the chair to let herself take in the sudden transformation her mother had somehow undergone, here in the hospital of all places.

On the drive home, Ellen was pensive. She couldn't get over how at peace her mother had been. She really didn't remember what they had talked about, perhaps they hadn't spoken much at all but it didn't matter.

Her father had died when she was so young that she had very few memories of him, and even those were rather faded. Her parents used to take her out in her baby carriage and, if there weren't many people around, they would stand apart and send her flying in the carriage back and forth between them. She loved the wind on her face and traveling at what seemed like tremendous speed. She also remembered her father taking her by the wrists and twirling her around in circles, while she laughed hysterically. Or at quieter times, reading her a story before she went to sleep. But that was about all.

Beverly raised her alone and it couldn't have been easy.

Over time, she began to take less and less pleasure from her life and developed the habit of always expecting more from Ellen. Whatever her daughter accomplished, it was somehow not good enough, not even when she got into Yale and did quite well there.

Now something had been cut loose from her mother's blighted psyche and that vague look of displeasure had vanished. Ellen noticed she had stopped calling her "dear," which had always grated on her nerves.

\*\*\*

When she returned the next day, she found her mother in an even better mood. "You know, when you left last night, your eyes were radiant. Are you surprised?" Beverly said.

"No, I guess not."

Beverly took the latest cassette from her daughter and laid it on the tray table. "You won't believe what I've got myself up to today. I don't know what prompted me to do it but I did a lot of thinking about my life, especially all my old sins."

"Mom, what old sins?"

Beverly waved her off before she could finish. "I even listed them all here, in chronological order." She flourished a sheet of paper covered with writing. "No, you can't see them, of course, it's just for me, but it doesn't matter, because in the end I came to the conclusion that what happened, happened. Nothing could be done about any of it, so I just let it all go." She ceremoniously ripped the paper up into little pieces.

Without it being necessary to say anything, something fundamental had shifted in their relationship. They were comfortable with each other, something Ellen realized that she had always wanted but had given up hope of ever having. Now she could sit quietly, holding her mother's hand while she dozed off, waking up now and then and looking at her daughter with a trace of a sweet smile before drifting off again.

How was it possible? Ellen wondered, over and over, as she drove home. What did Hugo do? All that nervousness, all that fear had vanished, replaced by an eagerness to get the operation over and done with.

She drove slowly, in no hurry to get back. Few cars were on the road. A few crazies, of course, zoomed by at eighty or ninety miles an hour, and she smiled when she saw one pulled over by a state trooper not far from Wellington.

*** 

The next morning, even while the operation was in progress, Ellen didn't feel unduly worried. In the afternoon, she went to Stelios's office to thank him.

He looked up from one of Seneca's tragedies. "I don't know what the hell I'm going to say about this tomorrow." He shook his head.

"You'll think of something. You always do." "It went well, the operation?"

"Unbelievably. I spoke to a nurse a little while ago. She's in Recovery now. No problems."

"You look beat."

"Exhausted. I have a day off from going there today, I think I'm heading home to crash."

"Good idea. By the way, who is this guy, Guez de Balzac?"

"He's a 17th century French B-list writer. Wrote mostly letters that were widely circulated around the salons like the Hôtel de Rambouillet. Why?"

"Because Foxwhistle keeps bugging me about him. Apparently he was influenced by Cicero, Seneca and Pliny. Foxwhistle assumes that since I'm teaching Latin literature I must know something about it. I tried to tell him no but it's the only thing Roy would let me teach, but he didn't want to hear it."

"People think that if you know Greek, you must also know Latin. So what does he want?"

"He wants me to tell him how Cicero and Seneca influenced this Guez guy. I told him I don't have a clue about Pliny."

"Guez de Balzac is all about style. He developed a way of writing that brought clarity and eloquence, even forcefulness to French prose and he combined this with an idiomatic, vernacular way of expression. Quite a feat, but for us the subjects he was drawn to seem pretty thin."

"I don't see what I can do. I don't know French that well but I don't want to get Foxwhistle ticked off at me."

Ellen thought for a minute. "I tell you what I'll do. Give me a paragraph or two from Seneca. Did he write letters?"

"Yes. He wrote a lot about death."

"Good, something from his letters, about death. I'll pick a couple of passages from Guez de Balzac and I'll do an explication de texte, tying them together."

"You don't have to…"

"It's okay. You helped my mother."

"I didn't do anything."

"You steered me in the right direction. It's okay. It'll be fun. I haven't done one for years but I used to be a whiz at it. I can't promise it'll be done right away."

"Don't worry. I can keep Foxwhistle at bay. Go get some sleep." She stopped at the door. "She went into that operation like a champ. I'm so proud of her. Her fear was just gone. How can that be?"

He laughed. "You expect me to answer that question? Take it up with Hugo."

"I intend to."

# Chapter Four

Ellen was in her office, sitting at her desk Serge popped in.

"You've heard, of course."

"What?"

"Todd Shipton. It's really quite amusing."

Serge had one of those attractively clipped European accents that was difficult to pin down. He no doubt held on to it because it conjured up all sorts of interesting qualities, not the least of which were suavely impeccable manners and the good looks to go with them, all of which gave him a continental charm irresistible to American women and irritating to American men. His background allowed him to be at home in a number of languages. A mysterious childhood suggested an old, aristocratic family, once prominent and powerful, now fallen on hard times. He was the department's only Russian teacher and Roy was counting on him to build up the program.

Todd Shipton had gotten a Masters in French at UC Santa Barbara, where he seemed to have done what studying he did on the beach, during those times when he wasn't surfing. While at UC, he had acquired a stunning Costa Rican girlfriend, Anita, who was also here at Wellington, as a graduate student in Spanish.

"May I sit down?"

"Of course. So what happened?"

"You're aware that Todd is taking the translation course with Prof. Jeanaud?"

"I am now."

"English to French, of course. Jeanaud is not really competent to go the other way. Well, it seems that young Todd has handed in a number of translations, all of which had came back covered in red ink with comments such as *plat* and *trouvez une autre expression plus évocatrice*. The grades he got were in the narrow range from C+ to B-. And I needn't remind you of the reputation Jeanaud has of preferring female students to male. Women tend to get A's from him regardless of what they turn in."

"Anita would be getting an A+ if she were taking the course," Ellen said. "Quite a few female students have lodged complaints of sexual harassment against Jeanaud, not that it did them any good."

"Or Jeanaud any harm. Anyway, since C for a graduate student is really a failing grade and Todd thought his translations were not that bad, he decided to conduct an experiment."

Serge paused for effect.

"As a French teacher yourself, you are, of course, aware

that Baudelaire's translations of Poe are acknowledged to be perhaps the best ever made."

"When Baudelaire first read Poe, he said he felt like he was reading poems and stories he had written himself."

"Precisely. So, Todd copied out a few pages of Baudelaire's rendering of Poe and handed it in as his own. Baudelaire posthumously received a C+."

Ellen laughed.

"The best is yet to come. Todd explained to the good professor, not privately in his office but in class, in front of all the other students, exactly what he had done and why."

"Ouch."

"Yes, very embarrassing, since Jeanaud was unable to come up with any plausible defense of his indefensible actions. It's all over the department now, and, as fate would have it, there's the departmental meeting this afternoon."

"Do you really think Jeanaud will come?"

"He has no choice. You know how Roy is about these meetings. As he is fond of saying, in the case of absence, death is the only excuse."

"Todd will be there, as one of our two student reps."

"You don't think he'll bring it up at the meeting, do you?"

"No, why should he? Somehow, I don't think he'll be getting any more Cs, regardless of the quality of his translations. Nonetheless, it could be tense." Serge stood up. "Well, I know you have a class coming up."

"French Civ."

"So far, there's no Russian Civ., at least not yet. Who knows, perhaps never. Maybe the idea is that there is no such thing as Russian civilization and culture. I believe many Germans are of that opinion."

***

Ellen looked out from the podium over the packed auditorium and wondered how many of her students had any interest in French culture. Roy suckered her into teaching it on the grounds that she spent her junior year in France and, therefore, could bring recent, vital, first-hand experience to the subject.

Now she knew that he really didn't care about such things. He had only set up the course, and others like it in Spanish and German, as a compromise that saved the language requirement from being eliminated entirely. The subject of endless student complaints (too hard, irrelevant, etc.), the requirement had been reduced from two years to one and this course, taught entirely in English now, somehow fulfilled it. By tacit agreement, grading in these courses was less stringent than in the other language offerings.

Once she had agreed to teach it, Roy refused to let her out of it, claiming that she was the best person for the job and that her student evaluations were terrific. Ellen couldn't argue with that.

The lecture hall (the one where Steadman had held

forth) was always packed. Back in the far left corner sat the jocks. Always polite, if not particularly attentive, they showed up regularly unless it was a game day, did whatever they needed to do to pass and tried not to look too bored. Who knows, maybe they weren't, maybe they were studying play patterns.

Ellen hadn't known what to expect. She loved the material but that didn't mean the students would share her interest. However, many did. She showed lots of slides, so she wasn't always talking about abstract things. Gradually, students came to class looking, if not enthusiastic, at least not resentful.

Today, they were discussing Louis XIV and Versailles. She explained how expensive building the palace had been, during foreign wars in Europe and in India, and that it had pretty much broken the bank. Linking the past with the present, to be more relevant, Ellen asked the rhetorical question, "Sound familiar?"

Quite a few heads nodded.

One of the female students raised her hand. "Someone told me that there was no indoor plumbing at Versailles."

"That's right."

"With all that money spent, well…why not?"

"Strange at it may seem to us, apparently King Louis didn't think it was important."

"So what did people do?"

"Well, for one thing, they didn't bathe."

"Didn't bathe, ever? Gross."

"That all started in the Middle Ages. The Romans had public bathhouses, as did places like France that they conquered. I don't think the Romans were too concerned about what went on in the baths, but in the Middle Ages the Church was shocked to find that people went to the baths not only to get clean but also to get it on."

"You mean..."

"Yeah. So the bathhouses were shut down and bathing was declared the work of the devil. Due to the power of the Church, people pretty much stopped bathing, even in a place as opulent as Versailles."

"Didn't they, like, stink?"

"No doubt, but if everyone smells bad, no one stands out. The nobles at Versailles used to put pouches of fragrant herbs in their armpits."

"How did they go to the bathroom if there were no bathrooms?" "They went in the rose garden behind the bushes or used chamberpots in their rooms."

The bell rang. That was a discussion that Ellen had not planned on having, but it certainly got the attention of most everybody in the auditorium.

She had about half an hour before the faculty meeting. Sitting in her office, still feeling good about the class, she ate the sandwich she had brought and thought about Laxman. These days, he seemed to always be around somewhere in her mind. Like the rainforest, he had the lure of the exotic. She had been going to the home soccer games and they had talked a few times. It was obvious there was a mutual attraction. At the last game, after everyone left, he helped her up from her blanket, held her hand for a moment, and grazed her palm with his fingertips as he let go. Their eyes met and he smiled. Ellen was sure he'd be good in bed, though his being married was a concern. If she learned anything from her studies of shamanism, however, it was to not pay much attention to conventional morality. She wondered where, if anywhere, it would go.

She was one of the last to arrive in the departmental conference room. Todd was there, his usual relaxed, smiling, affable self. He always reminded her of The Beach Boys. Jeanaud, sitting at the far end of the table from him, appeared lost in thought, as if wrestling with a particularly irksome problem of translation.

Foxwhistle and Roy were in the middle of a conversation.

"I've never read *Le Père Goriot*," Foxwhistle said.

"Not even in graduate school?"

"Not that I can remember. I read *Illusions perdues*. That was enough for me."

"You didn't like it?"

"I didn't say that."

"You're talking about two landmarks in 19th century French literature."

"Spare me the lecture on what an important novelist Honoré de Balzac was," he snorted. "I'll take Guez de Balzac anytime."

"Guez de Balzac was a second-rate, maybe even third-rate writer." "How do you know? You've never read him, have you?"

"Well, I…"

"Careful. I might give you a pop quiz."

"Could we get on with the business at hand? Some of us have work to do," Oswaldo said.

"What work do you have that could possibly be more important than Guez de Balzac?" asked Foxwhistle.

"Let's get down to business," said Roy.

Apparently, word had come back from Paris of a certain laxity in both the curriculum and the student attendance. Various ideas were put forward, none of which seemed adequate. To everyone's astonishment, Foxwhistle weighed in with one. Ellen had never seen him so animated during a departmental meeting.

"Maybe we need to send someone to ride herd on the foreign faculty." The native speakers around the table squirmed and looked down.

"Perhaps you would like to take on that mission yourself, James?" Roy asked.

"Hell, no," Foxwhistle answered.

Ellen thought about volunteering but decided against it. Getting tenure was hard enough if you were on campus. Being away often proved disastrous.

No action was taken on the matter, and it was set aside for further discussion at a subsequent meeting.

The next order of business was a review of the policy

that all graduate students had to teach at least one year of beginning language classes. Until now, everyone had done so without protest but this year Todd had requested that the provision be brought up for reconsideration. Like a consummate card player, Todd laid down his ace stating when he and Anita were at UC Santa Barbara, their Teaching Assistantships required it of them.

The faculty had previously been in favor of the requirement, since it alleviated them of the need to ever teach those classes, leaving them free to have fun in the playground of literature, the place where reputations and careers were forged. Foxwhistle's point had always been that, "If they don't teach the classes, how would the faculty ever know if they're competent to teach or give them the recommendation they'd need when looking for jobs in this market?

"We can get all the recommendations we want from our profs who had close supervision of the TA's, unlike here."

Roy frowned but moved that students like Todd be absolved of the need to demonstrate classroom effectiveness.

The voting was unanimous, as always in meetings run by Roy. The "ayes" carried it.

"Thank you, sir," Todd said respectfully, brushing his blond hair back off his forehead, basking but not gloating in his success.

Ellen was impressed. Not too many people got what

they wanted out of Roy. It was almost always the other way around.

"As to oversight of our TAs which has been neglected, this year Michel volunteered to, as James Foxwhistle would put it, ride herd on them."

Foxwhistle reared his head up like a leviathan rising from the waters, bellowing as he breached, "Michel? Who the hell's Michel?" "Why, he's sitting right next to you, James. He's new to our department this year and teaches French, just like you. He's a specialist in *La nouvelle critique*."

"Hmpf."

Michel was fresh out of graduate school, pale-skinned, short and a little on the chubby side. He gazed up at Foxwhistle with a sheepish grin on his rotund face, at once amiable and apprehensive.

Foxwhistle looked him up and down several times with a distinct air of disapproval. During those few moments, it was impossible to know what might happen beyond the definite possibility that Michel might receive, at the very least, a severe tongue-lashing. But after considerable deliberation, during which a slight twitch appeared in Michel's left eyelid, the senior professor abruptly extended the hand of friendship.

"Foxwhistle."

# Chapter Five

Beverley's recovery from the operation was surprisingly smooth. As soon as she was able to do another phone session, Hugo made a third cassette, that she listened to religiously. Soon she was out of ICU and into a room she had to herself until she was ready to go home.

Ellen arranged for a nurse to come in daily and went to see her mother often, not out of a sense of duty but because she had come to enjoy it. She did not ask to listen to the cassettes, not wanting to disturb the impressive benefits Beverly continued to get from them. However, she was compelled to find out exactly what Hugo had done so.

So she decided to try to catch him after Stelios's yoga class. Weather permitting, Stelios began his own morning yoga practice at 6:30, on a flat, grassy area near the running track. Before long, a few students, out to exercise in the early morning, would stop and watch. He never seemed to notice them, just kept on with his routine, which included some pretty advanced poses like putting both feet behind his head, which he had learned from a Russian yoga teacher in Athens.

Gradually, Stelios became a yoga instructor. One by

one, students arrived with their mats and tried to follow what he was doing. His first students had some yoga experience and could do many, if not all, of the poses. More came, until there were almost 20 in various stages of proficiency.

Realizing his practice remained beyond many of them, Stelios started coming at 5:30 so he could tailor a class to the abilities of those who showed up. He explained poses, breathing techniques and made adjustments in the students' *asanas*. When the Blue Dharma yoga studio opened in town, the class moved there. So, before he knew it, Stelios became a yoga teacher. He kept classes on a donation basis.

Last year, Ellen had purchased a mat for herself and had gone quite regularly. She was flexible, had a knack for it and always felt better afterwards. This year she hadn't gotten back into it yet.

The first day she went, a little bleary-eyed from getting up so early, Hugo was there. She took advantage of an empty space to set up next to him.

He wasn't bad, and had obviously done yoga before (what hadn't he done?), although he still did a fair amount of huffing and puffing, going into child's pose when he needed to take a break.

At the end of class, as they were rolling up their mats, he said, "Not as young as I used to be."

"You do very well."

She was just about to invite him for coffee, when Stelios came over.

"I'm so glad you came."

"Me too. You still have a very loyal following." Chad and Jorge joined them.

"What a good thing to have one of my teachers doing yoga." Chad said to Ellen.

"You'd never catch any of mine out here," Jorge said. He was a graduate student in the math department and quite good, perhaps because the weed he smoked liberated his intelligence from the limitations of the rational.

She looked around for Hugo but he had slipped away.

\*\*\*

The next day she didn't let him off the hook so easily. Stelios had everyone do twelve straight sun salutations. Ellen made it through eight; Hugo had to spend more time resting in child's pose than usual and was up for coffee at the Java Hut.

"How's your mother?" he asked as they settled in at a table.

"Doing great. She's at home, starting to get around the house a little. You must come and see her some time. She wants to meet you."

"I'd like to."

"I'm trying to get her to sell the house. It's too big for her now, too much for her to keep up."

"She probably doesn't want to move. Anyway, she wouldn't be up to that for quite some time."

"No." She paused, as the waitress set down their coffees. "I want to thank you."

He brushed her thanks aside.

"I don't think you realize but you...you gave me back my mother. For the first time, she let me help her with something...important."

"Well that's a nice bonus."

"The operation was probably the second hardest thing she's ever had to face in her life. and together, we saw her through it. Now she trusts me. She's dropped all that mother stuff. She treats me like an adult and we can just be friends."

"I'm glad."

Ellen stared into her coffee cup. "You know, of course, that's not really why I asked you for coffee."

He shrugged, feigning innocence.

"I haven't listened to the tapes. I felt that, somehow, it would be an intrusion. They're hers."

"From the energetic point of view, you're quite correct."

"Even so, I want to know what you did to bring about that extraordinary transformation. Overnight, she changed from being a scared rabbit into a warrior. The doctors and the nurses have asked me what happened. They know about the tapes, of course, but that doesn't explain anything to them."

"I suppose not."

She finished her coffee. "Look, I've read accounts of incredible cures in my shamanism books. Heck, in Amazonia Yves witnesses a woman suffering from agonizing pelvic pain lie in a pit of near scalding water. After an hour, she's lifted out and immersed in a special herbal bath. The next day, only traces of her pain are left. And this is a woman doctors could do nothing for beyond pain pills."

The waitress came over and gave them refills.

"Here I am, writing on shamanism in *Amazonia*. I've written my diss on it, given papers, now I'm busy turning it into a book. Some people in academia consider me an expert but it's beginning to dawn on me just how little I know. I feel like a fraud."

"Don't be so hard on yourself."

"Look, we all know that books on shamanism are full of inaccuracies. Native people don't tell gringos the true story, especially if they suspect there's a book project involved. Some of that stuff is flat made up."

"I haven't read many of them."

"Anyhow, after being a minor part of the miracle that happened to my mother, reading about it in books doesn't cut it anymore."

She glanced away, took a deep breath, stared him in the eyes and said, "I want to know what you did and what you do."

He nodded then blew on his coffee to cool it.

He deliberated before answering. "Look, I'm not even sure what I do. I'm not even sure it's me who does it."

"Are all shamans as evasive as you?"

"Have you ever heard me claim to be a shaman?"

"Stelios calls you one."

"That's okay if he wants to."

"What does that mean?"

"That I know what apprentices in the Amazon go through to become shamans and I haven't done anything like that."

"And yet you did for my mother what no doctor could. Only a shaman. The doctors did the operation well, but you got her mind into it and through it."

"If you listened to the tapes, you'd see there's nothing special on them."

"Don't treat me like an idiot. Even I know it's not what's on the tapes. The really important stuff can't be recorded."

He took a sip of coffee. "I like this place. They make really good coffee."

"So are you gonna tell me what you've done?"

"Depends. I don't usually do that. How serious are you?"

She stared him hard in the eyes. "Very."

He looked at her for what seemed like a long time. Then he finished his coffee, tossed some money on the table and stood up.

"Okay. When's the next time you're going to see you mother?" "Friday."

"I'll come with you and on the way, I'll tell you my story. If you want to do what I do, you have to do what I've done. But you'll have to make your own journey. I'll pick you up here at four o'clock."

She sat for a while, as her coffee grew cold, wondering how she could possibly wait until then.

***

On Friday, when she came at four, she half expected him not to be there but there he was, waiting at a table by the window so she didn't have to go in.

They were just reaching the outskirts of Wellington when he started. "I guess you wouldn't be surprised if I told you that I haven't always been the way I am now."

"No."

"You hardly knew your father. I knew mine all too well. He was a war veteran with a severe case of PTSD. Years ago, they didn't know what it was and called it 'shell shock' and that was it. He was always angry, had a terrible temper, and I went from being happy and outgoing to a silent, frightened kid."

Ellen looked at the trees rushing by and wondered whether it was better to have a father like that or no father at all.

"Well, no need to give you my whole life story. That would even bore the hell out of me. So I'm gonna fast forward to the time when everything changed. I met an extraordinary woman who took me to Peru, and introduced me to *ayahuasca*, the grandmother."

"So you've done that?" Ellen glanced at him. "I've only read about it, but I've always been afraid to try it because I don't want to throw up."

Hugo laughed. "The point is it cleanses your body and unblocks your emotions and your mind."

Ellen nodded, her eyes on the road.

"The shaman, Don Pablo, who conducted the *ayahuasca* ceremony, later married us in Machu Pichu, in the Temple of the Stars. For almost twenty years, we walked the *ayahuasca* path together."

"Where is she now, this extraordinary woman?" He pressed his lips together. "Dead--from cancer." "I'm sorry."

"I can tell you that remarkable transformation in your mother happened because my wife was working with me. A bond like that can never be broken. And I mean never. When I die, she will be waiting there to take me across."

"How can you be so sure?"

"Because she's told me."

A tollbooth came up and after they had gone through, Ellen said, "Tell me about that *ayahuasca* ceremony."

"Well, we went from Pucallpa upriver and into the jungle for about a two-hour walk to Don Pablo's camp. We all gathered at dusk around a huge tree whose roots rose up out of the earth. The tree trunk started five or six feet into the air, and the roots formed a sort of cave where Don Pablo had lived for six years, before building the camp."

"Who was 'we'?"

"A group of about twenty 'seekers' from all over, the U.S., Canada, Europe, and other places I've probably forgotten. I don't remember much about the ceremony. The medicine really knocked me on my ass except for one vision that I still see with absolute clarity: it was a massive, brownish wall, made of something like smooth cement, with several ledges. Each ledge was far apart and on them stood a number of figurines, motionless, dressed in capes and wide-brimmed hats of a dark color, presiding over the ceremony."

"Did they move? Did they do anything?"

"They projected such enormous power that it made everything else seem diminutive. As I was staring at them, Don Pablo, dressed in dazzling white, came out from behind his *mesa*. He was in his prime and danced with tremendous agility all around the circle like a magical elf. I remember thinking that if he can summon beings from the other world with such immense power, he must be a powerful guy himself."

"I'd love to do a ceremony around Don Pablo's tree."

"Too late. That camp was trashed by the Maoist rebels or drug runners."

Don Pablo then set up another camp outside Iquitos."

They were arriving at the outskirts of Brentwood and it was getting dark.

"We'll be at my mother's before long."

He nodded and continued, "The next morning, I noticed I wasn't quite so afraid. Every time I drank in a ceremony, the medicine wrenched more fear out of me."

"How much of the *ayahuasca* do you drink?"

"One cup. My body chemistry is very sensitive so it doesn't take much to send me off. Once, I asked the medicine to break through the rest of my fear. When it came into my body, it asked if I really wanted to do that. Part of me was tempted to say no, but I knew if I didn't do it then, I never would. So I said yes. The next minute I was jumping out of my skin and couldn't stay in one position for more than a few seconds. I ended up on the floor, blacked out for five hours."

"I came around, about five hours later, and realized I had wet my pants.

"I was feeling pretty sheepish. Before the ceremony, Don Pablo had given a little lecture about not lying down, so I assumed he would be disappointed in me. I'd been doing this for a long time by then and there I was, crawling around on the floor. After a while, he came over and sat beside me and asked if I remembered anything about the journey. I told him no. He put a hand on my knee and said, "You've got a lot of courage."

He must've seen the surprise on my face. 'Even though you're unconscious, you still have to go through it. Listen, almost anyone else would've been screaming at

the top of their lungs, but you kept it all contained. That
took a lot of guts.'"

"What about the fear?" Ellen asked.

"Vanished."

"So it was worth it. Would you do it again?" "I
don't have to."

***

They arrived and Ellen let herself in. "We're
here, Mom."

Beverly was waiting in the living room. Ellen made
the introductions and, when her mother took the hand
of the man who had saved her life, Ellen felt herself
moved to tears. Her mom had prepared tea and cookies
and Ellen went to get it in the kitchen, lingering a few
minutes, letting herself savor the moment.

Hugo was at his most charming and Ellen thought
that he must have been very close to his mother. Mom's
face glowed as they smiled and talked for two hours.
When her mother said she was tired, they settled her on
the sofa and left.

After starting the car, Ellen turned to Hugo and said,
"She's a new woman. I know I can never repay you, but
I'll never forget what you've done."

On the way back, Hugo described some of the other
ceremonies he had participated in and before Ellen
knew it, she was driving past the darkened buildings of the university. Of course, she had read many

accounts of *ayahuasca* journeys in articles and books and had always found them interesting, if rather repetitive. As valuable as they were to her work, the descriptions had always seemed dry, as if all the juice had been drawn out of them. Hearing it directly from the lips of someone who had lived it was an entirely different experience. Ellen was blown away.

When she dropped off Hugo, he leaned in the window. "I've saved the best for last, that is, if you're still interested."

"What do you think?"

"Call me in about a week."

Even though it was late, she sat in her car in the driveway for a long time, letting herself take it all in.

As she got ready for bed, everything he had said was still swirling around in her brain and she felt too excited to sleep. She lay in bed, remembering the magical moment when her mom held Hugo's hand. She must have been more tired than she thought, because, all of a sudden, the phone was ringing and it was the next morning.

# Chapter Six

"I'm sorry. Did I wake you?" Carl asked

"It's okay," Ellen said, trying to focus her thoughts.

"You have to come to the Henri Vervet concert tomorrow night." "You mean…?" Ellen asked, still a little foggy.

"Yes. *The* Henri Vervet. Not much time to publicize it but word will get around. André Henri, the tenor, is coming with him. They tour together all the time. They're an item. André has a terrific voice that Vervet knows like the back of his hand and he's written quite a number of settings of French poems for André to sing."

"I'm in."

Even on short notice, the auditorium was packed with several fairly illustrious figures from the Music School. Ellen had announced the concert in all her classes and was pleased to see a number of her students, including several from French Civ. She caught sight of Todd Shipton's blond hair as he leaned over to whisper something to the beauteous Anita. Ellen looked around for Hugo but didn't see him.

She was delighted to find that the program contained four of her favorite poems: *L'invitation au voyage, Le revenant, Correspondences* by Baudelaire; and *El Desdi-chado* by Nerval.

Generally speaking, Ellen was not a fan of poems set to music, because although the music could be quite beautiful, the poem was too often lost in it. But Vervet and his French lover had a unique approach to the genre. He assigned a minimalist role to the piano, to underscore the expressiveness of the poet's language. Thus allowing André, with his limpid tenor voice, to at once sing and recite the poems, bringing out the meaning, feeling and music of each word. Ellen let herself be carried away by the sensuality of the setting for *L'invitation au voyage*, the icy coolness of *Le revenant* and the stark simplicity of *El Desdichado*, which she considered one of the most extraordinary, most movingly indecipherable poems ever written. As Andre sang its opening quatrain...

*Je suis le Tenebreux, - le Veuf, - L'Inconsolé,*
*Le Prince d'Aquitaine à la tour abolie:*
*Ma seule Etoile est morte, - et mon luth constellé Porte le Soleil noir de la Mélancolie.*

...a teardrop ran down Ellen's cheek.

The concert was extremely well received and the enthusiastic audience kept clapping for an encore.

"I...we...never do encores," Vervet said with a rather heavy French accent, but the clapping continued. André was by the piano, drinking Diva water.

"I can't ask André to sing anymore...no, no, no...it's

too much. His voice can be fragile and there are other concerts to come."

The applause, if anything, grew louder.

Ellen leaned over and whispered to Carl, "Zees Americans so eemposseeble."

"So much like children," Carl whispered back.

Taking a step or two forward, Vervet insisted, "I don't know any encores. What shall I play?"

"How about your most recent piano piece?" Beveridge suggested. "That way there won't be any undue strain on André's voice."

Vervet shot him a furious glance, then seemed to change his mind. Raising one of his eyebrows, he shot a quick look at André, who gave a little shrug of his shoulders and a slight nod of his head and retreated to the side of the stage. Vervet sat down at the piano and, despite his reluctance, came up with a piece that was very light, full of charm and scintillating humor. The audience was delighted.

The concert was followed by the inevitable reception. Ellen finally spotted Hugo, standing a little apart, having some cheese and crackers with red wine.

"So you were there. I didn't see you."

"I was in the back," he said, as if that was an explanation.

"Did you meet Carl at the reception for Steadman?"

"I believe so."

"Did you like the concert?"

"Very much. I think I could make it on a desert island

with a copy of Baudelaire, you know, one of those with a facing translation. You probably wouldn't need that."

He never ceased to amaze her. "Baudelaire, my favorite poet," replied Ellen.

"He was an owl."

Ellen gave him a quizzical look.

"Owls know everything." Hugo said. "Well, I'm off. You'll call me?"

"I will," Ellen said.

The small crowd that had gathered around Vervet and his singer had gradually dispersed, leaving them alone with Beveridge, the rather pompous Chair of the Music Department. Carl and Ellen moved to within earshot.

"In literature the sound is in the poetry, in music the poetry is in the sound," Vervet said.

"Quite so." He brushed his hair back. "I'm so glad you relented about the encore," Beveridge said.

"You made me break one of my cardinal principles."

"And a good job that I did. I was very taken by that little piece. Absolutely brilliant. A little gem."

"I'm glad you liked it," Vervet said dryly, taking a sip of the not so dry champagne Beveridge had set out for the occasion.

"It's only Californian, I'm afraid," Beveridge said. "We don't have it in England, of course."

"Californian wines can be…" Vervet searched for the word. "Adequate."

"No substitute for French but on short notice," Beveridge said.

"It's…okay," André said, then muttered "barely" under his breath. Ellen smiled realizing they were having a bit of fun at the Brit's expense.

"What do zee Breeteesh know about *champagne*?" she whispered in Carl's ear.

"What can they know?" he whispered back.

"Anyway, I was quite taken with that little encore. What did you think, André?" Beveridge asked.

"It was…er…okay."

"I'd say it's much more than okay. When did you write it?" "Not long ago," Vervet said, not designing to be more precise. "Well, let me weigh in. I found it impressive how, at one point, you literally attacked the piano."

"Venting some spleen, I suppose. A la Baudelaire."

"Then it goes quiet, almost lyrical. So many different moods." "What have you called the piece?" "It doesn't have a name."

"Oh. I like that. Very mysterious."

"It reminds me of some of your Etudes. The 5th and the 7th, for example."

Vervet dismissed the idea. "Those were written years ago." "Quite." Beveridge emptied his glass, set it down on the tray of a passing student waiter, grabbed a full one and asked hopefully, "Was this perhaps a premier?"

"You could say that," Vervet said.

"Marvelous. Another coup for the university."

Beveridge rubbed his hands together. "Do you have any plans to record it?"

"I'm afraid that would be quite impossible, because it's done. It's come and gone. *Ce petit morceau n'existe plus.*"

"I'm afraid you've lost me."

"I made it up as I played it, and could never recreate it again," Vervet said.

Beveridge gulped. André, who had just knocked back a sip of champagne, burst out laughing, spraying champagne onto Beveridge's face, which had taken on a stunned expression.

"*Mes excuses.*"

Beveridge wiped his face with a handkerchief.

"You must forgive Henri," André said when he had stopped coughing. "He must have his little jokes."

"It was, how you say…improvised."

"Well, I must say, that's quite impressive. Improvised, you say, just like that. Extraordinary. Well, you sure had me…me fooled. A great loss, nonetheless."

Vervet gave a little wave of his hand, as if it were a trifle not worth bothering about, that he could knock off a dozen more at concerts when boors like Beveridge insisted he give encores.

"Such a pity it wasn't recorded," Beveridge repeated, shaking his head as he moved away.

Carl and Ellen drew nearer.

"I hate talking about my music, "Vervet said to them. "In any case, *bonsoir.*"

"*Bonsoir*, M. Vervet," Ellen answered, happy that it came out in her best accent. They shook hands. "*Je suis très content de faire votre connaissance.*"

"Ah! *Vous parlez français?*"

"*Bien sûr.*"

"She teaches it," Carl said.

"In my limited experience in your charming country, just because she teaches it, doesn't mean she speaks it."

"At the moment, I don't actually teach the language, just the literature."

"Ellen is writing a book on *Amazonia*, you know, by Gervin." "Carl, please, I'm sure Monsieur Vervet has other…"

"No, no, no. Of course I know it. It's one of my favorite novels. André, too. It's like a *Treasure Island* for our time. A great adventure. I'm sure Stevenson would have held it in high esteem. I've read it several times and I almost never do that."

"At this point, I'm not sure how many times I've read it," she said, laughing.

André, who had been noisily blowing champagne out of his sinuses, joined them. "Have you been to Peru?" "No, I haven't."

"You really should. We have a concert coming up in Lima in the winter…well, summer down there," André said.

Instead of making excuses, Ellen surprised herself by

saying, "I think I'll be going soon. Who knows, maybe this summer."

Vervet turned to Carl. "And you, you speak French also?" "No, just Spanish. And not all that well."

"Carl teaches composition. He's our composer in residence." "Really? Would I know your work?" Vervet asked.

"No, I'm here on a grant for young composers. I've written quite a few pieces for the piano and some small chamber works. This is meant to give me a chance to produce something bigger."

"Carl is working on a symphony," Ellen said.

"Very ambitious, which is why I don't write symphonies. What is your approach to composing? What you are hoping your symphony to be?" André looked at his friend, startled by the question.

"I want it to put he audience into another world, like an *ayahuasca* journey does. I've been doing some research on Pico della Mirandola and his theories about how music should put the listener into a trance. The musicians of the Pléiade believed that and tried it at certain public events. History doesn't tell us if it worked. I guess we'll never know. I think some of the modern French composers have tried to do it, too. Like Jolivet and Sauguet."

As Carl was talking, Vervet and André exchanged glances.

"This is all very interesting, young man. I would like

to hear some of your music. Too bad our stay is so short and we leave tomorrow afternoon."

"Well, there's the morning," Ellen said.

"Hmm. I usually give myself the luxury of sleeping in after a concert, but in this case…"

"I'll make breakfast," Carl said.

"Oh? Nothing elaborate, please. Just some croissants and espresso. No weak, watery American coffee if we are to rise early. And you must come, too, *Mademoiselle Amazonia*. Unless, of course you will be there already," said Vervet.

"No. We're just very good friends. I'll pick the croissants up on the way over."

***

The next morning was sunny and crisp and Ellen was happy to have the walk to Carl's. He had a cozy little apartment on the first floor of a house in a quiet neighborhood. His upstairs neighbor, an Asian woman, was seldom seen or heard. The Frenchmen were already there, regaling their host with tales of concert touring that continued over coffee and croissants.

"You should have seen Henri in Cambridge at Harvard," André said, leaving the "h" silent. "There was a man in the first row, who went to sleep. He wasn't snoring. How did you even notice him, Henri?"

"I was outraged, it's as simple as that," Vervet said.

"So for the rest of the concert, Henri was banging on

the keys, using the piano like a percussion instrument, like Bartok did."

"It is a percussion instrument," Vervet said.

"Yes, but you do not use it like that in your songs. I had to sing twice as loud. My poor voice was almost ruined."

"But it didn't matter how hard I pounded, the man never woke up."

"Henri was furious. He left the stage without a bow."

"I was ready to slap him across the face with my glove. *"A cinq heures et demie devant l'église, monsieur."*

When the time came for Carl to play some of his music, there was no such banging. He had a grand piano that occupied the greater part of the living room. His elegant cat Taisha, a longhaired Persian, appeared as she always did whenever he sat down at the piano bench. When he played some selections from his *Images*, the sound of the soft notes seemed to somehow explode into the most delicate harmonies, as if he were ringing fragile, miniature bells. He had played them before for Ellen, but this time, even though she could tell he was nervous, he nonetheless managed to take the pieces to an entirely new richness of sonority, as if he heard things other people didn't.

The Frenchmen listened with great attentiveness. When Carl was finished, he put his head down. Everyone clapped, of course, but that would happen, regardless of their opinion of the compositions. Taisha jumped up onto the piano and began preening herself.

"Such a beautiful cat," André said.

Vervet remained silent a little longer. When he spoke, it was with unusual seriousness. "I never comment on the work of another composer. I know how hard it is to create something worthy of the effort."

He paused. Carl looked up.

"I will just say this: you are a very gifted young man. I sensed that last night. Whoever gave you this fellowship…"

"The Ardenburg Foundation."

"…was quite right to do so. I cannot think of a more deserving recipient."

"Thank you."

"No, no. It is for me to thank you."

"I'll tell you that no one was more surprised than me yesterday, when Henri agreed to hear some of your works. He never does that," André said.

"I don't know what to say. My symphony is progressing but I still have plenty of work to do. I'm planning three movements and am only into the second. I haven't figured out how to end it yet."

"That can be hard. Ravel couldn't figure out how to finish *Daphnis et Chloé*. It was driving him crazy, until he went to a rehearsal of *Le sacre du printemps* and there he found his ending. If you listen to the two works again, you'll see what I mean."

As they were leaving, Henri said, "I hope the grant includes a performance."

"It does. In the spring."

"Let us know. Maybe we can attend. I mean that seriously," Vervet said.

As soon as the door closed, Carl collapsed in Ellen's arms. "I didn't get much sleep last night. I was shaking like a leaf. Sweating bullets. I hope it wasn't too obvious."

"No one could tell. You brought your A game and I'm really proud of you! So is Taisha."

# Chapter Seven

It was after 7 o'clock in the evening and the auditorium, usually dark and deserted at this hour, was packed, not a seat left in the house.

Ellen had gone with Stelios and Val to see a movie on campus. They had come early to be sure to get a good seat. Ellen seldom went to films ordered by the student entertainment committee, since they tended to be standard Hollywood stuff, but tonight was different.

Someone on the committee had gotten wind of the Japanese movie, *In the Realm of the Senses*, which tells the real life story of a woman who becomes so obsessed with her lover that she ends up killing him as they have sex, cutting off his penis and wandering around her city completely disoriented for days, carrying it in her pocket.

Todd and Anita were sitting a couple of rows in front. Ellen wondered when, if ever, he studied. He was often in the library with Anita, who seemed hard at work, while Todd would be doodling or reading, but not necessarily the masterpieces of French literature. His French was above average, although it was a mystery where he had acquired it. Certainly not in the Bonzai Pipeline.

The back quarter of the hall had been turned into an

almost exclusively male preserve. It appeared that many of the frats had emptied out and a fair number of athletes had come, although none that Ellen recognized from her French Civ. class.

A kind of a tense buzz of pent-up energy filled the hall. Suddenly, Roy made an unexpected appearance on the stage.

"What the hell is he doing here?" Stelios asked.

Perhaps it was the whiteness of the screen Roy was standing in front of, but his face seemed unusually red. Looking ill at ease, he asked for quiet. He got some and forged ahead.

"I want to make clear that the Foreign Languages Department had nothing to do with bringing this movie on campus," he said.

Roy did not command the same respect from a bunch of frat boys that he routinely demanded from faculty in his department.

He was greeted by jeers.

"Who cares?"

"Who gives a flying fuck?"

"Get lost!"

"Give'im the hook!"

"We want the movie!"

"What in God's name was that?" Val said.

"Pretty embarrassing," Ellen said.

Undaunted, if a little more red-faced, Roy pressed ahead with a rerun of his statement. "The Foreign

Language Department did not, I repeat, did not, have any part in ordering this film or bringing this movie on campus."

This time his reception was even more unkind. He was roundly booed. Stelios burst out laughing.

"You think that's funny?" Val asked through clenched teeth.

Laughing even harder, "Yes."

Val was seething. "The hypocritical mother-fucker! Too bad we didn't bring any eggs to throw at him."

Someone in the back with a very loud voice yelled, "Get off the stage, Fatso."

Roy saw that there was nothing for it but to retreat ignominiously back into the wings.

By the time the lights went out, the testosteronic energy in the room was nearing a fever pitch.

The movie gets right down to it, starting in a brothel, where the appearance of women on the screen caused the air to be filled with catcalls, wolf-whistles and cries of "Hubba-hubba!"

Cries of "Please be quiet," and "Shh!" were of no avail.

However, once it sunk in to those in the back that all the women were Japanese, weren't blond and didn't display big boobs and asses at every opportunity, things gradually calmed down, only to erupt again anytime the two lovers went at it in bed, which was quite often.

After the movie, Val and Ellen went for a beer. Stelios went elsewhere, he and Val barely saying goodbye.

"Anything going on?"

Val didn't answer right away. "Pretty obvious, isn't it?"

"Want to talk about it?"

Val paused before she answered. "No. Not tonight. Some other time, maybe. Or he can tell you, if he feels like it."

The Wild Bore was crowded as usual and they were lucky to find a table.

"That was amazing," Val said, as they waited for their beers. "All they did in that movie was screw for weeks, months, years. How long was it?"

"Very long."

"Maybe tonight I'll fantasize about having a relationship like that with Masasato. Except I don't think he's the type."

The waitress came and set their beers down. Val drank about half her pint down. "Wow, guess I was thirsty. Must've been the movie. Speaking of Masasato, I've got something to show you." She fished around in her purse, pulled out a sheet of paper and, with a mischievous look on her face, handed it to Ellen.

"What's this?"

"Just a little haiku I came up with today in an idle moment. I thought you might like it."

Ellen read it a couple of times:

For ecstasy, computer much, much better.

Easy to turn on and user friendly

Mmm...never have headache.

"Uh…not bad."

"No, no. It's just a goof. Thought I'd show it to Masasato." Ellen threw her a questioning look. "See if he gets it."

"Oh, I think he'll get it, all right."

"Yeah, but will he laugh?"

Chad appeared out of the crowd with half a glass of beer in his hand and sat down.

"Can't stay but a minute but you gotta hear this." "What now?"

"Foxwhistle." He took a hit of beer. "You know I'm taking his seminar on Molière."

"Lucky you. I mean it. That must be just about as good as it gets." "Lucky, yes, probably nobody knows Molière like him and let's just say his lectures have yet to disappoint. Anyway, last week we were doing *Les femmes savantes* and he delivered an absolutely brilliant lecture. No notes, just shooting from the hip. When it was finished, he didn't take any questions, just got up and left and we all sat there without saying anything, mesmerized, until some-body said, "Wow!"" "I wish I'd heard it," Ellen said. "Was it in English or French?" "Foxwhistle seldom favors us with his French, except when he gets really pissed off. Anyway, here's the kicker. Today he came in and it was pretty obvious he'd had quite a bit more to drink than usual. He wasn't staggering around or anything but… guess what? He gave the same damn lecture on *Les femmes savantes* and the amazing thing is he gave it pretty much word for word. It's not like he had it memorized or anything. But no notes, no nothing."

"Well, he wouldn't have been able to read them anyway," Val said. "During the whole class, he had a cigarette dangling in his mouth and a lighter in one hand. Every once in a while, he'd make as if to light it, but then get distracted. We were all on the edge of our seats, hoping he wouldn't or his breath would ignite." "And nobody said anything?"

"Who's going to say anything? Who's going to inter-rupt such an amazing tour de force? Sure as hell not me. Something like that only happens once in a lifetime, and it was just as fascinating the second time around. You heard stuff you didn't get the first time." He finished his beer and stood up. "Okay, gotta run. Gotta get up for yoga tomorrow. You're not coming to yoga, I suppose?"

"Maybe," Ellen answered.

They watched him head out the door. "Only Foxwhistle could do that and get away with it."

"Yeah," Ellen agreed. She caught sight of Masasato in the crowd at the bar. Val did not seem to notice him.

For a little while, they were silent.

"I think we need more beers," Val said.

To her surprise, Ellen agreed. Val quickly signaled the waitress.

"How's your mother?"

"She's doing fine."

"How's the work on your book going?"

Ellen took in a big breath. "You want the truth?"

Val nodded.

"It's not."

"I thought you were going to be finished by spring." "So did I. Doesn't look that way now." "What's wrong, some flaw in your research?

"No, nothing like that." The beers came and this time it was Ellen who took a big pull. "Something's happening to me, Val. You know how I used to love to hole up in my carrel and lose track of the hours, getting lost in my work?"

Val nodded.

"Not anymore. I never go there."

"Never?"

"The truth is I haven't been up there since the Dalí/ Lorca lecture."

"Wow, that's not like you."

"Part of it was my mother getting sick. She's okay now but I just can't bring myself to go up there again."

"Don't worry, it'll pass."

"That's what I thought at first but now I don't think so."

"I'm sure you could get it published."

"I agree."

Val's hand tightened around her glass. "Is it Roy? Has that son-of-a-bitch been harassing you again?"

"Well, yeah, he has. He's been hitting on me since I got here, and it's just been getting worse. He keeps putting pressure on me to go to the MLA convention. I kept putting him off, using my mother as an excuse, but now that she's doing well…"

"He thinks if he can get you there, he'll steer you into his hotel room. God dammit, somebody ought to…"

"He's putting a full court press on me. He's even got me a slot to give a paper in a section run by his friend Gwendolyn."

Val gave a low whistle. "Now you're really talkin' A-list. How would a guy like him get to know a biggie like her?"

"I don't know but she called to invite me onto her program. When I didn't jump onboard, she even did a little arm-twisting."

"What did she say?"

"Oh, the usual stuff: great opportunity, don't take too long to decide, others dying to get into the section, something like this usually leads to other things. She hinted at my paper being included in a critical anthology she's putting together."

"Jesus! That by itself would just about get you tenure." Val thought for a moment. "I don't get it. Why would she…?"

"I have my theory."

"You don't think…?"

"Yeah. Strange as it sounds, I think she and Roy had a fling a while ago and they've remained buddies. I know it sounds unlikely but maybe in his youth Roy wasn't so unattractive."

"Well, he's unattractive now," Val said, rolling her napkin into a tight ball. "Have you accepted?"

"No, but I probably will. I don't want to make an enemy out of her. I'm not quite ready to burn all my bridges but I'm getting there. On the surface, she's extremely nice, helpful, claims to be interested in my work, even to have read my diss."

"Well, maybe she is, but boy, he's really maneuvered you into a corner."

"He's expert at that. Lots of practice, I suppose." She sipped some beer. "All that aside, what it really comes down to is that doing research just isn't enough anymore. I don't want to analyze the adventures Yves had in *Amazonia*. I want to have them myself."

"Go to the rainforest?"

"I know it's a terrible job market and I should be happy having a job. But before at the movie, when those guys in the back were yelling, 'Hubba, hubba!' and making wolf whistles, I was sitting there thinking, "What am I doing here? What am I doing with my life? I'm almost 30 years old. And the students, well, most of them don't even care about learning. Don't get me wrong. I still enjoy teaching, and have some great students."

"Everybody needs to take a break sometimes. Stelios mentioned you'd been going to the soccer games."

"The games are fun. I sit with the Indonesian women who bring great food, and I'm picking up a little Indonesian. And…"

"Yeah?"

"One of the players is interesting too."

"Oh?" said Val. "Who?"

"Laxman."

"I've seen him. I know who he is," Val nodded. "Tall, lithe, commanding presence on the field. I wouldn't mind getting my hands on him."

"I don't really know him. Sure we've talked a little bit after the game, but I can't stop thinking about him."

"He's not a bad-looking guy. So you're hot for him?"

"He has the air of someone who's done unusual things, maybe legal, maybe not. He's been on the sea and looks kind of weathered. I get the feeling his life hasn't been easy but he's come through it strong."

"So what are you gonna do?"

"I don't know. This isn't like me. He's married and I know his wife. She comes to the games and I like her and their sweet little boy."

"Yeah, I've seen the little guy. Are you gonna make a move? Soccer season ends soon."

"I haven't decided."

Val finished her beer. "Well, I have some news you might like to hear."

"What's that?"

"He's coming to Stelios's birthday party."

"Really?"

"He asked to."

# Chapter Eight

After a week of anticipation, Ellen called Hugo to meet again at Java Hut; instead she received an invitation to his home that Friday afternoon.

Although sparsely furnished and comfortable enough, his apartment was the kind of place that could be easily abandoned at a moment's notice. Shamanic implements rested on the tables and walls, rattles with bright red feathers at the top, several drums of different sizes, brightly colored fans made from blue, yellow, green and red macaw feathers, elaborately carved pipes, crafted from light or dark brown hardwood and shaped into owls, snakes and the heads of figures from the spirit world. One pipe bowl consisted entirely of a coiled serpent. On the walls hung a headdress made of soft, red feathers, and many beaded necklaces.

"The beads are little pods and berries that drop off the trees and bushes."

"Mementos from the rainforest, I presume."
"Pretty much."

He also had two paintings. One had an enormous full moon in the center and buildings all around the edge of the canvas, making a rectangular frame around the moon that stood out, stark white against a black sky. The building's thatched roofs pointed toward the moon no matter where they were located. They were set at odd angles, as if they might be floating in the air. A large structure dominated the lower right corner.

The moon was split evenly in two on a diagonal. Coming off the ground at the bottom of the painting, a wooden ladder narrowed as it got higher, where it rested on the bottom of the moon. A nude woman perched on the third rung from the top, facing the moon. In her right hand she held a needle and thread and was sewing together the two halves of the moon.

Ellen had no idea how long she had gazed into the painting before Hugo, who had gone to fetch a pot of tea, came up beside her. Pointing at the large building in the lower right hand corner, he said, "That's the iron building in Iquitos and about halfway up on the right that's the steeple of the church in the Plaza des Armas. They're still standing. The iron building was invented by Gustave Eiffel, the same guy who built the Eiffel Tower. But you know that."

Ellen nodded, still lost in the painting.

"It was designed as a modular structure to provide indestructible housing for representatives of the French Government who were often sent to some inhospitable climes in various outposts of the empire. The structures were shipped in pieces, to be assembled on site in Indo-China, French Guyana and places like that. Two full floors served as both office and residence. All very practical."

"What was it doing in Iquitos? As far as I know, the French never colonized the Amazon," Ellen said.

"No, but anybody could buy these. During the rubber boom Iquitos went from being a tiny outstation on the Amazon to an incredibly prosperous city. It had an opera house where Sarah Bernhardt performed. Fitzcarraldo passed through. The Iquitos rubber barons were so wealthy they shopped in Europe and sent their kids to Madrid, Paris and London to be educated. One of the rubber barons saw the iron house at a Paris exposition, bought one, and it's still in great shape today. Pretty much indestructible."

"I like this one very much," said Ellen, moving over to other painting. "Is this what I think it is?"

"Yes, it's an *ayahuasca* vision."

The dazzling portrait of a woman with reddish brown skin, dark, expressionless eyes, deep red lips, and white teeth, stared back at her. Ellen found her beauty to be not exactly human. She wore a headdress of macaw feathers, red, yellow, green and blue and leaves of all different shades of green surrounded her. To her right, a green snake with white horizontal lines hung from a branch. In the lower left corner, a blue and white bird with a long black beak had taken up residence in the hollow of a dead tree trunk. In the upper left, stood an egret. In the lower right, a black and yellow frog sat on a bright red flower, shaped like an open oyster shell.

Ellen looked at the painting for some minutes before saying, "Well, aren't you just full of surprises today?"

"Why do you say that?"

"Because I'm almost certain I've seen her before. I've been having dreams about the rainforest and she's in them. I always see her from far away, running through the jungle, swimming in a lagoon or climbing a tree like a monkey, so I've never seen her face clearly."

"I told you the rainforest is calling you."

"Yes, it is, but it's more than that. *She's* calling me. And, even more, it's almost like she is me, or some part of me. Does that sound crazy?"

He smiled and shrugged. "Not to me. Anyway, there are no coincidences."

Ellen's eyes lingered on the woman's eyes, trying to see into them, to find an answer there. But she wasn't sure of the question.

He poured the tea. They sat cross-legged on the floor on pillows. "Okay, time for the rest of my story."

He took a big gulp of tea and lit a candle. If you get hungry, let me know."

He settled back down again. All the jungle paraphernalia, the drums, the rattles, the pipes, the necklaces, made the room like a cozy little jungle enclave in the dim candlelight. He refilled their cups.

"Now I'll tell you 'The Tale of the Wandering Irishman.'" "Not the legend?"

He laughed. "No, this actually happened. It all started one night, deep into a ceremony, when I realized I needed to pee. I roused myself, stood, put on my boots, and with an unsteady step, went into the underbrush. Now, *ayahuasca*, in addition to making you throw up, can also give you diarrhea. Although this rarely happens to me, no time for a dash to the outhouse, I just squatted down on my haunches. In the process of standing and pulling up my trousers, I stepped in my shit, so I decided to walk around in hopes of getting most of it off my boots. I probably succeeded but also went further into the jungle than I realized. The medicine can be very disorienting and I had no idea how to get back to the temple. Anyway, while trying to find my way back to the ceremony, I drifted deeper into the forest and got myself hopelessly lost."

"Did you call for help?"

"Yes, but by that time, I had wandered too far afield. Nobody came. Later, I found out several search parties were dispatched but finding someone in the jungle is just a matter of luck."

"You must have been pretty scared."

"Well, I wasn't. You see, the forest that night was very different. It was luminous. The light was soft, a kind of transparent greenish-grey, as if illuminated by the moon. The trees were not close together and had long thin trunks, with no branches, except at the top. There was very little in the way of ground cover. Quite deserted, otherworldly and strangely welcoming. I had never seen anything remotely resembling this. It drew me in effortlessly and I ventured forward without the slightest feeling of resistance. Then, after this luminous world had taken me into her embrace I began to hear the forest sirens singing to me. Sometimes seductively without words, other times: 'Hugo! Hugo! We want you! We want you! We want you!' When they sang, it was almost irresistible, like what you've always yearned for, women who full out desire you, no questions asked, calling you in the most sonorous, ethereal otherworldly voices, at the same time dripping with sensuality and lust. 'Come to us! Come to us! We love you! We're waiting for you….'

"I felt they would take me in and permeate me with a love so soft it would soak away a lifetime of cares. The sound of the few leaves in the wind and everything around me was infused with a soft, damp, powerful sexual charge. And the idea of being so completely desirable and desired was overwhelming. 'Come to us, Hugo! Follow the sound of our singing and we will give you everything you have ever wanted…and so, so much more.'

"It was all incredibly seductive. My blood, every fiber of my being was on fire. But Don Pablo had warned me about the sirens. 'If you hear the sirens calling, never answer them.' I asked him what would happen if I did answer them. 'You don't answer them,' he'd replied."

"So what did you do?" Ellen asked.

"I crouched down behind a tree and closed my ears with the tips of my index fingers. They didn't give up easily but I stayed where I was, huddled in the obscurity. It wasn't like I was hidden. They knew where I was, hunkered down for God knows how long, assailed by seductive murmurings, lured by thoughts of irresistible caresses and the most seductive songs in the universe. But even their persistence had its limits and suddenly I was enveloped by the sweet sound of silence."

"If you had gone to them, what would've happened?"

"I'll never know. But one thing I can say with absolute certainty:

I would never have come back."

A car horn honked on the street outside.

"By then morning was beginning to break. I started walking down the path I had been on, a simple forest trail, indistinguishable from the maze of others that crisscrossed all through the jungle. Having been stripped of all sense of direction, I had absolutely no idea of where I was but sensed somehow that it was okay. I had become lost in a dark forest."

"You wouldn't be the first one. Dante did and he came out okay." Hugo smiled. "I wandered, inconsolable, around the forest for who knows how long, until early one morning, when the leaves and the earth were still moist with dew and you could still see large spider webs between the trees, illuminated by the sun's horizontal rays, I caught sight of something on the path some distance in front of me, veiled in mist.

"I could see that it wasn't very tall. I thought it might be a tapir or an anteater or something of that sort, and I assumed it would scurry off into the underbrush. As I drew closer, I began to make out the body of a little girl who stood without moving, as if she were waiting for me. When I got fairly near, I half expected her to bolt away. Instead, she stood her ground, not in the least alarmed, her dark eyes watching me, her brown face impassive, her black hair catching a ray of sunlight.

"Hello," I said.

She stared at me for a moment and then asked, "Can I borrow an egg?"

"An egg? I don't have an egg."

"Yes, you do," she said, looking me in the eyes with the pouty indignation of a little girl having caught someone in a lie.

"I'm sorry, I don't," I said.

"You're not sorry! You do! Look in your pocket."

I was astonished to feel my fingers close around an egg that certainly hadn't been there before. I took it out gingerly it and handed it to her. Her face broke into a broad smile.

"You see!" she said, "Now I can have breakfast. Take

that path," she said, pointing to a little trail I hadn't noticed that went off to the left and she ran away.

Hugo sipped his tea.

"What was that about?" Ellen asked.

"I don't know, but it was a game changer."

\*\*\*

"It took days to find my way out of the forest. I always made sure I had enough water and monitored my urine to make sure it never became dark.

"I was beginning to lose hope of getting back to civilization and had begun to think I might be another of the many gringos who penetrate so deeply into the rainforest that it engulfs them forever.

"My pouch was growing heavier by the hour, but I was determined not to abandon it. I was feeling particularly forlorn and desperate when I, bursting though some underbrush, suddenly found myself in a small clearing, face to face with a young woman.

"I can't imagine what I must have looked like to her—some kind of appalling apparition with long and tangled hair, a full beard, and dressed in filthy, tattered clothes. My eyes were probably wild and bloodshot.

"If she found me threatening, she gave no indication. In fact, it was impossible to tell what, if anything, she thought of this wild creature who had suddenly burst from the underbrush. She must have heard me coming. It had become impossible for me to move surreptitiously, since the path I was on had disappeared. She could have ducked into the forest yet there she stood, showing not the lightest alarm. On the contrary, she welcomed me with the most breathtaking smile. I literally felt my breathing, which had grown rather labored, come to a halt.

"She had light brown skin, jet black hair, cropped so that it fell over her forehead, and brilliant white teeth. She was wearing nothing on her upper body. Her breasts, although rather small, were firm. At her waist were two squares of dark fabric, one in front and the other in back, suspended from a cord. She was sitting on a rock, in a shaft of sunlight beside a spring that flowed from some small boulders.

"Despite my exhaustion, I felt my penis grow hard, but wasn't berserk enough to wrap my arms around her, sink her to the ground, cover her astonishing body with kisses and take her. Even in my half-crazed state, I knew, despite how incredibly captivating she was, this encounter had nothing to with sex and if I acted on my almost overwhelming urge, the spring would dry up and I would be committing an act for which there was no rehabilitation, no absolution, that the Furies would be unleashed upon me for the rest of my days and I would come to know the true meaning of the word transgression and its consequences.

"So I stood still, transfixed by her smile, and felt my breathing start again. Then I realized, to my chagrin, that my erection, still rock-hard, had pushed itself through a hole in my pants. Although it would have been difficult for her not to have noticed it, she gave it no importance.

"Reaching down, she picked up a half gourd, filled it with water and held it out to me with the most warm, welcoming, friendly and lovely smile, saying a word in her native language that doubtless meant 'drink.'

"I had worked up a powerful thirst crashing through the jungle and my mouth was parched. Closing my eyes, I brought the gourd greedily to my lips and gulped in a mouthful. The water tasted clear, cool, pure and delicious. I drank it all. It was as if all women, the great mother even, had poured the essence of femininity into me and I could feel it finding its way into every cell. I suddenly felt all my longing and seeking was over. Exhausted, lost in the jungle, a profound sense of contentment stole over me. I left my eyes closed for a while to appreciate it all. When I opened them, the little clearing, the shaft of sunlight and the little spring were there, but she was gone.

\*\*\*

Outside, darkness had fallen and the street lights were on. Hugo got up and stretched. "Well, I've been talking for quite some time. What do you think?"

Ellen didn't answer or move right away.

"I felt like I was listening with my eyes wide and my

jaw dropped." He took the last sip of his cold tea and thought for a moment. "I probably should add one thing."

"Yes?"

"Ever since, I've been unable to love a mortal woman."

"Not even me?"

He smiled.

"Just kidding."

"Not even you." He got up and went over to the window. "So there it is. That's what I've done. Everything I am now I owe to *ayahuasca*. What about you? Do you want to step on that path?" Hugo faced her. "Those were my experiences, yours will be different. Just a word of caution, when you lift the veil between the worlds, anything can come through anytime. Whenever you go into the unknown, you never know what's going to happen, and it's not always good. We have no control over the spirit world."

Taking a deep breath, Ellen said, "I understand." "So?"

Without hesitation, Ellen answered, "I'm ready."

# Chapter Nine

The Faculty Club was a gloomy place full of dark hardwood walls, floors, tables, chairs, doors and, of course, the bar. Ellen never went there but this afternoon she made an exception since Foxwhistle, who was a regular, had invited her for a drink.

He was waiting for her when she got there around 5:30, a bourbon and water in front of him. He stood and pulled out a chair for her.

"I've got just one thing to say: *explication de texte*. I could never get the hang of it but you're a pro, brilliant on Seneca and Guez de Balzac. Just what I was hoping for. I can't thank you enough, except maybe to ply you with bourbon, if that's what you drink."

"How's the white wine here?"

"I wouldn't know."

"Let's find out."

As he was ordering, Ellen looked around and was surprised to see Todd sitting at another table, talking casually with, of all people, Pierre Jeanaud. Ellen wondered whether Jeanaud had reached out to Todd, as a defensive move to diffuse an extremely embarrassing situation; or if Todd, with his instinctive grasp of how academic politics are played, had taken the initiative to smooth things over. And why not? Although Ellen didn't particularly like Jeanaud, he wasn't a bad guy. Anita was there as well, looking, if possible, even more mysterious and ravishing in the half-light. She seemed to be drinking some kind of awful-looking, grayish mixed drink. Todd had a beer and Jeanaud a glass of red wine.

Ellen kept fiddling with her glass.

"How's your mother?" Foxwhistle asked.

"She's doing amazingly well, thanks. The operation was a great success."

"Glad to hear it."

"And how are you?"

Ellen realized that he actually wanted to know.

"Well..." she hesitated.

"Go ahead. I see something's bothering you and if it's not your mother..."

She took a deep breath. "Okay, it's Roy." "I shoulda known."

She took a sip of her white wine. It was, as André would say, okay. "You know, when I came here for the interview and read my paper, Roy seemed to like my work. I was flattered. That's how dumb I was. But since I've gotten here..."

"Yeah?"

"He just keeps hitting on me any chance he gets, and he makes sure he gets a lot of them."

Foxwhistle slammed his palm down on the table,

which was solid, so it withstood the blow without spilling any of their drinks. "Goddarnit, I knew it. I knew there was something."

Anita and Jeanaud looked over in alarm. Todd settled back and reached for his beer.

"He's been pressuring me to go to the MLA convention. He thinks it will be easier there to maneuver me into his hotel room."

"Damn him." Foxwhistle gulped down the rest of his whisky. "I should have it out with him."

"No, don't do that."

"Shoulda done it a long time ago. Right in the department corridor. Just yell at 'im, 'Come out from behind that desk you're hidin' behind, you sidewinder. I'm callin' you out, so we settle this once and for all, *mano a mano.*'"

Todd, Anita and Jeanaud grinned at each other... "He'd never come out,"

Foxwhistle slumped back in his chair. "That's just it."

"You know, I'll never figure that guy out. He's such a tyrant in the department."

"Like to save postage, he won't let us send any mail out unless the secretary reads it and decides it's departmental business. I never heard of such a thing. It's humiliating."

"It's his way of sucking up to the dean by keeping the department budget low. He took hold of his drink but didn't lift it up. "Anyway, he may be a tyrant in the department but he sure isn't at home, where I hear he gets pushed around."

Ellen finished her wine and Foxwhistle signaled the ever-attentive waiter to bring another round.

"So. Are you going to New York for the convention?" Foxwhistle asked.

"I don't want to go but he's manipulated me into a corner. He arranged for me to give a paper in a session chaired by Gwendolyn Stinton."

"Gwendolyn, eh?"

"I suspect they once had a thing going."

The waiter brought their drinks.

"As much as I am in favor of free love, the idea of those two making it together is not an image I care to spend any time with," Foxwhistle said.

"You can see it would be difficult to refuse," Ellen said.

"But not impossible."

"She's already called me once." Ellen sipped her wine. "I used to think I'd be happy teaching when I had a job in a reasonably good place..."

"There are worse."

"...get tenure. Write a few books. Teach some interesting courses. Now I don't know."

"It's kind of a weird way to make a living," he said finishing his drink.

"You seem to do okay with it."

"Where else could I get paid a pretty decent salary and get away with being the way I am? Speaking of which, I've got to go teach a seminar now."

Ellen was startled. Not knowing his schedule, she'd

assumed he'd just be heading home. She'd wondered how long he'd been there and how many he'd had.

"If you just get me in front of the library, I can take it from there." Ellen felt apprehensive at the idea of abandoning him at the library steps but didn't see what else she could do. Outside, it was already dark. A few scattered snowflakes were falling, an early warning of winter's approach. When they reached the entrance, the library's lights were ablaze.

"You okay? You want me to come with you up to the classroom?" "I'm fine, thanks. Don't worry."

He turned on his heel, climbed the stairs and disappeared into the revolving door, only to be unceremoniously expelled back outside with an abruptness bordering on impertinence. Snowflakes fell upon his slightly numbed, craggy visage and he exhaled plumes of frigid air into the unfriendly coldness of the night. There he stood, looking bewildered for a few moments. Then, with singular determination, he returned once more into the breach. This time he was subsumed into the quiet, scholarly fastness of the building, where, despite Ellen's apprehension, he presumably managed to negotiate his way to the 7th floor, where he delivered teachings of sufficient quality for the required several hours to ward off any complaints to higher authorities and to ensure that the class would gather together at the same hour in the same place the following week, as was the custom at that time in higher education.

# Chapter Ten

Two weeks later Ellen accepted an invitation to Hugo's apartment around seven on Saturday for her first experience taking *ayahuasca*. On the one hand, she couldn't wait for the time to pass, on the other, as the weekend drew near, she grew more and more anxious.

Hugo had instructed her to avoid certain foods during the week before: red meat, pork, citrus fruit, tomatoes, walnuts, sugar, spices and salt, cold drinks, dairy products, alcohol, beans, vinegar, sauerkraut, pickles, anything fermented, protein and vitamin supplements, a regimen easy enough to follow, although she began to feel weaker as the day approached.

On Saturday, having slept later than usual, she found herself at loose ends. After puttering around her apartment for a while, she ate a muffin for lunch and went to see some of the soccer game, one of the last for the season.

She sat, as usual, with the women, who kept trying to get her to eat some of the savory dishes spread out on a tablecloth. Her excuses were not very convincing and they were a little offended, but she couldn't do much about it.

To be honest, these days she really came to watch

Laxman, whose little boy had taken a shine to her and always sat next to her. It was a close game. Chad scored on a feed from Jorge. Chad was quick and could accelerate really fast, had exceptional balance, and an uncanny sense of how to put himself in scoring position. As usual, Stelios made some stellar saves and at halftime the score stood at 1-0. During the second half, the other team began putting more and more pressure on the Indonesians on the back line, but they—particularly Laxman—were up to it. He seemed to have a knack of stripping the ball off attacking forwards, particularly their best scorer.

Oetomo watched his father's every move with excitement yelling and grabbing onto Ellen every time his father made a clutch play.

"Your Dad's good, isn't he?"

"The best!" Oetomo answered. Ellen herself found it increasingly difficult to take her eyes off Laxman and hoped it wasn't becoming too obvious to the rest of the women, especially to his wife.

The game ended with the score still 1-0.

Ellen said goodbye to Gema.

"Are you sure you won't take something home with you? You didn't eat anything?" Gema asked.

"No, thanks. I'm not going home now and am on kind of a diet. No spicy foods."

Gema looked puzzled.

"It's just for this week. Next time."

"Okay," Gema said, smiling. Ellen was relieved not

to feel any tension in the air. Maybe everyone was too elated at pulling the game out, and most of the players, Chad, Jorge and even Laxman, were pretty done in.

*\*\**

   By the time she got to Hugo's front door, she was fairly nervous, and once inside, she blurted that out.

   "Don't worry. It's normal. In fact, I'd be surprised if you weren't," he said, leading her into the living room. He motioned her to take a seat on one of the pillows on the floor, facing each other, the one that had a red plastic bucket, a box of Kleenex and a little bottle of spring water next to it. He smiled as he took his seat opposite her. "Look, every time I take *ayahuasca*, as the moment approaches, I always get restless and uneasy and start asking why I keep doing this to myself. Of course, I know why, and although it does get easier the more you do it, for most people there are always butterflies beforehand."

   The room was warm, even cozy. All the shades were drawn and the only light came from a few candles. Around his seat, he had various shamanic tools spread out: his pipe, his drum, his rattle, feathers from different birds, some brightly hued, others grey and brown, depending on the need for camouflage in the jungle. He was wearing some simple bead necklaces and bracelets with bright red feathers around his wrists.

   Beside him was a bottle about half-full of a dark

liquid, the *ayahuasca*. Just seeing it jacked the fear quotient up a few notches.

He looked at her for a moment and said, "It's not too late to take a rain check."

She shook her head. "If I'm going to do it, this is as good a time as any. I can't imagine it will get any easier."

"It won't."

"Remember, I don't want to throw up."

Hugo burst out laughing.

"What's so funny?"

"That's the whole idea. Not just to get rid of what's in your stomach, but to break through mental and emotional blocks, let go of bad habits, that kind of thing. But you know that."

Ellen nodded. She hesitated before continuing. "There's something else."

"Oh?"

"Once, in college, I had a bad LSD trip. I'm afraid to experience anything like that again. An angry, nonsense voice came into my head and didn't go away completely when the acid wore off, but then it diminished. Still, sometimes I can hear it in the back of my mind. I'm afraid of making it worse."

Hugo thought for a while before answering. "Ayahuasca is a natural substance, the greatest healing plant on the planet. LSD is synthetic.

I stay away from things like that."

"You're sure it won't get worse?"

"When you go into the unknown, there are no guarantees but…quite sure. It might even get rid of it."

"Okay."

He lit some sage in a large clamshell and waved the smoke all around her to clear any negativity out of her energy field. When he finished, he put the shell in the kitchen sink, letting the sage burn itself out.

He picked up the bottle and shook it. Then, unscrewing the top, he took a small silver cup and filled it about three quarters of the way full. Holding the cup in his hands for a few moments, he stared intently into it before lighting his pipe and blowing smoke onto the *ayahuasca*.

Then he handed it to her. "Who knows. Maybe the grandmother will be gentle. Or maybe not."

With shaky hands, Ellen drank it down. The quantity was manageable and she didn't think it tasted as dreadful as she had expected.

"It will take about 30 to 40 minutes before you notice any effect." He got up and blew smoke in all four directions, starting with the south, followed by the west and so on, whistling as he went, not melodies just tones that were often minor. Then he sat down to wait with her.

In due course, she began to feel the *ayahuasca* entering her system and got fidgety and restless. Little tremors began to spread through her body.

"Breathe deeply and stay with your breathing."

She did and that helped. Hugo began to sing *ícaros*, songs *ayahuasqueros* sing to call beings from the spirit world into the ceremony. They seemed to intensify the effect of the medicine. Ellen began to see geometric designs with bead-like formations strung out across them in neon-bright colors, which took little, irregular jumps up. Her nerves felt as if someone had sandpapered them. It became hard to stay in any one position. She had never felt anything so intense and was pretty sure that, if any more sensory input came in, something major would happen, and it wouldn't be good.

"Keep breathing deeply."

She did, and the intensity began to wane. Soon it had calmed down to where she knew that, although it might continue to be difficult, she would be able to handle it. After a while she realized that the geometric designs were gone and figured the worst was over. She had no idea how much time had passed but was glad to be able to relax a little. Her body had become quite tense, so she used *ujayi* breathing, a technique she had learned in Stelios's yoga classes, and did a little stretching to loosen up.

She heard Hugo moving and opened her eyes to see him leaning toward her, holding a small rattle in the shape of a snake.

He shook it all around her and it had a remarkably soothing effect, although if he had used it sooner, when things were really intense, it would undoubtedly have driven her right over the edge. Now it put her into a quiet place, where she could just be with herself and her breathing.

And that was when she heard a man's voice in her mind.

She knew it was the *ayahuasca* speaking to her. She asked about Roy.

"Don't worry about Roy."

"Should I go to the MLA convention and give the paper?" "You can."

"So now I have to write it."

"That will be easy."

"It's important to my career?"

"Lot's of changes are coming."

"Yes, I can feel it."

"Changes will happen fast. It is good you are doing this now. It will take you to another level."

Ellen took a deep breath and let out a long sigh.

"You will do this many more times. You will do what you have always wanted to do. And much more."

Ellen was letting that sink in, when the voice continued. "You will burn your family's karma for seven generations back and seven generations forward."

She sat with this last idea for a while, wondering what she could possibly do to accomplish such a feat. She kept shaking her head saying to herself, "Little me. Little me."

"Be strong."

With that the voice left and she went off somewhere beyond the reach of her conscious mind. She had no idea how much time elapsed before she opened her eyes to see Hugo shaking a *chalapa* all around her. And that was when things got interesting again but in a totally different way.

All of a sudden, she found herself in a house, not one she had ever seen but she knew it was hers. The phone rang and she answered it. Some guy with a heavy Latino accent started talking.

"Hello. This is Estéban with the Cuban Man Escort Service." "The what?"

"The Cuban Man Escort Service. We gonna provide you with a Cuban man."

"I don't want a Cuban man."

"You gonna see this Cuban man we gonna send. You gonna like. You gonna forget all about your hospan, you gonna forget all about your boyfren. We gonna send him right over now."

"No. Don't do that. Hello? Hello?"

But he was gone. She had hardly put the receiver down, before the doorbell rang. She opened the door and there stood the Cuban man looking good, with black wavy hair combed straight back, brown skin, rather tall and thin, dressed in expensive clothes: a turquoise silk shirt open at the collar, an off-white linen suit with not a wrinkle in the crisply pressed jacket and trousers, and white leather shoes. His features were sharp, his nose long and angular. He was wearing a Panama hat, and smoking a long, thin Cuban cigar. Not what Val would call a hunk, but dashing nonetheless.

He tossed the cigar in the bushes, doffed his hat and with a sweeping, courtly bow, said "I'm gonna show you a real good time."

"But…"

"We're goin' dancing."

"But I'm not dressed."

All of a sudden, she was dressed in a stunning, soft red gown. He offered his arm and with a smile brimming with warmth and self-confidence, escorted her down the front walk to his waiting car, an enormous maroon Cadillac convertible with leather seats and huge fins.

They drove down a sunny boulevard lined with palm trees, the wind blowing her hair. Every now and then, he would throw her a smile that said: "I have nothing but fun."

Suddenly it was dark and they were walking into a salmon-colored nightspot with a gaudy neon sign that read: CLUB AYAHUASCA.

Everyone there seemed to know the Cuban man, whom they treated with great deference. They were led to a table right on the dance floor, which, to all appearances, was reserved for him. He ordered champagne.

"Is this where you bring all your other women?"

He opened his palms and smiled with all the good-humored innocence in the world. "What other women? There is only you."

They clinked champagne glasses and drank.

"Shall we dance?"

"Oh, I don't think so. I'm not a good dancer."

But there they were, all alone, out on the dance floor. He was, of course, an expert. Before she had time to feel embarrassed, she found herself doing all sorts of Latin dances, some of which she didn't even know the names of. But it didn't matter. He led her with such grace and precision that other patrons of the club gave them several rounds of applause. She began to let herself go in a new way, feeling free, her body opening up. She had never had so much fun.

Then, all at once, she was lying on what she could only assume was his bed and he was beginning to undress her.

"*¿Se puede?*" he asked.

She just looked at him, almost unable to breathe, as he expertly slipped off her clothes.

He lay down beside her and caressed her hair and her cheeks with his long, thin fingers. Surprisingly—or perhaps not—he turned out to be a very tender, considerate lover. Whenever he touched her, no matter where, he sent shivers through her entire body. And he kept caressing her for a long, long time. And, as soon as he slipped deep inside her, between her welcoming thighs, the movement radiated out to the tips of her fingers and toes, making her shudder.

The sleazy guy on the phone had been right. She couldn't even remember if she had a husband or boyfriend.

\*\*\*

Some time passed and she found herself at a beautiful deserted beach on a sunny afternoon swimming in the surf. The ocean was cool and invigorating, the sun warm without being too hot.

She was playing in the waves like a little girl, diving under them, riding them in, when she heard some voices on the beach. A group of guys had appeared. There were seven of them and they were fooling around, chasing each other, playing some kind of game like tag.

As soon as they saw her, they came running into the water, splashing each other. They all looked very much alike, relatively short, trim, with brown hair. They all wore identical tight, sky-blue bathing suits, and they were all named Herb.

They frolicked in the waves with her for a while, splashing her and ducking her under and then they began steering her gently toward the beach. They seemed so harmless, in such high spirits that she didn't resist.

They carried her ashore and laid her out on the sand. Nor did she object, when one of them undid the top of her bikini while another whisked the bottoms off. Then they were kissing her and licking her all over her body, while one of them slipped inside her. They were enjoying themselves immensely. And so was she.

One after another, they took her, while others sucked on her fingers and toes, nuzzled their face into her hair. Out of the corner of her eye, over to the right, she saw two of them, apparently too exited to wait their turn, fucking each other.

She closed her eyes, listening to the breaking of the surf. When she opened them, the Herbs had gone, taking with them the beach and the waves whose sound had morphed into Hugo, shaking his rattle.

After some time, she became aware of a mild feeling of nausea. Then all of a sudden bile rose in her throat. She opened her eyes, groped around, grabbing her bucket just in time. A large spurt of dark green, acidy, foul-tasting liquid burst out of her mouth. She kept heaving, holding her head over the pail, as less and less came out, giving her a chance to catch her breath.

It took a lot of strength out of her and she heard herself groaning. She thought it was over, sat up and put the bucket aside. In a little while a second round of vomiting erupted, with more of the repulsive liquid spewing up, her eyes watering and tears streaming down her cheeks. The vomiting seemed to come from somewhere very deep inside her, making her stomach muscles spasm so that the vile stuff heaved up with great force, filling her sinuses and causing her to gag.

When it was over, and she straightened up once again, Hugo pushed the box of tissues closer. She grabbed a handful, spat out the remnants of the puke and wiped her lips and blew her nose. Unscrewing the top, he handed her the little bottle of water.

"Rinse your mouth."

That helped, although it didn't get rid of the foul taste completely. Her whole body felt limp and she was pretty weak. She had an almost over-whelming urge to lie down but she resisted, knowing that to do so might cut her journey short. And she was glad she didn't.

\*\*\*

After a while, when much of her strength returned, she found herself in front of an incandescent full moon that was so close she could reach out and touch it.

It was as if she had stepped into the painting hanging on Hugo's wall, the one she had liked so much. Everything was there: the rickety ladder, the moon split down the middle and partly sewn together with thread, the iron house, the cathedral and the other dwellings framing everything. The nude woman was now her.

She stood there for a while, staring at the moon with bulging eyes. And then, without really thinking about it, she began to climb the ladder. Each step seemed to take her not only up but further out into space. It was all very scary and exhilarating and she was aware of the rapid beating of her heart.

She remembered not to look down. She was feeling light as a feather and she hung onto the rungs tightly. As she got higher, she ran out of rungs to hold onto and leaned in against the moon, holding on as best she could to whatever purchase she could find.

And she kept going until, standing on the last rung,

she grasped the top of the moon. Then, without thinking how she was going to get down, she hoisted herself up off the ladder, onto the moon itself, and sat down.

It was pleasantly cool and breezy. From her perch, she couldn't see the earth. She tried out of the corner of her eye, but that didn't work and she didn't want to lean over.

She was struck by the silence. She yelled a few times but the sound was absorbed into the vastness of the universe. No echo came back.

She could see the stars, shining with an astonishing brightness. After a bit of hunting, she found the Southern Cross. Bringing her legs into lotus pose, she sat for some time, just breathing softly, soaking in the vastness of the silence surrounding her.

Then, she noticed something. She couldn't understand why she hadn't noticed it before. She looked more closely. No, there was no mistaking it. She could see paths, skyways between the stars. Not between all of them, by any means, but a fair number. They took on the appearance of broken lines, similar to the kind that are painted on roadways to divide lanes, only, of course, there were no actual roads. And they were perfectly straight.

She wondered what determined how they were set up. Presumably, they went between solar systems, between inhabitable planets. Those stars that were left out of the network probably didn't have any. She didn't see a route to our region but she thought she might not, even if there were one. And she wondered what it would be like to travel from place to place in the universe and if she would ever be able to.

Maybe, she thought, after all, I'm sitting on the moon.

She liked it there and stayed a long time. She loved the silence and felt as if she were wrapped in its embrace.

But most of all she had the sensation of being connected to the immense reaches of the universe, of being a tiny part of its gigantic organism, as if it were breathing and she were breathing with it.

She knew with absolute certainty that she never wanted to come down. And she never did climb back down the ladder but at some point the entire scene dissolved. After a while, when she opened her eyes, she found herself sitting in the nude in front of Hugo.

He tossed her a robe.

He smiled. "How are you feeling?"

She yawned. "Tired."

"No doubt."

"Content."

"Good. How's your stomach?"

"Okay. Can I drink some water?"

"Sure. Do you think you're finished with the bucket?"

"Probably."

"I'll rinse it out but you best keep it handy, just in case."

As she passed it to him, she was surprised to notice how relatively little there was in the bottom. She was under the impression she had thrown up copious amounts of nasty stuff. Just looking at it started her stomach going and she threw up a little bit more.

He took it to the bathroom, emptied and rinsed it out and set it back down by her side. "Are you hungry? I have some fruit."

"Oh, I don't know."

"I'll get you an apple and an orange."

She heard him in the kitchen, cutting up the fruit.

"So now you know there are other worlds besides the one science has put all it's chips on."

She nodded, biting into a piece of orange and letting the juice wash away the remnants of bad taste.

"And you don't need any proof, because you've been there." He ate a piece of an apple. "Want to talk?"

"Maybe tomorrow." She reached for another slice of orange. "I will say it wasn't what I expected, although I'm not sure exactly what I did expect."

"Every journey is different. Best not to expect anything. You can sleep in my bed. I'm fine here on the floor."

"I don't…"

"I'm used to it, believe me. Go ahead."

She fell asleep as soon as she crawled into his bed and didn't wake up until late morning.

She felt rested enough but a bit strange, as if she hadn't made it all the way back yet. He assured her that was normal.

"I'm embarrassed. About taking off my clothes last night."

He laughed. "In the jungle, everyone jumps into the watering hole naked."

Over a light breakfast, he told her, "It's a good idea to stay with the diet for a few days. Steer clear of alcohol and sugar."

"I still don't feel ready to talk about what happened."

"That's okay, and you may not need to, but if you do, I'm at your service. That's part of the deal. Oh, and you may start seeing things."

"What? What things?"

"If your third eye has opened enough, you may begin to see animal spirits, or human. Spirits that are around us all the time, but most people never see them."

"What does it mean if I see them?"

"Sometimes it doesn't mean anything, but if they have a message, they'll let you know."

*** 

Out on the street, it was strange seeing people going on about their regular lives, as if nothing had happened. She couldn't help feeling a little smug, as if she had a secret. She felt different in a way that was hard to put her finger on but she suspected that whatever change had occurred was permanent.

After she had gone a couple of blocks, she began to realize even the way she walked was not the same, as if her body had somehow loosened itself up, as if everything, not just her legs, was involved in walking.

She liked it.

As she was strolling home, a man came out of a building, walking toward his car, a red BMW. His skin was swarthy, his hair black and rather oily. His shirt was open at the collar and he had a gold chain around his neck. Not her type. Or perhaps it would be more accurate to say that, even a few days ago, he definitely wouldn't have been. He still wasn't, but today, his swagger caught her eye. As he opened the front door on the driver's side, he looked at her and smiled. In the past, she would have tossed him a dirty look and hurried on, but today, she smiled back.

# Chapter Eleven

Ellen spent the remainder of Sunday in bed resting, not thinking too much about her journey, giving it time to settle in. She didn't have to teach on Monday, so she pretty much took another day off, although she did put in an appearance at the department.

She sat at her desk and spent a good hour just looking at the papers waiting to be corrected before packing it in. On the following days, she taught her classes and before she knew it, it was the weekend, time for Stelios's birthday party on Saturday night.

\*\*\*

During the whole day, her anticipation at seeing Laxman increased, so that by the time she drove up to their place, she was trying to think of something clever to get the conversation going. Stelios and Val lived in a little village, in a log cabin outside of town. At the bottom of their hill was a small stream that could fill up quickly after a heavy rain. Smoke from their wood stove was curling out of the chimney when Ellen arrived.

As soon as she took her coat off she looked around for

Laxman, but he had not yet arrived. Hugo spotted her and came over.

"How are you?"

"Different. Very different."

"Tell me more."

"My whole body has loosened up and I seem to know a lot more about people just by looking at them."

"I'm not surprised. Remember, when you throw up, you're breaking through deep, long-standing psychological and emotional blocks, all that stuff finds its way into the physical body."

"And I'm seeing things."

"*Ayahuasca* opens up the pineal gland."

"Like people's auras. I see yours now."

"What's it like?"

"Big. Much bigger than most. Probably the biggest one here."

"Do you see colors?"

"Yes. Yours is purple."

"Purple is good."

"Don't be modest. It's the best. And like you said I would," Ellen looked around then back at Hugo, "I see spirits. Animals and humans. Yesterday, I was walking in a little woods and I saw a tall, balding Elizabethan man.

"What was he up to?"

"Nothing special. Maybe gathering herbs."

Ferguson, from the English Department, joined them. He was tall, somewhat thickly built with jet-black hair and a deep voice that allowed him to put forth his opinions with more authority than they merited, a very useful trait in the profession.

It seemed that he was teaching a course on modern world literature and wanted to pick her brain on existentialism, particularly the works of Sartre, which he pronounced so that it rhymed perfectly with "fart." He spoke the name forcefully, one might even say explosively, looking around menacingly as if daring anyone to correct his pronunciation. There was no getting him off the subject. Hugo drifted away and by the time Ellen was able to extricate herself, a small group had formed around Serge and Elena, a graduate student from the Dominican Republic.

Elena was a gifted psychic and somehow they had gotten into a discussion of the paranormal. Apparently Serge, always of a practical, rationalist bent, had been, in his urbane way, debunking such things.

"Come on. We've all been to mediums at one time or another. I know the drill." He closed his eyes, pretending to go into a trance. "I'm getting the letter A. Who do you know whose name starts with an A? Well, most people know someone whose name starts in A. Don't you?"

"Yeah, my husband, Alberto. You know that. So what?"

"Or if that doesn't work…And D. I'm getting a D. Do you know someone whose name starts in D?…How's his health?…He's not well…no, no, I don't know if it's serious but it might be."

Serge was getting more and more laughs and was enjoying his little bit of theater immensely.

"And, by the way, you have a good sum of money set aside, don't you? You can tell me. I know you do. How much?"

Elena was becoming increasingly annoyed. After this last remark, she'd had enough. "Okay, suppose I give you a little demo?"

Even though Serge was a very skilled chess player, he hadn't anticipated that move. "What kind of demo?" he asked warily.

"I'll tell your fortune."

"Well…" He paused, evidently looking for an acceptable way to bow out.

"Come on, Serge, it'll be fun," someone said. Others urged him on.

"All right. Let's set up a time," was the best he could come up with.

"No time like the present." She looked around at the others.

"Right?" Everyone agreed.

"Right here? You don't mean that, do you?" "Why not?"

"In front of all these people?"

"Sure, why not?"

"Because I'm a very private person."

"Well, if you really believe what you've been saying, it won't make any difference."

"And why is that?"

"Because there's no way I'll be able to come up with anything about you that I don't already know or they don't already know. Which isn't much, because you're such a private person."

Serge, who wasn't used to being maneuvered into a corner, had to agree. Ellen was surprised to see him squirm a little. He was trying to maintain a skeptical smile, but his unflappable self-confidence seemed on the verge of abandoning him.

"Give me something of yours."

"Like what, my wallet?" He got some more laughs.

"Your watch will do."

He took it off and put it in her outstretched hand. "I want it back. It's a Rolex."

Elena smirked and shook her head. "I'll make this short. Maybe not sweet, but short." She held the watch and concentrated for a moment, her eyes closed. "You're an orphan, right?"

Under ordinary circumstances he might have denied it, but he was caught off guard.

"So your early life wasn't easy. Wasn't easy at all. In fact it was downright unpleasant."

Serge's smile faded, along with his habitual veneer of casual nonchalance. "No need to go into details."

"You've never gotten over it, have you?"

He didn't answer. His eyes narrowed.

She closed her eyes again and said nothing for what

must've seemed to Serge a very long time. Then she opened them.

"You're a Scorpio, aren't you?"

"I think so. Maybe."

"You know you are. In fact, I would be surprised if you weren't a double Scorpio. So you like secrets."

"What of it?"

"You have one now, one secret…no, you have two secrets, yes, two secrets. And I'm not talking little, inconsequential bullshit secrets. Biggies, yes." She rubbed her hands together with relish. "Very big ones."

Serge blanched. His lips, already thin, got thinner. He stood.

"Going somewhere? Afraid I might let the cat out of the bag?"

Ellen had never seen Serge so rattled. She wouldn't have thought it possible. He stammered something inaudible, pulled out a handkerchief and wiped his forehead.

"You look like you need a drink. Maybe you better get one," Elena said.

"Maybe I should," he said and abruptly headed for the bar. He poured himself a liberal belt of vodka, what looked like a triple, which he knocked right back.

"I love parties," Elena said. Several people crowded around her, asking her to read their fortunes but she was through for the night. "Nope, sorry. Show's over."

Not long after, when Ellen looked around for Serge, he had unceremoniously left the premises.

\*\*\*

Ferguson was holding forth on the sofa on the subject of Gabriel García Márquez, whom he referred to as Márquez. Every time he did, Val would gently say, "García Márquez," and Ferguson would glance over at her as if to say, "What's the difference?" and go right on talking about Márquez, whose work he apparently esteemed highly, so much so that he had included *Cien años de soledad* in the curriculum for his World Literature course.

Val leaned over to Oswaldo, who was sitting next to her on the sofa and said, "You tell him. Maybe he'll listen to you."

So Oswaldo took the next opportunity to explain that the correct way to say the author's name was García Márquez, rather than Márquez. At first, Ferguson seemed on the verge of becoming put out. But then he decided he had come into possession of a rather little known fact that, when he shared it with his students, could only make him look good. So he took it graciously, even going so far as thanking Oswaldo.

Val put her arm around Oswaldo's shoulders and gave him a squeeze, "I knew you could do it."

In an instant, Damaris, Oswaldo's wife, an attractive, refined woman who was quite high-strung, swooped in out of nowhere, leaned over the back of the sofa and said, "Don't tosh my hospan." Oswaldo habitually brought her to parties and then ignored her. "Damaris, please, don't start. This is a birthday party. We are all here to have a good time."

But it was clear that Damaris was not having a good time. "Why you even bring me to these parties. To just humiliate me?"

"*Que no Damaris, que no!* Nothing could be further from my mind."

"Don't act so *inocente*. You fool no one." Addressing the room, "Do you know that he believes that being faithful to one woman is, in fact, bad for a man? That it could even make him *impotente*. As if it was the woman's fault. He has told me so, many times."

"I was speaking in general terms. Theoretically, *mis ojos*. You always take everything so personally."

There was no stopping her now. "You know what he calls his female students?"

"Damaris, *por favor.*"

"*Una fuente inagotable.* In fact, I have just had the pleasure of being made aware, by accident, of his latest conquest among his student body."

Oswaldo's eyes flashed. "Who told you such a thing? I have a right to know, tell me, so I can confront them, right here if necessary."

"I will not tell you. The person did not intend to tell me. The person thought I already knew, that everyone knew. Of course, as usual, everyone does know, except me."

"This is ridiculous. No complaints have ever been

lodged against me, unlike other faculty members whose names I shall not mention. You have only to ask Roy."

"Roy? He is as bad as you. I would say worse but that is not possible."

"Please, Damaris, he is my chairman." Foxwhistle was enjoying the exchange immensely.

"Your chairman? What a laugh. He has even tried to seduce me, on many occasions. And you know, if he were the least bit *atractivo*, I might have gone to bed with him, just for the pleasure of getting even with you. Not that I could ever really get even with you. You have much too great a head start."

"Only in your imagination, I assure you, *tesoro*."

"Is that so? You know something, all of you? He has reached the point, this hospan of mine, that he is unable to perform his marital duties without Viagra."

Oswaldo's face darkened. "Now you are going too far, Damaris. You are embarrassing me in front of my colleagues."

"Become a friend of the little blue pill, have you, Oswaldo?" Foxwhistle asked.

"Certainly not."

"Maybe we should frisk him. See if he's holding," Foxwhistle said. "He has become the victim of his own debauchery," Damaris said. "This is intolerable. Would you like to know the truth, Damaris?

It is only with you that I am obliged to have recourse to such pharmaceutical aphrodisiacs. And do you know why? Because you no longer excite me. That is why. Are you satisfied now?"

"Good. You have admitted it, that you are with other women. You disgust me. I am leaving you here."

"Can I give you a lift?" Foxwhistle asked.

Oswaldo glared at him. "I beg of you, Damaris, please do not go, please do not go in his car. It is not safe."

"I am taking our car and I hope no one gives you a ride home. I hope you have to walk."

"If necessary, I will call a cab."

Damaris grabbed her coat, slamming the door as she left.

"I apologize. I don't know what's wrong with her anymore. She's so overwrought. The least little thing sets her off."

An embarrassed silence hung in the room, so Carl and Stelios broke out their instruments and started jamming. Carl, with his love of all things Spanish, was not bad on the guitar but Ellen could see that he was hard pressed to keep up with Stelios who was amazing on the bouzouki. Stelios would go off on long, improvised solos that were beyond anything Carl could conjure up. Nonetheless, they were great together and their playing provided a welcome distraction from Ellen's growing suspicion that Laxman might be a no-show.

Then somebody put on some music and soon the little space for dancing was full.

Ellen grabbed Carl's hand. "Let's go."

"I'm no good at dancing."

"A musician who can't dance?"

"Composer."

Todd came over and led her onto the floor. Needless to say, he was full of interesting moves and fun to dance with.

Ellen asked him how he had learned such fluent French. "You never studied in France, did you?"

"The next best thing. I had a French girlfriend for a couple of years, an au pair in Santa Barbara. I taught her to surf and, among other things, she took my French to a whole new level. It was a real win-win." The answer was so obvious she might have guessed. "Alas, she had to return to France."

"Soon to be replaced by Anita."

He gave a good-humored shrug. "I upgraded."

"How's your Spanish?"

"Getting better."

What an operator, she thought, not without a certain grudging admiration.

On the sofa, Jorge had begun to enlighten Carl on the virtues of his favorite subject. He held the bottom of his shirt out to Carl. "Feel this, man."

"Nice. Very soft."

"Hemp. Makes the best clothes. So much more comfortable than cotton. Lasts forever." He whipped the shirt off. "Here. Try it."

Carl did. "I see what you mean."

"Just molds to your body."

Carl started to give it back.

"No, you keep it man."

"But…what about you?"

"I'll borrow one from Stelios. Take it, man." "Thanks. I will. I like it." "Hemp, man, hemp."

After a while, Chad and Jorge turned the music down and started herding everyone out onto the front lawn. Someone had placed a car on a tilt and turned on the headlights, so that they shone on the roof, whose peak formed a horizontal line facing the lawn.

At the exact moment when *The Walk of Life* by Dire Straits began blaring through speakers on the front porch, Stelios appeared at the top of the roof. He had changed out of his jeans and T-shirt and was now wearing a light grey suit with wide pin stripes, cut in 1920s gangster style. On his head was an off-white Panama hat and he was holding a thin bamboo cane.

He performed a funky dance routine straight off the vaudeville stage, raising his knees high, bending back and waving the hat as he crossed the roof, pretending to lose his balance, waving his arms as if he were about to fall. Although he made it look easy, it was very dangerous, but he seemed not to care. The full moon was in the sky, illuminating the show from behind, and their cat, Micci, came up and sat on one end of the rooftop. Ellen couldn't tell if Stelios had rehearsed the act or was just making it up. Either way, it was an amazing performance, full of agility, wit and terrific dancing. The high point of the night. Watching him up there, so nimble, so creative and free, having such a good time, she wondered if there was anything he couldn't do.

*** 

The time came when Ellen was about to leave. She had looked for Stelios to say goodnight and wish him happy birthday again, but he was nowhere to be found and nobody seemed to know where he was.

Before leaving, she went to use the bathroom but found the door locked. While she was waiting, she heard a tearing sound coming from the bedroom. The door was ever so slightly ajar, so she peeked in and there, on the floor beside the bed were Oswaldo and Val. Val was on her hands and knees. He was removing a condom from its wrapper, which he threw on the floor, already littered with their clothing. Ellen watched as he entered her and began moving slowly inside her. Ellen had intended to just take a quick look but she found it impossible to pull herself away.

"Talk to me," he said.

"What do you mean?"

"Talk to me."

"About what?" Val asked in an irritated tone.

"Anything."

"You want me to talk dirty?"

"No, no. Not that. You have a very sexy voice,

did you know that? Just talk about anything. No matter what. *No importa.* It's the sound that counts. The melody of your voice."

So Val began to talk about the various preparations she had made for the party.

"That's perfect, *perfecto.*"

Ellen heard the toilet flush and the bathroom door open. Anita came out. She was just about to say something, when Ellen put her index finger to her lips. Anita moved to her side. She peeped in and Ellen heard her intake of breath.

A bedside table stood to Oswaldo's right, with a cigarette burning in an ashtray. Perhaps a whiff of smoke drew his attention to it, but he paused, stopped thrusting and reached for it. The twisting motion made him slip out of Val. He took a long drag and blew out a long stream of smoke. As he was dropping the cigarette back in the ashtray, he noticed the glass of whiskey beside it, made a little expression as if to say, "Why not?" and picked it up and took a large gulp.

Val began to grow impatient. "What's the holdup? Getting tired?" "Perhaps. But since I am Venezuelan, it is my duty to fuck you,

regardless of how tired I might be."

Val turned her head around almost in slow motion to look back. Ellen could tell she was very drunk. Her eyes passed over Ellen and Anita but their presence didn't seem to register. "Waiting for the Viagra to kick in?"

Fire came into his eyes. "There has been no Viagra, as you well know. Now I'm going to show you everything I am capable of."

With that he plunged hard into her asshole. She gave a gasp and her eyes bulged out almost as widely as his. It was difficult to say what prompted him to attack with such renewed vigor. Was it to prove how macho he was, or had he somehow surreptitiously popped a Viagra which was only now making its presence known, or was it the severe lashing of whiskey he had just belted down, pure lust, or all of the above? Whatever the inspiration, he gave it all he had, which looked fine to Val, as if she was glad things had turned a little rough.

Ellen could feel Anita's warm breath on her shoulder, the closeness of her body. She inhaled the exotic fragrance of Anita's perfume and asked herself for the first time what it would be like to make love with a woman, especially a woman as stunning as Anita. She wondered what would happen if Todd were not around and she lured Anita back into the bathroom or back to her flat. Was Anita having similar thoughts? She stole a glance at her out of the corner of her eye. Was her bosom heaving more than usual? Difficult to tell but one thing was certain: Anita was completely absorbed in the scene before her. More than likely Todd would be the recipient of some passionate lovemaking that night which would, like so many things, simply fall into his lap.

***

Ellen was searching for her coat when she felt a presence behind her.

She turned around and there he was. Laxman.

"Oh, I thought you weren't coming. The party's pretty much over."

"I know. Something came up at work. I had to stay late."

"Does that happen often?"

"That's just it. Almost never."

"Just our luck."

"What shall we do?"

"Let's just go. We can take a walk in the park, the one near my apartment."

The park appeared deserted. As they were ambling along, he took her hand and she felt comfortable with him, as if they had been together for years. The full moon flooded the walkways with light and the air was pleasantly crisp without being cold. She knew him to be a man of few words and they kept meandering a while without saying anything, almost as if everything was already understood.

Well, not everything. Ellen had one thing she had to get off her mind, so finally she just came out with it, hoping it wouldn't ruin everything.

"What about Gema?"

"What about her?"

"Well, she's my friend. And she's your wife."

"Gema doesn't care. The days of passion are over for us. We're more like friends and partners bringing up Oetomo. That is very important."

"Are you sure?"

"It's different for us. We're Muslims. I could have more than one wife, if I wanted."

"Does she know? About me…us?"

"No. It is not our custom to tell each other everything. But if she did, she would be happy it was you, not, I don't know, some woman from a bar."

"You like women from bars?"

"Not particularly."

At the same time, they both noticed something up ahead.

"What's that?"

"I don't know."

As they drew closer, they could see a silhouette in the moonlight; someone sitting, his back against a tree.

"That's Stelios."

"Isn't he at home, at the party?"

"He left before we did."

"Left his own birthday party?"

"So it would seem."

Because there he was, calmly smoking a joint, still dressed in his suit. They sat down beside him.

"What are you doing here?" she asked.

"Thinking. Waiting for someone."

"Where did you get that amazing retro suit?"

"In a used clothing store in Vienna. Made in Prague."

She thought Serge would have appreciated it, if Serge had stayed around long enough to see it.

He passed the joint around. It was rumored that Stelios had a mistress, although no one knew who she was. At first, Ellen had dismissed the idea. After all, no one had ever seen her, so no one knew anything about her but it was obvious something had gone very wrong with the marriage, so...

The joint was almost finished when Ellen heard a soft footstep behind her and she thought, so I'm actually going to get to meet this mysterious lover. She turned and saw the figure of a woman coming slowly toward them through the trees. At first, it was hard to see her distinctly, but as she emerged like a wood nymph out of the semi-darkness, it became clear that she was beautiful, with black curly hair, large dark eyes, very white skin. A large lower lip gave off more than a suggestion of sensuality.

She went straight to Stelios, bent over and gave him a long kiss, sat down beside him and said, "Happy Birthday, darling."

"This is Derya."

Were she and Stelios in love? Perhaps. It was evident they were happy to be together. Derya was doing a post-doc in Physics and spent most of her time in her office, producing an endless stream of paper filled with numbers, comprehensible only to her, from her computer.

As dull as that sounded, Ellen was fascinated to learn that she was born in a village high in the mountains in Daghestan in the Caucasus, a part of the world Ellen knew almost nothing about except that it made her, like Laxman, a Muslim.

Soon Stelios stood up to leave. "It will no doubt be better if Laxman and I both put in an appearance at home before morning."

"Alas," said Derya.

Once in Ellen's apartment, no time was wasted on the usual niceties like:

"Nice apartment."

"Oh, I'm glad you like it. I'll show you around." "Have you been here long?"

"Would you like something to drink?"

She took his hand and led him straight into the bedroom and into the bed.

"Let me just hold you for a while," she said. And he did. When they threw themselves into making love, it was without any of the usual nervousness of a first encounter. She was happy to see that he was taking his time and without any conscious decision, her body opened up in a way it never had before. Whenever he touched her, she quivered and couldn't kiss him deeply enough. He wasn't doing anything out of the ordinary, just being himself, calm, powerful, as much at ease in bed as he doubtless was on the deck of a ship, but that's all it took for her to sail away with him on a longish voyage to a very exotic place, a voyage that had a very, very happy ending.

Afterward, she looked at him as they were lying peacefully next to each other. There was no question that, even though he was leading a quiet life, he still had the allure of adventure about him.

"Do you miss your country?"

"Every day. I miss the heat, the tropics. I miss sweating all day. I hate the winter here. But the money's good."

"Don't you ever go back?"

"I can't." He wasn't going to say anymore but saw she wanted to know.

"Someone started a fight in a bar."

"Over a bar woman?" she asked, teasing.

"No, no. He didn't like me, for a long time he didn't like me and he just wanted a fight. And he got one. He hit me here," he said, pointing to the scar on his face, "with a broken bottle. He tried to put out my eye. Blood poured into it. I could only see out of the other eye."

"And?"

He hesitated before answering. "Well, let me put it how your lawyers here like to say: he did not prevail and I had to get away fast."

"Are you saying…?"

He nodded. "I had to leave."

"But wasn't it self-defense?"

"Yes, but the police, it's not like here. I didn't want to

go to jail. I couldn't risk that. I got out on a boat with my family and we came here."

"Just like that?"

"Oh, no. No visa. I had a friend who was the captain of a ship that was going to Mexico. From there we made our way here."

"How?"

"By water. Let's say I borrowed a boat I forgot to return. I've been a smuggler. I'm very good at making boats invisible."

"I always fantasized that you were a pirate."

He laughed. "In my country, sometimes there's not much difference."

After a while, they fell asleep and sometime before morning, he slipped away.

# Chapter Twelve

When Ellen took her seat on the plane to New York for the MLA convention, she was relieved to see that Roy was not on board. She thought of sitting next to him all the way to New York, or him waddling down the aisle in mid-flight to talk, and she shivered.

When she arrived at her room in the Sheraton, she was not surprised to see the message light blinking on her telephone. It was Roy asking her to call him, to meet for a drink before retiring, no doubt to his room. She put the phone down without calling him back. He would be at her session tomorrow afternoon; that would be plenty soon enough.

To be well rested for her talk, she turned in early. The next morning, she looked up some friends from her graduate school days and, while it was nice to see them, she was surprised to find she didn't want to spend much time with them. She had developed other interests, but they hadn't.

By the time she arrived for the session, Gwendolyn, a tall, not unattractive businesslike woman in her late forties was already there.

"Good to see you. I think we have some very strong

papers. Why don't you sit there? Then we'll be in the order of presentation."

"Oh no," Ellen said. "You mean I have to follow you?"

"Don't worry. Your paper is quite distinct enough to stand on its own."

She met the other presenter, a man named Tom from Weslyan. He was giving a paper on Le Clézio, who had spent considerable time among the Ebera-Wounaan tribe in Panama, so he professed a keen interest in Ellen's work. "We'll have to talk more sometime," he said.

Ellen had given papers at other conferences but never at the MLA. Unlike other times, she found herself quite composed. She looked out over the room that was filling up. Soon there would be no seats left, something that in the past would have raised her anxiety level, but she remained almost detached. She had prepared well, rehearsing her paper several times, but she always did that. Something else was going on and she knew what it was: her *ayahuasca* journey. Had the vine taken her to the place beyond death, as its name suggested? She didn't know, but it had taken her somewhere and, when she came back, nothing had been quite the same. The experience had opened the door to a whole new way of being in the world.

At five past the hour, Gwendolyn started by welcoming everybody, and expressing pleasure at the good attendance. She introduced Tom, who gave an excellent paper on *Le chercheur d'or*, which Ellen had always considered to be Le Clézio's best book.

Gwendolyn, who built her reputation on controversy, had chosen the most provocative topic: Sexuality and Freedom in Huellebecq's *Platforme*, seen through the lens of queer theory. Ellen's delivery of her paper went smoothly and there was a lively discussion afterwards. Many of the questions were directed at Gwendolyn and her rather outré subject, but Ellen got quite a few, as well, inquiries about her personal experience and her analysis of *Amazonia*.

"Have you been to the Amazon?" a woman in the row three asked.

"No, but I'm planning to go."

"Have you taken *ayahuasca*?"

Ellen didn't answer right away, so Gwendolyn turned to her with a penetrating look and replied, "No."

"So when are you planning to take the plunge?" "Who knows? Maybe this summer," Ellen smiled.

The last remark got a laugh and Gwendolyn seemed satisfied, but then a dark-haired, scowling young man sitting in the front row proclaimed loudly, "*Amazonia* is inner space. It's inner space."

"I don't recall saying it wasn't," Ellen said.

This only made the young man more agitated. "It's inner space. Inner space," he repeated. He stood up and it looked for a moment as if things might get out of hand, when someone in the back of the room broke in. "Inner space. That's a phrase so general as to be utterly meaningless. It can easily be said of many works. Madame Bovary, for example. Madame Bovary is inner space. So what?"

The voice, quietly authoritative, seemed familiar, and after a moment, Ellen realized that it was Steadman, the man with the missing page 17.

Gwendolyn jumped in. "Quite." She glared at the young man. "Perhaps you will chair a session next year on inner space. I'm sure we'll all be eagerly awaiting it. Now, I'm afraid our time is up. Thank you all so much for your attentiveness."

As Gwendolyn was gathering her papers, Ellen leaned over and said, "Well, that was unfortunate."

Gwendolyn dismissed it with a wave of her hand. "Annoying is how I'd put it, but don't let it bother you. There's one in every session. Your paper was quite well received, as were they all. We must do this again."

Steadman strode to the front, sweeping his hair back from his forehead.

"Fascinating stuff, your paper."

"Thanks for coming. And thanks for shutting that guy up."

She could see Roy, halfway down the aisle, making his way up, but Gwendolyn intercepted him.

"You look like you could use a drink. I always can after these things. How about it?"

"That would be great. But we just have to get past Roy." "Don't worry. I'll take care of it." And he did.

As Steadman whisked her passed him, Roy said, "Oh James…Ellen…"

"Good to see you, Roy. We'll talk." Steadman called back over his shoulder.

Leaving behind a very peeved-looking Roy, they went to Rosie O'Grady's. It was crowded but they found a table. "Guinness?" he asked.

"What else?"

He came back from the bar with two of the dark brews, sat down and loosened his tie. "I hate these things. I try never to wear them, even when I'm teaching."

"Did you know that when I was at Yale, they did a study in the sociology department on the effect of wearing a tie?" Ellen asked. "It lowers your IQ by 15%, on average."

"Wow, that's…15% is a lot."

"It's huge. It was a rigorous scientific study, too. The amazing thing is that men at Yale, where intelligence is supposedly at a premium, still wear them."

"Did they explain why? In the study, I mean?"

"No, but it must have something to do with cutting down the flow of blood to the brain. Maybe that's why women seem smarter than men. Sorry. Couldn't resist."

"That's it, never again." Steadman whipped off his tie. "Hungry?" "Starved."

They ordered some food.

"You'll never guess what's developed from the paper on Lorca and Dalí. I worked it up into an article and sent it to PMLA."

"Boy, you go right to the top, don't you? And they accepted it?" "Well, not at first. They liked it but sent it back suggesting I add references to people like Barthes, Foucault, Derrida, you know, the usual suspects."

"That's a little behind the times, isn't it?"

"Well, maybe the reader or readers were caught in a critical time warp. Anyway, I stuck in a few references and a quote or two, sent it back and it was snapped right up."

"Congratulations. They'll like that at Princeton. You're off and running for tenure."

"Maybe, but I've still got to produce a book."

For a moment, the thought of her book project languishing in the stale air of her carrel popped into her mind but she chased it away. Her paper had gone well and she wanted to have some fun.

Their food arrived with a couple more beers and, before they knew it, they found themselves in his hotel room, snuggling in bed. They lay there for a while, ready but in no hurry to make love, and Ellen felt good wrapping herself around him, just talking. She told him about her problem with Roy.

"Guys like that should be taken out and shot." He thought for a moment. "Maybe you should turn the tables on him."

"How?"

"Oh, I don't know. Lead him on and then stiff 'em. No pun intended." He ran his hand through her hair and began the first overtures to lovemaking. "Roy would give his eye teeth to be where I am."

"Make me forget about Roy."

And he did, because this time he brought along all his pages.

***

When Ellen got back to her room, the message light on her phone was blinking, and once more she chose to ignore it. The next morning, when she went to the session where Stelios was giving a paper, Roy was lying in wait for her.

He took her aside. "That was a very good paper you gave yesterday. Gwendolyn was very pleased. She likes you, she likes your work. You've made yourself a powerful ally." He lowered his voice and came closer to her. "Hmm…so here we are, Ellen. No place to run, no place to hide."

"From what?" she said acidly.

"Hmm…I think you know exactly what I'm talking about." She glared at him without answering, hating the way he started sentences with "Hmm."

"Let me lay it out for you. I needn't remind you that your contract is coming up for renewal this year. Once you're over that hurdle and your book is out—it is coming along well, isn't it?"

"Yes," she lied.

"Good. You've already published quite a good article, so you'll be in a strong position to apply for tenure. All things being equal."

"Meaning?"

He looked around, moved even closer and said firmly, "I would like to come to your room tonight, to discuss all this further."

"Oh, I don't know about that. Why my room?"

"You're at a critical point in your career. Hmm…at the eleventh hour, Erica took a sudden interest in attending the convention, which she never does, so your room will afford us the uninterrupted privacy we need."

"I see."

"Well…?"

The doors to the room were closing. "I think they're about to start."

"Very well, think about it. Let me know. You have my room number?"

"I can get it," she said, moving off. Roy didn't move. "You're not coming in?"

"No."

Stelios's paper was on Theo Angelopoulos and Italian Neo-Realism. Ellen had seen one of his films, *Vlemma tou Odyssea* with Harvey Keitel, and had liked it a lot.

But still fuming over Roy, she couldn't focus on the paper, which seemed excellent.

When the session was over and the crowd around Stelios had thinned out, she went up to congratulate him. She was just about to say something, when a young man came up to him.

"Professor Pelitos, I'm so glad to meet you. I couldn't get here until today and I just made it to the session, straight from the airport. Great paper."

"Thanks."

"Oh, my name is Peter, by the way. I was in the NEH summer seminar for college professors this year on Modern Greek literature and we used your book as our main text."

"Oh, really? I hope it was useful."

"It certainly was. It really got me into Modern Greek poetry, which is absolutely amazing. Where are you teaching now, Professor Pelitos?"

"Well, I'm teaching at Wellington, but that's only for this year. I'm actually looking for something for next year. Where are you? Maybe there's something in your department."

Peter's face, which had been full of admiration, as if he was meeting an academic rock star, clouded over in confusion. Surely Stelios would have long since secured a position way up in the academic hierarchy but here he was scrounging around for a job like a grad student without a dissertation. In that instant, Stelios came crashing down off the pedestal Peter had placed him on. Ellen looked away, not wanting to watch Stelios' embarrassment.

"Ah, no. Actually, I don't think we have anything open at the moment…I'm afraid…in your field." He backed away and there was an uneasy silence. "If I hear of anything, of course…"

"Thanks."

Peter extended his hand awkwardly and said, "Well nice to meet you." "Nice to meet you, too."

After Peter departed, Stelios said, "Well, that was what my mother would have called mortifying. I would say damn depressing."

"What can I do?"

"Get me out of here. Get me a drink."

She took him to the hotel bar, which, at that hour, was not particularly crowded. Stelios ordered a tequila, a double. Ellen ordered white wine, which she barely touched. He sat there, staring morosely off into space.

"It's not important, Stelios. You'll probably never see that guy again. He really wanted to meet you. And he loved your book."

"That's just it. Everybody likes my work. When I give papers at conferences, I'm treated like a celeb. But I can't get a job."

"I know Roy has this thing about nepotism, about not hiring a husband and wife," Ellen said.

"Just my luck."

"But I thought he told you to apply for the opening in the department this year, and that this time he would hire you?"

Stelios finished his tequila and ordered another. He looked at his hands for a moment. "Okay, I might as well make my morning of humiliation complete. There's more to it than that." He took a deep breath. "You have no doubt noticed that Val and I aren't exactly getting along."

"Yeah."

"Well, one night last summer Roy had us over to dinner. Erica was off somewhere, Germany I think. After we'd all had quite a lot to drink, he made us a proposal."

"What?"

"Do I have to spell it out?"

Ellen raised her eyebrows and shrugged.

Looking down at his glass, he continued. "After a few more drinks, Val motioned for me to go. And I did. That's what I did. I didn't go over, grab her by the arm and take her away. I got up and left. I got in my car, put the key in the ignition, started the engine and drove home." The waitress came with his tequila. "A simple quid pro quo. Only he got the quid and I'm beginning to suspect I'm not getting the quo."

Ellen didn't know what to say. She put her hand on his arm. "What kind of a man pimps out his wife so he can get a teaching job?"

Ellen didn't have a good answer. Perhaps there wasn't one.

He took a sip and looked at her. "Not much of a man," he said. "Can you imagine how degrading it is to sit across the desk from this guy who blackmailed you into letting him fuck your wife, who you'd like to reach across the desk and strangle? But you just sit there and smile and say stuff like, 'That's great, Roy. Thanks, Roy. I'll get my letter of application right in.'"

"You'll get the job."

"I'm not so sure. I was at first, but lately, without actually saying it, he's been giving me signals that he's changed his mind. He's having this woman in from Montana for an interview." "Any idea why he would change his mind?"

"Maybe just because he can. Just being his usual bastard self." Stelios grunted. "My gut tells me he's all set to renege. Look, my life is a mess. I've pretty much destroyed my marriage. Val and I had a horrendous fight the night before I left."

"I'm not surprised."

"I know, I know, I did a really stupid thing. Worse than stupid." Stelios twirled his glass and looked down. "After we screamed at each other, she drove off and didn't come back." He took a while before continuing. "I perforated a door." He made as if to take another sip but didn't. "Later, I took off all my clothes, got into the bathtub and poured ketchup all over myself."

"You did what? Stelios, that's pretty weird." "It felt like something I needed to do." "Doesn't sound like you…are you okay?"

He took a deep breath, leaned back in his chair and said, "Sure, sure, I'm okay."

Ellen pressed her lips together and thought for a minute or two, while Stelios consumed more tequila. "I have an idea."

"What?"

"It's something Roy won't like. He won't like it at all but you gotta help me."

"You got it."

*\*\**

On her way to her room, Ellen ran into Todd and Anita. "How are the interviews going?" she asked him.

"I don't…actually, I haven't had any." "Really? I thought you were graduating?"

"I am. Guess I just didn't get my application letters out in time." Ellen frowned. A smooth operator like him not getting his interviews lined up, now that was passing strange. She looked at Anita.

"Me, neither."

They didn't seem to be particularly concerned, even in a bad job market. Or maybe, as she sometimes thought, he really never had any intention of teaching at all. Or maybe they were planning to move to Costa

Rica to teach. In the end, it too had it all: abundant sun, gorgeous beaches, endless waves.

Back in her room, the message light on her phone was blinking again. This time she returned the call, telling Roy to come to her room at eight o'clock.

At the appointed hour, he was at the door. She quickly let him in. "You've made a very wise decision, one that is sure to affect your career in a very positive way."

"Let's hope so," she said dryly.

He came close to her. "I've been waiting so long for this." He ran the fingers of his right hand down her cheek and leaned forward to kiss her, but she pulled back.

Stomach churning, she asked, "Would you like a drink?"

Roy was not to be delayed. "Hmm…no thanks. I had a few drinks with some colleagues. Err, no one you know," he hastened to add.

"Well, look, I'm going to get undressed in the bathroom," Ellen said. "You get ready out here."

From behind the door, Ellen heard the rustle of clothing, his belt buckle jingling, and grunting.

After a few minutes, Roy asked if she was ready.

"Almost."

Just then there came the sound of someone rattling the hallway doorknob, followed by soft, insidious tapping, just loud enough to be heard.

Ellen, wearing a robe, poked her head out the

bathroom door. To her disgust, Roy stood there naked opening the foil of a condom.

"Roy, someone's at the door."

Roy, his senses focused elsewhere, appeared not to have heard it. "What? What's the matter?"

The rattling came again. "There it is again. Don't you hear it?" "Probably someone with the wrong room. Just ignore it. They'll go away."

"There it is again. Do something."

"Ellen, don't get hysterical."

More rattling, more banging.

"Stick your head out and get rid of them."

"The door's locked."

"I won't be able to relax until you do."

"But…"

"And I don't need to tell you what that means."

Roy threw up his hands and went to the door. She followed behind him. He opened the door and poked his head out. "You see? There's no one there."

Before he could shut the door, she jerked it wider, pushed him into the corridor and slammed the door shut.

There followed many knocks, many entreaties, ending ignominiously with, "At least give me my pants."

Ellen didn't answer.

"You can kiss tenure goodbye. Is that what you want?"

Smiling, Ellen turned away from the door and drew herself a hot bath. Settling into the tub, she imagined Roy out in the highways and byways of the hotel, or taking the elevator down to his floor. She saw him crouching in the corner of the elevator, the horrified faces of people waiting to get on as the doors slid open, revealing a naked, fat man. Or maybe he took the stairs, furtively descending and asking a maid to open his door, who would probably run off screaming.

Still smiling, she ducked her head under, pleased with herself like Julia Roberts in *Pretty Woman*.

# Chapter Thirteen

One Friday afternoon, Ellen stood neatening up her desk before having dinner with Carl, when Serge popped in.

"Oh, sorry, you're on your way out."

"That's okay. I'm not in a big hurry."

"Good…may I sit down?"

"Of course."

"Because I've come to say goodbye."

Ellen sat down hard. "Goodbye?"

"Yes. I'm leaving."

Ellen's jaw dropped. "Leaving Wellington? Why? What happened?"

"I was discovered."

"Doing what?"

"It was inevitable, although I was hoping it would last a little longer. One of my better students transferred somewhere. When she sat down in her first Russian class, she knew something was very wrong."

"Was she behind the other students?"

"If it were only that." He looked out the window. "Someday, if we ever meet again, we'll probably sit around and laugh at it. These two years, my students thought they were learning Russian."

"What do you mean 'thought'?"

"I was actually teaching them Bulgarian."

Stunned, Ellen shook her head. "What? Why?"

"Because it was easier."

"Don't you know Russian?"

"Of course. I was born in Bulgaria. Everyone in Bulgaria speaks some Russian. But, as you realize, knowing some and teaching it are two different things. Russian grammar is extremely complicated, you have no idea. I might have managed, but it would have been a hell of a lot of work." He paused. "Don't look at me like that. My formal education was pretty spotty."

He pulled out a cigarette. "Do you mind if I smoke?" Normally she would have, but under the circumstances…

"I'll stand by the window." He inhaled deeply. "Anyway, I'm not the first person to engage in such a deception. Ever hear of George Psalmanazar?"

"Who the hell's that?"

"Well, this might interest you as a teacher of French culture, because, despite his rather peculiar name, he was a Frenchman from Provence. Lived in the 18th century. He fell on hard times and to better his lot, he went to England where he pretended to be from Formosa, now known as Taiwan."

"Of all places."

"Because few people knew anything about such a

remote island he did quite well for a while, became a celebrity. He invented a fake Formosan language, which he taught to future missionaries. I can only imagine the consternation of his students when they stepped ashore on the island and engaged the natives on the subject of the Lord."

Ellen laughed. "So you're Bulgarian?"

"Perhaps."

"What does that mean?"

"A lot of people are born in Bulgaria. Most are Bulgarians but many are not. I don't know who my parents were or anything about them."

"So you could be anything."

"Pretty much. I could even be Russian. Wouldn't that be a hoot? Or, Formosan."

"But…what about your credentials?"

"All faked. A made-up university in Moscow. Even if they bothered to check, I could have told them it closed down when the Soviet Union collapsed. Anyway, Roy was so anxious to hire what he thought was a native speaker, whose English was good, I bet he never checked. I was counting on that."

"So what happened?"

"Dean Hairheart got an irate call and Roy got an even more irate one, summoning us both to his office."

"That must've been unpleasant."

"Not really. Believe me, I've had to deal with far more intimidating people than the Dean. He let me know immediately that we were in a terminal situation. He had a letter to that effect prepared for me to sign. I didn't object. Then he let me know, in no uncertain terms, that he didn't appreciate my little scherzo à la russe. When I yawned, he yelled that I had given the university a black eye and that I would never teach again in any university. When I shrugged and said 'So what?' he gave up on me and lit into Roy, who got red as a beet. I thought he might have a heart attack."

"What did he say?"

"Oh, you know, the usual stuff. How embarrassing it was for the university. How could he not have done a thorough background check, a full vetting, etc. Then Hairheart really went off on Roy about the MLA convention. I couldn't make out what he was talking about."

Ellen chuckled. "Apparently, Roy made an appearance in the lobby dressed only in a dirty towel."

"Did he? What will he think of next?"

Serge finished his cigarette.

"So what will you do?"

"Oh, don't worry about me. It's been a good couple of years." He stood up. "I have a lot of practice landing on my feet."

"So that was the first secret…"

"Secret?"

"Elena, the psychic…she said there were two." "Oh, that, yes, the Bulgarian gambit was the first." "And…do I have to ask?"

"So you won't be satisfied until you hear the second one, too? Well, why not? I'm out of here anyway, although I'd still prefer that you keep it to yourself."

"Okay."

"As you probably gathered at the party, I had a rough childhood. I was afraid Elena was going to come out with the whole sordid story that night, but mercifully, she was discreet."

"Sordid?"

"I mean, among other things we needn't go into, I was a rent boy. I really didn't have much choice. I had to eat, but I never really got over it." He paused. "You see, I'm gay. So there you have it. Had you guessed?"

"Yes. And none of that is sordid. You did what you had to." "And I continue to do so."

"As far as being gay, Serge, it really doesn't matter." "Thank you."

Serge came over and kissed her cheek. Ellen placed her hand on his forearm. "I'm very sorry to see you go. I'll miss you. Keep in touch."

"I will," he said, but she knew he wouldn't.

\*\*\*

When she got to Carl's, he had the table neatly set for dinner and everything was ready.

"Sorry I'm late."

"That's okay. Let's eat while it's still hot." They sat

down at his little table. "Nothing fancy. Just spaghetti with a very good bottle of wine."

"That's fine." They started eating and Ellen took a sip of wine.

"Oh, yes, that's really good."

"Spanish. Organic. One of my recent discoveries."

She explained about Serge's hasty departure from campus.

Carl leaned back in his chair. "Well, he pulled off a stupendous con."

"One that blew Roy's years of sucking up to Hairheart right out the window."

"Makes the department look pretty bad."

"Exactly what Dean Hairheart said."

"What's your feeling about it all?"

"Well, I'm in favor of anything that makes Roy squirm. I don't know. Maybe a year or so ago I would've been upset. For the students, for the department, for myself as a member of the department. But now, I just don't care enough anymore to muster up much righteous indignation. I like Serge, despite what he's done. Such an intriguing guy." She took a sip of wine. "You know, I almost think he did it as a goof."

By the time they did the dishes and Carl played some piano pieces for her by Albéniz and Debussy. It was getting to be time for Ellen to think about leaving. She didn't really want to go, since it had been such a pleasant evening. Just as she was about to say something, the front door to the house burst open and a heavy-footed person tramped up the stairs to the second floor.

"What's that?"

"My new neighbor. The Asian girl moved out. I was hoping he wouldn't come back while you were here. He usually clomps in around three in the morning, waking me up."

"Have you spoken to him?"

"Oh, yeah. One night he came in around three, turned his TV on and went to sleep. I woke him up and got him to turn it off. He did but he didn't seem to see any need for me to bother him about it. I guess I was just supposed to lie in bed and listen to the audio on his TV, until he got around to shutting it off."

"Who is he?"

"I don't know. He claims to be some kind of student but it's hard to imagine him ever doing any studying. He's on the phone a lot, especially at night and of course he has a deafening voice. He seems to have plenty of money, and at first I thought he might be a drug dealer. He's certainly a user. He might be a gambler. Or maybe he's just a royal pain in the ass. I've talked to him a couple of other times about the noise, explained I work at home and require quiet."

"A guy like him is the last thing you need."

"I was having enough trouble figuring out how to finish my symphony…and now this?"

"What does he say?"

"Okay, I'll keep it down.' But then he just does what he pleases." Without warning, the guy upstairs started screaming at the top of his lungs. "You're a whore! Say it! You're a whore!"

"He's on the phone with his girlfriend. This goes on all the time. You can substitute any word you want, he eventually gets around to them all."

"What kind of a girlfriend would put up with that?"

"A very mousy one. When he's up there screwing her, you think the bed's going to come crashing through the ceiling."

He started in again and Carl yelled, "Shut up!! Shut the fuck up!!"

In an instant the guy was down the stairs, pounding on Carl's door.

"Don't answer it."

"He won't go away."

No sooner had Carl opened the door than the guy was yelling at him. He was much taller than Carl, thin but well built.

"Never, never yell at me! Don't ever tell me to shut the fuck up. If you have anything to say to me, you come upstairs! You hear me? You come upstairs and you knock on my door."

"I've tried that. It didn't do any good."

The guy ignored him. "You get it, you fucking moron, come upstairs!"

Carl slammed the door and the man stomped back upstairs and continued yelling at his girlfriend.

"Well, that was embarrassing. I'm sorry you had to hear it." "Oh, don't worry." She put her hand on his arm. "You're shaking all over." She drew him into her arms. "That guy is a sociopath." "You're telling me?"

"Look, I'll stay with you tonight. I'll sleep on the couch." "You don't have to. He's my problem." "It's okay. I want to."

She woke in the middle of the night and it took her a moment to remember where she was. She saw the silhouette of Carl, sitting in the armchair by the window. It had started snowing and outside the trees and the ground had a covering of white. She went over behind him. Taisha was on his lap, purring. "It's beautiful."

He nodded his head. Then she realized that there were tears streaming down his cheeks. She came around and knelt beside him. "Oh, sweetie, don't let that guy get to you. He's not worth it."

He put his hand on hers. "It's not that. It's not that at all. I finally figured how to end my symphony. I've got the last movement! I can hear it!"

She enveloped him in her arms and they stayed for a long time, watching the snowfall.

# Chapter Fourteen

Stelios had been looking forward to watching *Les enfants du paradis*, which he had, of course, seen before but not recently. He was particularly fond of the work of its director, Marcel Carné, especially *Quai des brumes*, and it was always good to watch Jean-Louis Barrault and Arletty, some of the best French actors of the mid-20th century. He had no idea who had the extraordinary good taste to have booked it (certainly not the Foreign Language Department) but had been telling all his friends not to miss it.

He was killing some time in his office when Roy appeared at the door.

As the chairman sat down, Stelios wondered if he had somehow found out it was he who had rattled Ellen's doorknob at the MLA Convention. But it wasn't that at all.

"Just taking a break from some paperwork and I was hoping I might catch you. I'm afraid I have some bad news."

Stelios's stomach contracted and his mouth went dry. He felt himself go numb. "Yes?" was all he managed to get out.

"I'm afraid I won't be able to offer you the position that's open for next year."

Stelios felt dizzy. "But you said…"

"I know, and nothing would give me greater pleasure, but you know, it's not completely up to me. The problem is the other people in the department were against it."

Stelios knew that the people in the department had nothing to say about it and, given the choice, they would hire him in a minute, but such a bold-faced lie left him speechless.

"So we'll be giving the job to Miss Wight, you know, the woman from Idaho we interviewed recently." Roy made a gesture of helplessness. "I'm afraid that's it."

Stelios didn't say anything.

"She's going to write a book," Roy said, as if that made all the difference.

A strange sort of paralysis crept over Stelios. Going to write a book? Stelios had already written one, one which had been used as the textbook in an NEH summer seminar for college professors.

Roy got up to leave and Stelios heard himself asking, "Will there still be the possibility of work, you know, like this year?"

"Of course. Of course. Shall I close the door?"

Stelios didn't answer and then Roy was gone. He sat there feeling as if he'd been hit by a truck. Even though he'd been suspecting this, to have it actually spelled out was entirely different. He hadn't realized how much he'd still been hoping.

He had only been sitting there in a daze for a few minutes, when Sondra, one of his graduate students, came by.

"Oh, good, you're here." She sat down and began talking enthusiastically. A weird feeling came over Stelios, as if he wasn't really there but off somewhere at a great distance, watching. He tried to concentrate. Apparently, she was planning to do a master's thesis on Marcus Aurelius and wanted him to direct it.

She stopped and looked at him, waiting for him to answer. He cleared his throat. "I…I don't know if I can."

"Oh, that's disappointing. Can I ask why?" "Well, I won't be teaching here next year." She was stunned. "Oh. We all assumed…" "Roy just informed me."

"I'm sorry. You're such a good teacher." There was an embarrassing silence. "Maybe you could ask him. About my thesis, I mean. Maybe he could make some kind of special arrangement."

"I doubt it."

"I'd really like to work with you."

Stelios nodded.

"I'm sorry. I guess I've come at a bad time. I'd better go." And Stelios was alone again and it was all he could to do to not to burst into tears.

After a while, he roused himself and, not knowing what else to do, decided to go to the movie, even though little was left of his enthusiasm. When he got outside, he noticed a group of graduate students standing over by the street. Elena, the psychic, was with them. He wondered if she had known he wouldn't be hired. She waved to him to come over. He wasn't sure he could maintain his composure, but there was no away around it. He spent a few minutes talking to them but he had no recollection of what was said. As soon as he could, he extricated himself, saying that the movie was starting.

***

After a light dinner at home, Ellen had come back to campus to take in *Les enfants du paradis*. She had already seen it twice, but it was the kind of film you could watch many times.

She would be passing Morey Hall but she had no plans to stop at her office. As she drew close, Foxwhistle issued forth from the front door, marching down the outside stairs, shaking his head, muttering to himself, looking quite put out. He stalked off in apparent disgust to the faculty club, no doubt to consume a number of stiff bourbons.

After a several moments, Tom Prent, a graduate student, came out and collapsed in a heap on the stairs, his shoulders shaking. Ellen didn't know him very well and, although she realized that most professors would just walk by, she decided to stop.

"Tom?" At first he didn't answer. She laid a hand on his shoulder. "Tom?"

He looked up at her, tears running down his cheeks. "I don't know what to do. I give up. I give up."

"What is it?"

"Foxwhistle. I never should've taken his class. Now it's too late. He'll probably fail me."

"I realize he can be tough, but…"

"You know he has this crazy idea for a book that would make clear for the first time what people in the 17th century meant by *l'honnête homme*? His point is that everybody used the phrase as if everybody knew what it meant but no one ever defined it."

"Maybe that's because it's undefinable."

"Yeah, but that's not good enough for Foxwhistle. He wants to nail this down once and for all, so he's assigned an author to everyone in class and we're supposed to read the guy, find out what he meant by *l'honnête homme* and report back to the class. Chad was the first and he lucked out. He got Mme. de Lafayette."

"Mme. de Lafayette was not a guy."

"No, she wasn't. Anyway, Chad came back with his findings and it seemed all right. He stuck me with Guez de Balzac. I did my best." Ellen turned when she noticed Stelios some distance away talking with a small group of students and thought, oh, good, I can go with him.

"I was about two-thirds of the way through my report when all of a sudden Foxwhistle jumps up and starts yelling, 'No, no, *ce n'est pas ça! Allez cherchez encore!*' in that horrible accent of his, you know, like 'No, no, ce nay pahr ça! Allay shairshay encore!'" Tom put his head in his hands. She hoped he wasn't going to start crying again. "It's like I don't know what else I can do."

"You knew when you took the class that Foxwhistle takes no prisoners."

"Yeah, but I kind of liked the 17th century."

Tom was just a plodder. Maybe the whole thing was beyond him. She looked at her watch. "Look, Tom, I have to go. Just pick something. Narrow it down."

He tried unsuccessfully to smile. "Thanks, Professor Metran. I'll try to do what you said."

She left him looking less despondent. She wondered what Guez de Balzac would have thought if, hunched over a few pages of manuscript, quill in hand, a candle by his side, he had had any inkling that he would steal across the considerable expanse of four centuries to haunt the nightmares of an unfortunate American student?

The cluster of students was still there but Stelios was gone. "Damn," she said.

***

The movie had drawn a pretty decent crowd, although not as big as *In the Realm of the Senses*. No jocks or frat boys, no cat calls or wolf whistles. No need for Roy to make another disclaimer. She looked around but couldn't find Stelios.

She loved the film. Afterwards, in the hallway, she spotted Stelios with a crowd around him and was walking over, when Oswaldo came up to her.

"I loved it. Especially the pantomime. Stelios was right."

"You should tell him."

But Stelios was gone.

\*\*\*

Early the next afternoon, Ellen was vacuuming her apartment when the phone rang. It was Val.

"Ellen, Ellen. Come to my house! Please!" "What's going on?"

"Come right away! Please! Please!"

"Val. What's wrong?"

"Just come!"

When Ellen pulled up, an ambulance was parked in the driveway.

Val was outside, sitting on the picnic table, her head in her hands.

"What's going on, Val? What happened?"

She looked up, her eyes filled with tears. "It's Stelios. He killed himself."

"What?" Ellen's breath caught in her throat as if she had been punched.

"He committed suicide."

Ellen turned to run into the house, but Val grabbed her arm. "It's no use. There's nothing you can do. He's gone."

Disorientated, Ellen shook her head, "No, no," she said, remembering the conversation at the bar when he was so distraught. She looked at Val, frowning, eyes tearing, "When? How?"

"I don't know," Val sobbed. "He was asleep when I got up. I went shopping…I…I…didn't get to say anything…goodbye." She shook her head. "When I came home, Micci met me at the door. She was crying and I knew something was wrong. She led me to the bathroom. He was lying in the tub in this cold, bloody water."

With an intake of breath, Ellen thought of the ketchup. "Oh God, oh, no." She felt her legs give away, held the table to steady herself and sat down. "What can I do?"

Val looked off into the distance. "He knew what he was doing. This was no cry for help. He went vertical, not horizontal, with the razor." She reached into a pocket and handed Ellen a piece of paper. "Here. Read this."

At first Ellen struggled to focus on the paragraph. She recognized

Stelios's handwriting:

*I can't please the emperor anymore. I don't know how to please him. I can't find him. Hell, I don't even know who he is. I don't know where to go from here. I don't see any light anywhere anymore. The emperor welched on his agreement. Emperors can do that, I guess. Even worse, I let myself down and even worse, I let you down. I don't even know how you feel about me anymore. I'll see you on the other side.*

*If you want to. Meanwhile, I'll go out quietly...stoically...
like Seneca.*

Ellen looked up. "Like Seneca," she mumbled.

"Yeah, like Seneca."

The paramedics came out rolling a gurney, which they carried down the steps. A sheet covered the body. As they lifted it into the ambulance, Val gestured over toward Micci, who was sitting at the edge of the bushes in front of the house. "Look at her. She knows. She knows she won't ever see him. He loved that cat so much."

"You know what he told me, when we first got together? He said,

'I've come to love you like the gods and the angels love.'" She looked at Ellen. "And now it's all come to this."

The doors of the ambulance slammed shut and it drove off.

***

The next thing Ellen knew, she was running down the department corridor, screaming, "They killed him! They killed Stelios!"

Foxwhistle came bounding out of his office and roped her into his arms. "Hey. Slow down, little lady. Who's they?"

"Roy. Everybody," she said, her jaw clenched.

He took her into his office and sat her down in a big, comfortable chair. She watched as he opened a desk drawer, took out a bottle of bourbon and filled half a glass. "Here, drink this. Drink it all. It'll do you good."

"I'm surprised you're here?"

"Expecting a phone call."

He waited while she emptied the glass, then poured her another.

She drank more slowly and Foxwhistle let her finish the second.

"Some more?"

She shook her head.

"So tell me what happened."

She told him what she knew. "I feel guilty. There were signs. I should've realized…done something."

"Don't beat yourself up. It's not your fault." He stood and went to the window. Pounding his fist into his palm he said, "God damn that Roy! This just ain't right."

The phone rang. "Hello? Yes, yes, I'm interested… what?…Okay, but I want it understood I have free reign…good…what?…forget that…I mean just what I said. I don't do interviews…that's exactly right, you heard me right…look, you called me. Either you want me or you don't. Okay, call me here. Yes, this number. No, I don't have a damn cell phone." He hung up.

Ellen looked at him. Under any other circumstances, she would've been smiling. "Should I have left?"

"No, no. It was just Harvard."

"Harvard?"

"They want me to direct their graduate thesis program."

"Will you accept?"

He narrowed his eyes, teasing. "It's always nice to be wanted, especially when the price is right."

She stood. "I have to go."

"Are you okay to drive?"

"Better than I was when I drove here."

He took her in his arms again and she let her head fall on his shoulder. "You call me, anytime you need me, you hear? I don't care if it's the middle of the night, you call me."

"How?"

He leaned over his desk, scrawled on a piece of paper, and handed it to her.

"What's this?"

"My home phone number."

"I didn't know you had one."

"I don't. This is just for you. The university doesn't even have it." He smiled. "Neither does Harvard."

# Chapter Fifteen

The following week, Roy asked Ellen to stop by his office.

"Please sit down."

"I'll stand. What do you want?"

"Hmm…I wanted to talk to you about the memorial service."

"It's not a service. It's a ceremony in his honor."

"I see. But there'll be speeches?"

"I wouldn't call them speeches. Some of his friends will say something by way of saying goodbye."

"Hmm…as chairman I suppose I should say a few words."

"It would be better if you don't speak."

"What?"

"It would not be appreciated." She turned on her heel.

"Believe me, I'm as distressed as anyone about this," she heard him call after her. She kept on walking.

\*\*\*

The day of the ceremony was sunny and crisp. On her way, Ellen drove past the green where Stelios's yoga class first started. His students were doing sun salutations, holding a leaderless practice in his honor.

At the university chapel, a good number of faculty and students had already gathered. Chad and Jorge were acting as ushers. The Indonesians and the Africans from the team sat in the back, the faculty members in front. The doors were about to close when the members of his yoga class arrived, still in their yoga clothes. When they were offered seats, they refused and went to stand in the side aisles as a sign of respect.

One of the students from his academic classes got up from where she was sitting and went to stand with the yoga students. Then another, and soon all his students were standing in the side aisles.

According to his wishes, Stelios had been cremated. An urn holding his ashes stood on a table in front of the podium.

Chad was the first to speak.

"Stelios once told me that ancient peoples, maybe it was the Greeks, I don't remember, believed that in the earliest times we could see the angels. Then, they made themselves invisible to us because they didn't want us to see them crying." He paused and took a deep breath, trying to get control over his emotions. "The angels are crying now.

"You were my teacher, my teammate and my friend and I will miss you for all the remaining days of my life. You will never be forgotten, *o adelfos mou. Poté.*" He looked down for a moment. When he raised his head, his eyes were flashing. "I have this to say to you: Sing your death song like a hero and go home with your head held high."

Ellen came up to the podium next.

"Val has asked me to speak in her place. She feels too emotional to speak. I can stand in for her, but I can't speak for her. I can only speak for myself." She paused, collecting her thoughts.

"I really don't know what to say, I'm so overwhelmed with losing him, someone who I guess was just too sensitive to make it all the way through his life in this world." She felt tears well up in her eyes and start running down her cheeks. She didn't bother to wipe them away.

"This is such a…such a waste. He was so, so talented. I've never known anyone who got such an enthusiastic response from his students. His students loved him." There was a murmur of assent from among them. "The thing he wanted to do the most was to teach. That's all he asked." She paused, gritted her teeth and felt a surge of anger well up inside her and she said to herself, "Okay. Screw it. I'm going to say it." And she went on. "But that was too much to ask from this fucked up, so-called profession. Even though he jumped through all the hoops. He was an amazing teacher. I hear administrators blowing air around all the time about how important good teaching is. And research, well, he also wrote a brilliant book that was used in a NEH summer seminar for college professors, but none of that got him anywhere. Never got him a real job. I could go on, but I won't. I will just say that I love him and I miss him terribly and I will always love him. I wish him Godspeed and peace at last."

She didn't go back to her seat but went over to the side aisle to stand with his students. She felt someone press a tissue into her hand and say to her, "You go, girl!"

Hugo was next. He walked slowly to the front, accompanied, Ellen saw, by a spirit eagle on his left and a spirit jaguar on the right. They were, she assumed, his power animals. Before her *ayahuasca* journey, such a vision would have been startling but she was getting used to them.

"I knew Stelios as an inept student in his morning yoga classes and as a friend. Like most of you, I am immensely saddened by his death. Our world is a shabbier place without him. That is pretty much all I want to say but I do want to read you a prayer from the Lakota.

*"Take care of the elders*
*For they have gone a long way*
*Take care of the children*
*For they have a long way to go*
*And take care of those of us who are in between For we*
*are doing the work.*

"Stelios was doing the work and we did not take care of him enough."

Val let out a wrenching sound of utter anguish, as if an ice pick had plunged into the deepest regions of her heart. The jaguar, who had been licking his front paw, washing his head and shoulders, stopped abruptly, the paw in mid-air, and fixed Roy with a murderous gaze that, if translated into words, might have said, "You will be wiped off the face of this universe." Ellen thought she never wanted to be on the receiving end of a look like that. The eagle, too, spread his wings and rose menacingly off of Hugo's shoulder. Ellen thought he might swoop down on Roy and rip his face apart, but the eagle settled back down.

Hugo was about to leave the podium when he looked at Val, who was sobbing inconsolably. "And to Val, the depth of whose grief I can only begin to imagine, on behalf of my beautiful friend, Stelios, I offer this blessing from the Mewa Puebla.

*"Hold onto what is good*
*Even if it's a handful of earth*
*Hold onto what you believe*
*Even if it's a tree that stands alone*
*Hold onto what you must do*
*Even if it takes you a long, long way from here*
*Hold onto your life*
*Even if it's easier to let go*
*Hold onto my hand,*
*Even if I've gone a long way from you."*

And with those words, the ceremony came to a close. Chad took the urn with Stelios's ashes and walked down the aisle. There was a look on his face that Ellen had never seen before, one that was, well, beyond anger. The yoga students joined their hands together at their chests, fingers spread wide, thumbs at the heart center, in *anjali mudra*, the ancient gesture of gratitude, and bowed their heads. The other students, some a bit shyly and awkwardly, did so as well.

Afterwards, there was a gathering at the log house, for which Ellen had arranged some food. Roy must have figured he wouldn't be welcome, because he didn't show up. Derya, who had sat in the back at the ceremony, did, coming hesitating at the door. Val greeted her warmly.

"Come in, come in. Of course, you're welcome. You gave him some happiness in these last months, which is more than I did."

For the first time that Ellen could remember, Jorge didn't seem to have any grass with him.

***

A few days later, Ellen was driving to the post office when she noticed Val sitting on a bench in a little triangular park nearby, reading through a pile of condolence cards in her lap, and she was weeping. Ellen thought of stopping but decided it would be best not to intrude. Anyway, she didn't know what she could say.

She noticed two red-tailed hawks circling above Val, high in the sky. Real ones, not spirits. She went to the post office but when she got there, she realized that she had forgotten the most important thing, an overdue bill that she had to get in the mail right away. So she went back, got it, and came back. Val was still sitting on the bench and the hawks were still circling in the sky over her. There was a line at the post office and someone in front of her was sending an endless number of boxes. When she drove by the park again, Val was gone. So were the hawks.

She asked Hugo about it. "What were the hawks doing?" "They were there for protection." "Protection?"

"For all I know, Stelios sent them."

"You mean if someone bothered her, like tried to mug her, they would swoop down on them?"

"I don't know. It's unlikely that anyone would while they were there. But I wouldn't want to be anyone who did."

# Chapter Sixteen

A week or so later, Val stopped by Ellen's office. She looked a little better and Ellen told her so.

"Well, I've been getting a little sleep. Are you going to be around? I'm on my way to Roy's office to pick up some paperwork. I'm trying to tie up all the loose ends regarding Stelios."

"You don't have to do that yet."

"I want to. I need to get it done. Is Roy back?"

"Oh, yeah, he's back. You can't keep a control freak like him away for long."

"How is he?"

"Bad. Someone literally kicked the shit out of him."
"Good. Who did it?"

"No one knows." Ellen suspected Chad, but kept her suspicions to herself.

When they walked into Roy's outer office, the secretary said, "Just a minute. I'll see if he can see you."

Val ignored her and went directly in. Roy was seated at his desk leafing through his mail, swathed in bandages and wearing the neck brace.

"Oh, Val. Sit down."

"I came for the paperwork on Stelios. I understand there are some things I need to sign. Insurance forms."

"I haven't had the chance to express to you personally how sorry I am. I can only imagine what a terrible loss this is for you. If there's anything I can do, please don't hesitate to tell me."

Val stuck out her hand. "You can give me the papers."

"Hmm…this is a bit premature, Val. They're not quite ready." "What the hell does that mean?" "I mean I haven't gone over them."

"What the hell do you need to go over them for?" "Well, to see if everything is in order, for one thing."

Val looked as if she was ready to slug him. "Look, Stelios didn't just step away from his desk. When I go home tonight, he won't be there. He's never fuckin' comin' back. Now give me the goddamned papers."

Roy still hesitated.

"Or I'll kill you."

Roy stared at her for a moment, his mouth open. Then, without further comment, he handed them over.

When they got back to Ellen's office, Val was still breathing hard. "Just give me a moment to get it together."

"Take your time."

"I should've smacked him."

"I'll make you some tea, some really good chamomile." "That'd be great."

"I think I even have some biscuits."

When they were sitting down, drinking their tea, Val said, "This is yummy."

"Comfort tea. I put a little honey in it."

She put her cup down. "Can I tell you about a dream I had?" "I'm listening."

"It isn't very long." She took another sip of tea. "Stelios and I were in a car, going down this road. He was driving. The radio was on to the classical music station we used to listen to. Whatever was on came to an end, and they announced they were going to play *Dawn over the Moscow River* by Mussorgsky. 'Oh I love this,' I said and turned up the volume. 'So do I,' he said without looking at me. In fact, now that I think about it, he never looked at me."

"Keeping his eyes on the road?"

"I suppose. Anyway, the piece came on. Do you know it?" "Yes."

"He's one of my favorite composers. Too bad he drank himself to death. Anyway, it was amazing. As we were listening, I put my hand on his thigh. 'That's maybe the thing I miss most,' he said. 'Not being able to touch you.' That could've made me sad but it didn't. So we listened. I wish I could say that the landscape we were driving through was beautiful but I don't think there was any landscape. Everything around us was just kind of grey but it didn't matter."

She put down her empty cup.

"We didn't say anything else. We were just grooving

on the music and there was nothing between us, none of the shit that accumulates living in this world, because even though we were driving our car, we weren't in this world. We were somewhere else. I don't know where. And all I felt between us was this pure love."

"That's what Jung used to call a big dream," Ellen said, pouring her more tea.

"Yeah. But there's something else I'll tell you, because I know you won't think I'm crazy."

"Go ahead."

"I feel like I left a part of me, part of my soul, maybe, in the car with him."

Ellen said without thinking, "You did."

"Somehow we're still driving down that road together. I don't know if I mean that literally or not. I'm here, but I don't feel as though I've lost anything. On the contrary, if anything, in a strange way, I feel stronger. Like I lost him here but, in the big picture, I'll never lose him."

"You won't," Ellen said, wondering what made her so sure. "Somehow, that dream really cleansed me." She paused for a moment. "Ever since I slept with Roy—you knew about that, didn't you?"

"Yeah."

"I felt disgusted with myself. Unclean. Now that's all gone. It's over. I'm okay. Well, I'll never be okay, but…"

"Better."

She sipped her tea. "I'm feeling like I can lift my head up again."

# Chapter Seventeen

When Ellen met Carl outside the music hall on the evening of his performance, he was looking pretty nervous.

He handed her a program and there it was: *The War Symphony* by Carl Miller. "I'm so proud of you."

"They're coming," he said.

"Who?"

"Henri Vervet and André Henri. Remember they said they'd try to come? Well, they had the chance to do something in New York and arranged their schedule to be here."

"Great."

"Yeah. But what if they don't like it?"

"They will."

And, as if on cue, the two Frenchmen appeared, a little out of breath. They did the two-kisses-in-the-air routine with Ellen. "So good to see you again, *Mademoiselle Amazonia*. I hope we're not late."

"No, but we should be going in," Carl said. "I've saved us some good seats."

Ellen noticed that Carl's voice was shaky. "On edge?" "Very."

"It'll be fine."

"You don't understand, it's really political. A lot of people won't like it."

No one had been let into the rehearsals. Perhaps because of that, word had spread around campus that the concert was not to be missed so the hall was full. Coming down the aisle, Ellen was surprised to see Foxwhistle's head, several inches above the people surrounding him. As they were taking their seats, Beveridge looked around and, after getting over his shock at seeing Vervet, waved to them.

Huge screens had been hung at the back and sides of the stage. The orchestra, a combination of students and faculty, was already seated. The violins had finished tuning up when the conductor entered and tapped on his music stand. Ellen heard Carl take a deep breath; she took his hand.

The first movement, which, for the most part, seemed jittery and tense, also contained one of the most hauntingly beautiful melodies Ellen had ever heard. So far, so good, she thought.

She had never listened to anything quite like the second movement. It was, following tradition, the slow movement, but that was about as traditional as it got. It consisted of a number of notes played as a solo by a series of different instruments: a viola, a clarinet, a trumpet and a marimba. Each of the instruments played their solo part twice. The notes, although pleasant enough

to listen to, didn't add up to much by themselves until
the four instruments came together and, all at once,
the random sounds coalesced in a dazzling series of
connected chords. When the whole orchestra took them
up, their effect was, Ellen thought, something like what
Scriabin intended with his mystical chord.

After the usual round of coughs, the conductor
launched into the third and final movement. It began
innocently—if rather dissonantly and menacingly—
until, a few minutes in, the orchestra seemed to get
stuck, like a needle on a vinyl record, repeating a single
phrase over and over with a driving rhythm. Then,
softly at first, almost imperceptibly, it started to gather
around itself the sounds of weapons being fired, beginning with pistols and rifles, then ratcheting up to attack
guns, machine guns and planes strafing the ground.
The few lights in the hall began to wink out, just as the
screens at the edges of the stage lit up. Projected images
began to appear, dimly at first, then sharper, war scenes
in the streets of a city, soldiers firing off rounds in the
streets, snipers shooting from the rooftops. The hall
went completely dark. Bodies of the dead and wounded
appeared on the screens. Sounds of mortars fired from
outside into the city, hand-held rockets discharged
at fighter planes zooming overhead, bombs dropped.
Some screens lit up with images of white phosphorus.
Pictures of women screaming, holding their dead

children, loomed up. All this time, the orchestra played a cacophony of notes.

Suddenly it fell silent, except for the percussion section, from which thunderous, bomb-like detonations blasted forth. Everything grew louder and louder, deafening, almost unbearable, until suddenly, all at once, the screens went dark, all sounds stopped and the lights came up on stage. The musicians, some standing, some crouching, were holding their instruments like weapons, the bassoon like a bazooka, clarinets like rifles, violins like attack guns all aimed at the audience. The conductor held his baton as if it were a knife he was about to hurl at the audience. Sounds of weapons firing started up again. The lights flashed off and on. Each time, the musicians moved into new stances, sometimes crouching, sometimes bolt upright, sometimes on one knee, their instruments held against the shoulder or waist high. At times they stayed still, at others they jumped around, as if they were taking cover or firing off rounds.

When the lights came on, the musicians were wearing combat berets. All sound stopped and the hall filled with silence. For a long time, nobody moved. The musicians were frozen in place, expressionless, still aiming at the audience, which also was motionless, too stunned to react.

Then a man stood, pumping his fist, screaming, "Yes!"

Shaken out of their stupor, some in the audience got to their feet applauding, others hissed and booed. The musicians laid down their instruments. Arguments broke out, people screamed at each other, and a few scuffles, some fairly violent, erupted. One man was punched in the nose and had blood all over his white shirt that had been ripped open. An education professor in the back of the hall cried out, "Shame, shame!"

Foxwhistle jumped up and yelled back, "That's enough out of you!" He made as if to climb over some seats. The education professor sat down.

Vervet leapt to his feet, fought his way into the aisle, sprang onto the stage and applauded the performance. The conductor and the musicians remained rigidly in place. Then he said to the audience, "We have all been present at the making of musical history." He motioned to Carl to stand and clapped. His efforts brought a modicum of calm to the hall. More and more people started to clap with him. Neither the conductor nor the musicians bowed or in any other way acknowledged the applause. A few people were still yelling at each other. Dean Hairheart was on his cell phone. Security guards appeared at the back of the hall.

After a while, things quieted down enough for the audience to file out.

***

The Dean did not attend the reception. Beveridge looked distraught. "I didn't know what to do. About the reception, I mean. Perhaps I should call it off."

"And why would you do that?" André asked.

"Well, because, for one thing, I don't want any more fights breaking out after people begin tossing back drinks."

Beveridge watched with some displeasure as two women were telling Carl how moved they were by his music.

That was too much for Beveridge. "That's not music. I don't know what it is, but it's not music. All those videos."

"What would you know about music?" Vervet asked.

"Now I understand why I, the department chairman, was not allowed into the rehearsals. I would have put a stop to it, substituted in some Beethoven and—" Beveridge came to an abrupt halt as he realized what Vervet had just said. His jaw dropped open and he remained too shocked to reply.

Carl suppressed a laugh; André didn't.

"As for the videos, if Wagner, whom I consider to be the greatest composer who ever lived, the only composer who, unlike all lesser composers—and I include myself in this group—speaks directly to the soul, if he were alive today, he would be using video, ambient sound and anything else he could get his hands on. Can you imagine what he would do with all the stuff that's available?"

Instead of answering, Beveridge sullenly slurped up a generous amount of red wine.

"I came all the way from Paris to hear this work and I am very glad I did."

"So am I," André said.

"It couldn't be more different from my own compositions," Vervet continued. "But I find it immensely powerful, inventive and innovative."

"Well I find it pretentious and bombastic. Even unpatriotic," Beveridge said.

"Unpatriotic?! What does that have to do with music? Who cares about that?" Vervet asked.

"I don't care," André said with a shrug.

"Well you're French. I wouldn't expect you to," Beveridge said. "It's people like you who didn't like *Le sacre du printemps*, when it was, how you say, debuted," Vervet said.

"Nobody's more patriotic than me and I found it engrossing," Foxwhistle said.

"You, of all people, what could you possibly see in it?" Beveridge asked.

"Well, I don't know much about music but I know what I like. Something with *cajones*."

"I daresay you slept through most of it," Beveridge said.

Foxwhistle laughed. "Not even I could sleep through that."

"See me in my office tomorrow at nine, Carl," Beveridge said as he moved off.

Carl watched him go. "Well, I guess we know what that's all about. I don't think they like me here anymore."

"Don't worry about it," Vervet said. "How would you fancy being in Barcelona next year?"

"Barcelona? That's one of my all-time favorite cities."

"We have a friend there who's important in music circles. I'll speak to him. He'll find you something much more suitable, and we'll get your symphony performed in Paris, won't we, André?"

"We will."

Carl leaned over and whispered to Ellen, "Barcelona! Oh my God! What better place to write my Lorca opera?"

# Chapter Eighteen

Word of the performance got out to right-wing circles, creating a buzz, and Carl was invited to be a guest on the Liam O'Higgins show.

Ellen was not sure that was a good idea. "He's a professional blowhard. A bully, like your upstairs neighbor. You'll be on his turf and he's used to browbeating guests, making them look bad."

"I know, I know, but I feel like I have to."

Carl left that afternoon for New York City. Before long, he was on the TV screen, sitting across from Liam O'Higgins himself. Liam appeared quite relaxed, if rather grim and disapproving. Carl looked nervous, but Ellen was amused to notice he was wearing his recently acquired hemp shirt.

"So I understand you've written a very controversial piece of music, a symphony, is it?"

"It's a symphony, but I don't know how controversial it is." "Well, you've managed to raise quite a few hackles." "Good."

"That was your intention?"

"Among others."

"You'll have to forgive me. Classical music is not one

of the subjects I'm most familiar with, but"—he looked hard across the desk at Carl—"since when has it become political?"

"At least since Beethoven. He was going to dedicate his *Eroica Symphony* to Napoleon, but he became disenchanted with his fascist ways."

"Fascist? Hmm. As a historian, I've never thought of Napoleon as a fascist. But let's talk about this symphony of yours. You've called it a War Symphony, I believe?"

"Correct."

Liam looked at his notes. "But you're not, as far as I can tell, a politically active person."

"Neither was Benjamin Britten."

Liam looked at him quizzically.

"He wrote a War Requiem."

"I see. But you went a little further. You named the third movement, where all hell breaks loose, *Faloojah*."

Oh boy, here it comes, Ellen thought.

"Correct."

"Now, I have to say, I haven't heard the symphony."

"It's only been played once."

"But my understanding is that it's very antiwar."

"Correct."

Ellen wished he wouldn't keep saying *correct*, but she put it down to his nervousness.

"You're against the Iraq War?"

"Yes. We were taken into it by a pack of lies, repeated endlessly in the media, I might add."

"Then you support Saddam Hussein?"

"No, I don't."

"You sure as hell do. You're not getting any free ride from me on this one. If you're against the war, then you're supporting Saddam Hussein."

"Are you trying to tell me that I support the government of any country I'm not ready to invade? That's preposterous."

"You support the troops, don't you?"

"That depends on what they're doing."

"Do you or don't you?"

"If they're bombing women and children in Baghdad, if they're rounding up men who haven't done anything and tossing them in jail, I don't support them."

"Americans don't behave like that."

"If you bomb a city, you bomb civilians."

"We do precision bombing."

"Be serious. How precise do you think you can be?"

"Surgically precise."

"Yeah, sure."

Liam looked furious. "The battle of Faloojah was a pivotal victory for us, a turning point in the war."

"Which produced hundreds of thousands of refugees and who knows how many deaths."

"You vilified it in your...what was it? Your symphony? Americans were dragged through the streets of Faloojah. We had to teach those people a lesson."

"What people?"

"Terrorists."

"How? By bombing them with white phosphorous? Women and children were hit, not just combatants. You know what that stuff does?"

"Americans don't use white phosphorous." "You know damned well we did."

Liam jumped to his feet and thundered, "I've had enough outta you! Why don't you just shut up?"

"What?"

Liam loomed over him, looking twice his size. For a moment Ellen thought he was going to take a swing at Carl. "You heard me.

Shut up!"

And there was timid Carl, jumping to his feet, standing his ground, refusing to be bullied. "You can't shut me up! I'm not a Dixie Chick!"

Suddenly the screen switched to a commercial for some prescription drug with a list of side effects that, well, just wouldn't quit. When the show resumed, Carl had disappeared and some other guy Ellen had never heard of had taken his seat across the desk from Liam, who was still fuming. She switched it off.

\*\*\*

Just like that, Carl was a celebrity, appearing on the morning talk shows, actually being asked tough questions—not the usual cream-puffs lobbed at prominent figures, but ones that questioned his patriotism or implied that he had composed a subversive work. Carl had found a way to put aside his shyness and answer the harshest criticism.

Then, abruptly, all the controversy in the media came to an end. Although all this earned him a certain amount of notoriety, even acclaim in certain circles, it didn't do him any good at Wellington.

As Carl had surmised, he wasn't being asked back.

Ellen, who expected to be let go, was surprised to receive a very favorable evaluation letter from the committee reviewing her status. She assumed that Roy had decided not to take revenge and block her being offered another three-year contract. Apparently there was no need for her to worry.

A few weeks later, she was teaching her French Civilization class, talking about the Impressionists and showing slides of Monet's haystacks. It was a subject she knew a lot about, having spent a summer in Paris at an NEH seminar in modern French painting. The class gave every indication of sharing her interest when, out of nowhere, instead of a haystack a slide appeared of her on the beach with the seven Herbs. Luckily, it was not one in which two of the Herbs were fucking each other on the side, but it was one in which they were fucking *her*. To make matters worse—if that were possible—she couldn't move to the next slide. Clicking the remote did no good; the mechanism remained stubbornly stuck.

A number of thoughts raced through Ellen's mind— *What the hell is going on?*

*Where the hell did this picture come from?*

*How did it even get taken?*

*How in the hell did it get into the presentation?*

*Should I just walk out? Leave?*

The students' first reaction was one of stunned silence, but they were beginning to get over that and some giggling could be heard here and there. She shut the machine off and the image on the screen vanished before any catcalls or wolf calls had a chance to break out.

"That's all for today. Sorry for the malfunction. Class dismissed." At this time she usually announced the theme for the next meeting, but in this case that seemed unnecessary. As the students left, some looked at her with alarm, some with confusion and some with disapproval, but a few smiled.

After class, students would often come up to ask questions, but today only one—a tall, young African-American man—walked down the aisle toward her. She had noticed him, sitting with the jocks who looked bored even when pretending to be listening, but he was always attentive. She didn't know what to expect.

"Professor?"

"Yes?"

"I just wanted to tell you how much I enjoyed this class." It didn't escape her that he used the past tense. "I'm glad you did." "I can see that you're very passionate about the subject. Oops, bad choice of words. I didn't mean..."

"That's okay. I'm glad you've liked it. You...you play a sport? I notice you sit with the athletes."

"Hoops."

"For most people, that's a long way from French Civilization." "Maybe, but listen, I'm lucky to be here. I may look pretty tall,

but I'm too short to make it in the pros. This is as far as I go, so I'm trying to learn as much as I can while I have the chance."

"Smart."

"Anyway, I just wanted to let you know I think you're a good teacher. The best I've had."

"Thanks. And thanks for reminding me why I became a teacher." She held out her hand. "Good luck."

"You too." He turned to walk away, then stopped. "Who knows, maybe I'll get to go to France some day."

"I hope so."

He smiled and moved away.

She picked up her mail, went into her office and closed the door. She felt like crying but didn't. A squirrel was on a branch outside the window, eating an acorn and watching her. It stayed there for a long time while she leafed through the latest issue of PMLA. There was Steadman's article, replete with the references to Barthes, Foucault and Derrida that the editor had requested. She tossed the journal aside. It teetered on the edge of the desk, then toppled over into the wastebasket. Happy as she was for Steadman, she did not retrieve it.

She sat for awhile, pondering her future. She took her ticket to Lima out of a drawer. She was going to use it that summer but...

The squirrel chattered and clicked its teeth. Ellen looked through the glass of her office window and into the branches of the tree. "Okay, it's time go."

Turning on her laptop, Ellen composed her letter of resignation.

She called up Hugo and told him what happened.

"I thought I was through with the Herbs. In fact, I'd pretty much forgotten about them."

"Well, you may have been through with them but apparently they weren't quite finished with you."

"Where did they come from?"

"Through the crack between the worlds, the portal between the realm of the spirit and ordinary reality. Remember I told you that once you open that door, anything can come through. Well, they did."

***

Toward the middle of the afternoon, she got the summons to Roy's office she had been expecting.

"Sit down."

"I'm fine standing."

"Hmmm...well, I don't need to tell you what this is about." "No. How many students complained?"

"I don't know. It only takes one. Dean Hairheart is furious. I've never seen him so livid. He was read the riot act by the Vice President for Academic Affairs. The Dean is at a loss to understand why so many extremely awkward—not to say, embarrassing—situations have arisen all of a sudden. First, we had Serge's, if that's what his name really is, Bulgarian classes, then this very unfortunate business with Stelios."

Ellen's face clouded over. She was about to go off on him, but he raised a hand, wincing as he did.

"Don't get me wrong, the Dean and I are as deeply upset about what happened to Stelios as anyone."

"No doubt."

"And, as if all this wasn't enough, James has announced with great glee that he is leaving us."

"Going to Harvard?"

"You knew? I guess I'm the last to find out. Yes, he's off to supervise, of all things, their graduate dissertation program."

"Do they understand what they're in for?"

"Well, they haven't asked me. Anyway, I doubt that they care. They just want his name. And now, as if all that weren't bad enough, today a picture of a female member of my department *in flagrante delicto*, having some kind of orgy on a beach, flashes on the screen in the middle of one of her classes."

"Are you implying it would be less…umm…damaging if it had been a male professor?"

"I didn't say that."

"Don't you wish you'd been there? On the beach, I mean."

"I do not. Of course, that very unfortunate business with that friend of yours in the music department doesn't help, either. I met Beveridge, looking ashen, coming out as I went into the Dean's office. Anyway, the Dean has let me know that I no longer enjoy his confidence in my ability to run the department smoothly. What he said to me was, 'A lot of things are going on in your department, Roy, and none of them are good.' Without spelling it out, he gave me to understand that my days as chairman were numbered."

"Does he want to talk to me? Maybe I should talk to him. Fill him in a little more on the MLA convention, now that I have nothing to lose?"

He picked up a paper that was on his desk and put it back down again. "I don't understand, Ellen. When you came here for an interview, you were such a nice girl."

"By nice, do you mean vulnerable?"

"Hmmm…no. I mean someone with a bright future in the profession. I don't understand what happened."

Ellen didn't answer.

"You do know what this means, of course?"

"I'll save you the trouble." She handed him her letter of resignation and walked out.

***

Then it was the time for goodbyes. As she was cleaning out her office, Foxwhistle came by.

"You've probably heard the news. Harvard actually hired me. With a big boost in pay."

"Congratulations. Now you can go raise hell in Cambridge." "That's my plan."

"You may have to fly out to Wyoming from there."

"Oh, I'll still rely on my trusty Chevy. Just may take me a little longer. Anyway, how can I get a trunk full of books onto a plane?" He gave her a big hug. "You're probably doing the right thing, you'll be much better off. Where are you going?"

"Peru."

He laughed. "You don't fool around, do you?"

"I'm setting off on a great adventure, something I've only dreamed about. No more just studying about the Amazon. Now I'm actually going to be there."

"Well you've got me beat. Cambridge isn't exactly the most exotic destination."

"Already have my ticket. I just have to move up the date."

He stopped at the door. "Come see me in Cambridge. Or Wyoming, for that matter."

"You never know," she said. The gesture was flattering, especially since, as far as she knew, no one had ever been invited to Wyoming.

She followed Foxwhistle out and found Val in her

office, looking sad and lonely. "When will you be coming back?"

"Dunno. Maybe never," she joked.

"Maybe I'll come see you."

"That would be great."

They both knew it would never happen.

A little later, Chad and Jorge came by. She gave Chad her laptop and all of her French books.

"Are you sure you won't want them?"

"Positive. I've had enough of academia, and academia has had enough of me."

They sat out on the lawn in a secluded spot and smoked one last joint together.

"Did you hear?" Chad asked. "Todd landed a job at UCSB." Ellen shook her head and laughed. "No wonder he never had any interviews. He had it lined up all along."

"Anita, too. Of course, it's just lectureships for both of them." "Todd won't have any trouble parlaying that into a tenure track

job, as soon as he finishes his diss, which I heard is well underway, although when he works on it is a mystery."

"Whenever the surf's not up," Jorge said and handed her a big bag of homegrown for the road.

They helped her load boxes into her car until her office was empty. She was about to drive home when she saw Carl coming toward her, all excited, waving a piece of paper.

"Vervet kept his word. I've been offered a job in

Barcelona, teaching composition at the Escola Superior de Música de Catalunya. There's even some talk about a commission for my Lorca Opera."

"That's great! I'm so happy for you." She gave him a big hug. He looked at the boxes.

"What's all this?"

She explained what had happened. He started to say how sorry he was, but she interrupted. "It's okay. It's probably the best thing that could happen to me. It's so strange the way life plays itself out, I mean, if Vervet's New York concert hadn't been canceled, you wouldn't be going to Spain. And if Hugo hadn't somehow washed ashore in Wellington, I wouldn't be headed for Peru."

She called Laxman, who called in sick to work so he could spend another night with her. It was a long evening of slow and sweet lovemaking, after which, she curled up in his arms and fell asleep, oblivious to all the uncertainties her future held.

As they kissed goodbye in the morning, she said, "Look at us. You're a fugitive from the Third World who's made a life for himself and his family in the First World. And here I am getting the hell out of the First World to try and find something better in the Third."

Laxman smiled and said, "Now we are both exiles."

Before her departure, she spent a pleasant weekend with her mother. Beverly had recovered very well from the surgery and had even acquired a gentleman friend (Larry, who seemed quite nice), all of which made Ellen feel a lot better about leaving. Her mother had even put her house up for sale so she could move into Larry's spacious condo.

When Larry went off to run errands to give them some alone time, the moment arrived that Ellen had been dreading. After her mother poured them some tea, Ellen took a deep breath. "Mom, I left my job."

There was no outburst of disapproval. Beverly put her cup down and looked at her, waiting for her to continue.

"It wasn't what I wanted. My chairman turned out to be a terrible man, a lech, and the university…"

Beverly reached over and touched her daughter's hand. "What will you do now?"

Ellen exhaled, relieved, "I'm…I'm going to the Amazon."

"For research?"

"Something like that."

Beverly took a sip of tea. "Well. I suppose you always wanted to. Sounds like an exciting trip. How long will you stay?"

"I don't know."

When the time came for Ellen to go, Beverly said, "Your father would be proud of you. I think if he could have had his way, he would have been an explorer of some kind." She placed her hands on Ellen's cheeks. "I only ask one thing, that you keep me informed. Write me, from time to time."

"I'll do my best. I'll be in the jungle and I may not always be able…" "You'll find a way."

Driving back, Ellen realized that her mother had somehow become a wise old woman and that she was leaving with her blessing.

She met Hugo at the Java Hut to say goodbye. He announced he was leaving, too.

"There'll be nobody left," Ellen said.

He stretched luxuriously. "My work here is done."

"What work?"

"You."

"Me?"

"Anyway, it's time for me to retire, as much as people like us ever retire, and become a beach bum. Something I've always wanted. I always feel better around salt water."

"Have you picked out a place?"

"Not yet. I'm going to scout around Central America." "Not Peru?"

"Water's too cold. But of course I'll always be visiting."

She sipped some tea. "Looks like Roy is gonna get replaced as chairman. Too many *scandales*." She put her cup down. "He deserves much worse."

Hugo drummed his fingers on the table before answering. "Roy's travails and tribulations have only just begun."

"You seem very sure."

"You saw the jaguar."

# Chapter Nineteen

The announcement of the first morning flight woke Ellen, sleeping in the Lima airport surrounded by Peruvians in sweaters and heavy coats headed for the Andes. She caught the morning flight for Iquitos.

Iquitos was as hot, muggy and tropical as Lima had been chilly. The airstrip and the airport were modest and provincial. In the grass and weeds that surrounded the runway, stood old, rusting airplanes. She remembered the story of Fawcett Airlines, named after Col. Percy Fawcett, an early aviator-explorer who, like Saint-Exupéry, plied his trade in Latin America in the pioneering days of aviation. Fawcett himself was lost on an expedition into uncharted territory in Brazil, searching for the mythical city of El Dorado, probably killed by hostile tribesmen. For years, the company owned a total of one plane, which made a direct flight, once a week, from Miami to Iquitos and back, always sold out, always late getting off the ground. They kept operating until the plane died of old age. In very Peruvian fashion, no replacement had ever been planned for; the company simply closed its doors and went out of business. Ellen wondered if one of the dilapidated aircraft was the legendary one of Fawcett Airlines.

Although she had gone through customs in Lima, some guy who didn't even seem to be a customs agent insisted on going through her bags again. Emerging from the airport, she picked a taxi driver out of the noisy throng clustering around her and went into the city on a three-wheeled motorcycle taxi. She stayed in a small hostel on a little street that ended at the water; very basic—no seat on the toilet—but perfectly adequate for her needs. It had a family feel to it, and she was glad she had chosen not to stay in an expensive hotel. She found that all her research on *Amazonia* had prepared her well. She knew what to expect in the Third World.

After a shower and a change of clothes, she walked to where she could look down at the river. Some small boats were moored at the muddy shore; long wooden crafts, each with a cabin. Little children were playing on a deck. Spotting her, they waved and she realized that the boat was their home. Technically she knew that the expanse of tan, silted water she was surveying was not the Amazon but a tributary, the Rio Itaya. Nonetheless, in only a short distance it would merge with the immense river she had read so much about. And now she was here. She breathed in the sultry air and found it exhilarating.

Like Yves, the hero of *Amazonia*, she ate dinner in the restaurant on the second floor of the Iron House. The menu offered many choices and she decided to go with something exotic, an unfamiliar rainforest animal. The waiter couldn't explain what it was. To any of the possibilities she suggested, like crocodile or boa, he just shook his head. "*No, no. No es eso.*" In the end, it didn't matter. It was delicious, and maybe it was better that she didn't know.

Afterwards she went out to stretch her legs, feeling she was walking in Yves's footsteps, strolling down the same streets. Because the sun was so hot during the day, people came out in force at night, filling the sidewalks. She was glad that they didn't seem to pay any special attention to her. Tired, she turned in early. As she lay in bed, listening to the sounds of the city, the distant music from a nightclub, she thought about how easily she was leaving behind everything she had worked so hard for all those years.

The next morning, she approached the group of moneychangers at the corner where they always hung out, calculators at the ready, to buy soles on the black market, just like Yves. She remembered that Yves had been cheated by one of them once and she made sure she wasn't. And she, too, spent time exploring the town, discovering a neighborhood of large houses with exterior walls completely covered in exquisitely colored tiles.

She went to the open Belén market and bought a pair of Wellington boots for when it rained, and some sturdy flip-flops. The market had almost everything you could think of, but she spent most of her time there meandering down the one dirt street filled with shops selling herbal remedies for everything from arthritis to impotence, one of the potions for which went by the name of *rompe calzón*, or rip your underpants.

Although one of the entrances to the floating city of Belén stood at the end of the street of herbs, Ellen elected to hire a boat to take her on a little tour. In some ways, this was the perfect way to go, because the waterways between the houses served as the town's streets. She glided past homes with two stories, painted yellow, blue and white, with front porches, often with clothes hanging out to dry.

"They have two floors because in the rainy season, the lower one floods out," her guide Juan explained. "They're built on a foundation of logs, so they rise with the river during the rainy season." Ingenious, she thought.

In addition to the houses, she noticed a small shop, a bar, even a school. Belén is sometimes called the Venice of South America, and Ellen had to admit that, even though she wasn't gliding by Renaissance palaces in a gondola, it had a certain charm. But only if you didn't look too closely at the water, which was dirty. But then, the canals of Venice aren't exactly pristine. She had wondered whether the people might resent being gawked at, but nobody seemed to mind and she saw a lot of happy, smiling faces, especially on the kids.

Yet Hugo was right. Iquitos must have been charming,

but now, with all the three-wheel taxis thundering through the streets, it was just too noisy. It still had some nice spots, like the promenade by the river where vehicle traffic was not allowed. She sat at the café for a long time drinking pineapple juice, watching the passersby and the sun going down. She decided that while the men looked okay, many of the women of Iquitos were exceptionally beautiful, quite comfortable and free with their bodies. As she was walking back to the hostel along the esplanade, past the cart holding an A-frame filled with primary colored balloons, a young woman was taking a picture of a girlfriend against the backdrop of the water. She yelled something at her friend and slapped herself on the ass. Although Ellen didn't understand exactly what she said, she knew it was a joke that was all about sex. She smiled and the young woman gave her a broad, conspiratorial smile back.

The next morning, she missed the *rápido* but found another boat going her way. Leaving Iquitos and civilization for the jungle was both exciting and scary. They left the city behind, passing a bank rimmed with thatch-roofed houseboats and blue, brown and red houses on stilts; the Peruvian Naval Base, an ornate old black and tan triple-decker riverboat with a sea horse on the prow; and a big lumber yard.

And then they were on the mighty Amazon itself. All sorts of boats were plying the river, many small craft carrying plantains, pineapples, even ice downstream to

market. Larger ones were ferrying people to and from
the city. Most of the time, low trees stretching out to the
horizon lined the shore. It took the better part of three
hours going against the current before reaching the small
town from which she could walk to Don Pablo's camp.
They passed little settlements scattered along the banks,
one with a *Bar de las Estrellas*, clothes drying in the sun,
families sitting on benches in the shade of a broad, leafy
tree, stairs carved out of clay leading down to the water,
and kids swimming and playing in small boats.

Stepping ashore, she was surrounded by children.
Everyone knew the shaman's encampment, and a little
boy attached himself to her, taking charge of her backpack (almost as big as he was), offering to show her the
way. It turned out that the main path leaving the village
went straight to Don Pablo's camp, but she was glad to
have company for the nearly two-hour walk, glad for the
chance to practice her rusty Spanish, glad to give him a
few dollars for his trouble.

The camp was very rustic, made up of wooden structures with thatched roofs. Since Hugo had shown her
pictures, she knew what to expect and she recognized
Don Pablo immediately. She told him that Hugo had
sent her, but he seemed to know already. Not a young
man, his exact age was difficult to tell. He was of medium
height, thin, agile, with brown skin and black hair.

He assigned her one of the *tambos*, one-room dwellings open on all sides that were scattered in an irregular

line beside the stream. It stood on the far side of the path from the water, on higher ground, and had a raised floor to avoid flooding during heavy rains. It came equipped with a bed with a thin mattress, sheets, a hammock, a wooden stool and a small table. In one corner stood a large plastic container of drinking water. There was a big bucket for fetching bathing water from the stream; a metal plate; a fork, knife and spoon; a plastic glass; a box of candles; and matches. Off down a little path was a basic open-air outhouse, a little wooden stand with a hole in the middle perched over a hole in the ground. That was her new home.

As luck would have it, a group of gringos had come in that same day, about an equal number of men and women from the United States, Canada, England, Spain and Ireland, where Don Pablo went about once a year to do *ayahuasca* ceremonies. They had come together the night before in Iquitos, so it was easy for Ellen to blend in. Don Pablo urged everyone to spend most of the time alone in their *tambos*.

Don Pablo told everybody to rest well that night, because in the morning they would be making the acquaintance of Dr. Ojé. Everyone, weary from traveling, retired early and, almost at once, Ellen entered into as deep a sleep as she could ever remember having, except as a little girl. She understood in a new way where the expression falling asleep came from, because she felt herself drifting far down into her slumber, almost in slow motion. In the middle of the night, she was awakened by a fairly loud beeping noise. Somebody had apparently set their alarm clock, or forgot to turn off their cell phone. She was furious and found it difficult to get back to sleep. She mentioned it to Don Pablo, but he just laughed.

"In every group, someone always complains about that."

"Well, it's very annoying. I was having the best sleep in years—" He interrupted. "It's a bird."

Ellen was stupefied. "But it sounds so electronic." "It's a bird. A high-tech one."

Hugo had warned her what to expect from Dr. Ojé. Often given to children who play on the ground and pick up parasites, *ojé* is the latex-like sap from a close cousin to the rubber tree which once made Iquitos a fabulously rich boomtown. Milky and rather thick, it tastes rather mild but it packs a wallop and is very caustic.

"Keep drinking water," Don Pablo said. "How much?" Jeanne, a Swiss woman, asked. "As much as you can. Eight liters." "That's a lot."

"If you don't, it will burn your insides out."

Despite the warning, an American named Dave, some sort of scientist, didn't think he needed to drink all that water and slipped off to take a stroll in the jungle instead.

Not long after Ellen drank her half-filled glass of *ojé*, she began to feel nauseated and lay down on the wooden floor of the walkway where they had assembled. There was a big container for water, which one of the local women kept full, and everyone had a large plastic bowl for drinking. She kept sipping the water, taking down as much as she could, feeling weak, finding it difficult to stay still, rolling around a lot on the wooden walkway.

All of a sudden her stomach lurched, and she knew she had to get to the rail fast. Jumping up, she made it just before cutting loose with an explosive stream of projectile vomit. That got rid of the nausea but then one by one, the *ojé* drinkers repaired to an open, sandy square with a trough running all around the edge, over which they all squatted, letting the *ojé* come gushing out the other end. Normally, it burns, but Hugo had warned her to bring hemorrhoid salve to put on in advance, which she had shared with any of the others who wanted to use it. A young woman with eagle vision came around and inspected everyone's shit for parasites, and Ellen was happy to learn she didn't have any.

When Dave returned from his walk, Ellen noticed he was staggering holding his swollen stomach. He went straight to Don Pablo, who was thinning out some underbrush on the edge of camp. The shaman hustled to his little house by the stream and returned with an antidote.

Ellen thought she would never want to eat anything ever again. Well, certainly not for days, but when the time for lunch came around, she realized she was rather hungry. So was everyone else except Dave, despite the fact that all that was offered was a thin, dish-watery soup and a boiled plantain. The really strict jungle diet had begun.

Over the meal, Don Pablo told the story of a Canadian woman who had arrived at the camp with terminal cancer. Her doctors had informed her that nothing more could be done.

"Coming down here was her last hope. After she drank *ojé*, we could tell she was full of parasites. I told her she would have to take it again. She didn't want to but she was desperate. After the second time, she fell into a coma that lasted for several days. People in her group began to get very anxious. There was even talk of calling in a helicopter to fly her to a hospital in Iquitos."

"Did they?" Ellen asked.

Don Pablo shook his head. "I knew she would be okay. After three days, she emerged from the coma and a day later was feeling fine. When she got back to Canada, her doctors found no trace of cancer." "This was the last communal meal until the diet ends," he announced. From then on, two workers brought the food around to each *tambo*.

Dave spent the day in bed and by evening the swelling in his liver had gone down.

"What would have happened if you didn't know the antidote?" Ellen asked.

"His liver would have exploded," Don Pablo said.

"It'll probably never be the same," she said.

"No. And he certainly won't be drinking any ayahuasca."

***

That evening, everyone assembled near the bathing hole around a very large basin filled with the clear and colorless juice from the fruit of the *huito* tree. The idea was for everyone to spread it all over their bodies, with one exception for the men.

"Be very careful. And I mean very careful," Don Pablo cautioned. "Don't let it get on your scrotum. If it does, it will cause extreme irritation that doesn't go away easily and there's no treatment for it.

One poor guy was careless, and after two days, he could barely walk, even bow-legged."

"You mean...?" José, one of the men, asked.

"Yes. But lucky for him, the inflammation gradually subsided. A few drops of *huito* won't do much damage, but more than that, look out."

The men were very, very judicious applying the juice near their crown jewels.

***

Ellen was okay with the spartan conditions of life in her *tambo*. She didn't mind the solitude and didn't really miss all the stuff she had accumulated in her former life: her car, cell phone, apartment, all her clothes. She had brought very little with her because everything you take, you have to carry: a few changes of clothing, a flashlight, batteries, a water bottle, some personal items, good walking shoes, a notebook and a few pens. Although journal writing was okay, Don Pablo urged everyone not to read anything. All cosmetics, tooth-paste, soap, anything with a fragrance, all vitamins, supplements and, of course, prescription drugs, were also off-limits, as they would interfere with welcoming in the *ayahuasca*. She realized that very little was needed in the jungle and it came as a great relief.

There were inconveniences. It seemed that there was a colony of large black ants by a big tree next to her *tambo*. As soon as she moved in, so did they. But, although they were all over the place, but they never bit her. There were generic jungle bugs in the bed that did bite her, but they didn't interrupt her sleep, and in the end were more of an annoyance than a problem.

When turning in for the night, Ellen always started out lying on her back. The bed was positioned so that her head was at the front edge of the *tambo*. She was sound asleep when something happened so fleeting and intangible that she questioned whether it had happened at all. She sensed a sudden presence of raw power, heard the slightest sound just above her head, and somehow knew it was a jaguar. The big cat glided past the top of her bed, so close that she could feel the unmistakable warm caress of his breath on her head. She didn't see it, because jaguars are masters of camouflage and move silently though the forest. But she did see it in her mind's eye, and she knew instinctively it was a male.

She sat up quickly and tried to catch a glimpse of the great cat as it melted into the night, but it was too late. She wondered if she should get up and tell Don Pablo there was a jaguar roaming around, but not really sure there was one, she lay back down and before long had fallen asleep again.

In the middle of the night, the terrified screaming of a man woke her. Oh my God, she thought, the jaguar is attacking someone. The screaming subsided but she heard other voices, presumably of some of the workers and Don Pablo himself, running to investigate. In due course, things quieted down and, figuring nothing too terrible had happened, she went back asleep.

Upon awakening in the morning, she was shocked to see that her hands had turned a deep, midnight blue. In fact, all her skin was now almost black. She looked at her face in a small mirror she had brought with her. She recognized her features, but her whole appearance had undergone a radical transformation.

When the two men brought around her breakfast of watery rice and dry, cardboardy plantains, they told her what had happened during the night.

"An anteater came into Aníbal's *tambo*, jumping down from the roof. He had no idea what it was and was terrified. Don Pablo heard him and found the guys who were supposed to be standing guard still asleep, so he ran over to Aníbal's *tambo* himself."

"Was the anteater still there?"

"It was long gone."

"How do we know it was an anteater?"

"Don Pablo recognized the smell it left behind." "So he calmed Aníbal down?" "And fired the guards."

Aníbal had to pass by Ellen's tambo to get to the stream to wash, and when he did, she called out to him.

"Things got pretty exiting last night, huh?"

"Yes. Already before bedtime, I am apprehensive. This is not my environment. All of a sudden I heard this loud thud. I get out of bed and saw this black thing with a long nose and a long tail, bigger than a dog, walking on the crossbar under the roof of my *tambo*. I thought I was as good as dead. I tried to shush it away but it didn't go. I screamed like hell and it ran away. I had no idea what it was. I thought maybe it was a jaguar. Or a monkey."

Ellen laughed. "But it was just a plain old anteater." "Why are you laughing?"

"Well, they're pretty harmless unless you're an ant." "How am I supposed to know that?"

"If he comes back, send him over here. I've got lots of ants, big black juicy ones."

"I had no idea the jungle would be like this, so hot, so far away from everything, so full of strange animals. There are monkeys around here, aren't there?"

"Yes. You can hear them at night. They howl."

"They won't hurt you," she said, wondering why he had come. "No?" He seemed unconvinced. "Well, I better get down to the stream for my morning bath, before the sun gets much higher." He made as if to brush some invisible bugs off his forearms. "I still feel creepy from last night."

She watched him walking stiffly toward the stream, wondering why someone who knew so little about the jungle would decide to come here.

As she went through her day, she noticed another, subtler effect of the *huito*. To say that she felt different would be an understatement. Somehow, the *huito* had stripped away the veneer of how she thought of herself, allowing her to begin to blend in with the forest. When darkness fell, she became indistinguishable from the night.

# Chapter Twenty

Sometime that afternoon, two boys came by her tambo carrying a long, thick brown snake. The snake was twisting around trying to escape, but one of the boys grasped it firmly below its head.

"Good afternoon, señora. You like to buy snake skin?"

"What happens to the snake?"

"We kill snake, take skin and sell to you."

The snake's tongue kept darting out. It looked terrified. Ellen thought for a few moments.

"We make bracelet, belt, purse. Whatever you like."

"How much?"

The boys looked at each other. Then one blurted out, "Five dollar." The other boy said, "Good price. Cheap." The snake wriggled around without making any headway.

Clearly this was not the first time these boys had put a snakeskin on the market. "I have a deal for you," Ellen said.

"Five dollar?"

"Yes. I give you five dollars." The boys' eyes lit up and she realized they expected to be bargained down for less, but she didn't care. "And you let the snake go."

"Let go?" They looked at each other, astonished.

"Yes, but you have to promise me you won't go after it, you won't catch it again and sell it to someone else. If you do, I'll know. It's a better deal for you. Less work and I get what I want, and the snake gets to go back into the forest and enjoy a happy life."

Although this was a strange concept, they seemed to get the idea. Their faces became serious. One boy nodded and said, "Okay." He stuck out his hand.

"I'll have to get it." She went over to her bag and pulled a five-dollar bill out of her wallet. She would just have to trust that they wouldn't come back and rob her or tell someone else who would. She thought it was unlikely. Anyway, everyone knew all the gringos had some money with them.

*\*\**

Shortly after nightfall, Don Pablo began beating his drum, the signal to gather for the first ceremony.

With some trepidation, Ellen got her things together: a flashlight, her little pillow, her water bottle and some toilet paper to double as Kleenex. She noticed her hands were a little shaky. Even though it was still hot, she pulled on an off-white, long-sleeved shirt for protection against mosquitoes and in case it got cooler. Then, with a last look around, she joined the procession up to the temple.

As she arrived, she noticed a tall, lanky blond man sitting on a bench outside the entrance. He was slouching comfortably, his arms draped over the back-board, looking so relaxed and confident it was intimi-dating. "Sit down for a moment, will you?"

"Okay."

He looked at her with a friendly smile and said, "I had a dream about you last night." He spoke with a German accent.

"How could you? We've never seen each other before."

He leaned toward her. "Nonetheless, you were in my dream. I recognized you right away as you walked up."

"I don't know what to say." Ellen sized him up and decided he was being friendly and he seemed as sincere as a European can ever be.

"Listen, I've been down here for a while. I've even bought some land from Don Pablo and fixed up a little camp where I've begun holding *ayahuasca* ceremonies. Oh, don't get me wrong. I have no pretenses toward being a shaman. I don't lead them."

"Where's the land?"

He waved his hand vaguely. "Not far from here."

"What was the dream?"

"You know, I really can't remember the details. I just remember you. Quite clearly. What do you think this means?"

"I don't know." Although it could easily have appeared otherwise, this didn't seem to be some New Age way of coming on to her.

The drumming started up again to bring in any strays. "Well, your ceremony is starting."

"You're not coming in?"

"No, no. Not tonight. I just needed to talk to Don Pablo about something"

As she got up, he looked at her intently. "Enjoy your ceremony. I'm not sure *enjoy* is the right word, but you know what I mean."

"Thanks. It's my first. Here in the jungle, that is."

"The first one is always special, just because it's the first." He smiled again. "Okay, we may never know what the dream means, but I'll tell you what I think now, having met you." He made a deprecating gesture with his hand. "For what it's worth."

"Yes?"

"That you belong here. In the jungle. We both do." He stood with a courtliness that reminded her for a moment of Serge. "Perhaps we shall meet again. Or perhaps not, but I think we will both be down here for a very long time."

Inside people were checking out everyone's new *huito* look. Lots of oohs and aahs and people saying "Oh, look at you!"

The temple was a circular building with a thatched roof and individual places around the edge for sitting on the floor. Each one had a bright red, blue or green potty beside it for throwing up, which Don Pablo called color televisions. The only light came from a few candles.

Directly opposite the entrance the shaman had his *mesa*, with all his bottles, stones, feathers, stones and some instruments (Peruvian pipes, small drums and rattles). His guitar was resting against the wall behind the table. He was decked out in ceremonial finery: a brilliant white shirt and pants with black embroidery, and a hat that fitted closely around his head, also white with black trim, all of which looked quite dashing on his slim frame. He was at ease, looking forward to doing his work.

There was no mistaking the *ayahuasca* bottle standing among the many objects on his *mesa*, not far from the Agua Florida, and Ellen felt a shiver of nerves. By the time she picked her spot and settled in, darkness had fallen and the only light was from a few candles. Ellen was glad to see that some of the local people had come in unobtrusively to take part in the ceremony.

Don Pablo told the group not to drink any water until the ceremony was over, and if the journey became difficult, to keep breathing deeply and stay with their breath.

Taking his seat behind the table, he shook the bottle of *ayahuasca* and set it in front of him. He unscrewed the top, leaning over it, focusing his full attention on it, speaking to it, singing to it in a low voice, whistling into it, praying to it, infusing it with his power. He lit his pipe and blew mouthfuls of smoke into it, whistling in a minor key. He leaned back for a few moments, perfectly still, before filling a small glass and calling the first person up.

Everyone went up in turn. When Ellen's time came, she drank her glass down and handed it back to Don Pablo who smiled at her. She tried to smile back, but the taste of the *ayahuasca* didn't let her, conjuring up memories of when she threw up during her first journey at Hugo's. As soon as she got back to her place, she grabbed her water bottle and rinsed her mouth out, spitting into her bucket. That helped, and after spitting a few more times and blowing her nose, she was able to settle in to wait for the medicine to take effect.

After everyone had gone up, Don Pablo and his two apprentices, Julio and Fernando, drank and immediately began sneezing. Ellen wondered if they had developed an allergy to the medicine from having taken it so often. The sneezing fits didn't last long. Then the shaman stood in the middle of the floor and blew smoke in the four directions. Then he extinguished the candles, leaving everyone to sit quietly in the darkness with their eyes closed.

The night was filled with the sounds of cicadas and croaking frogs in heat, setting up quite a din. Other than that, the forest seemed remarkably hushed. Ellen thought she sensed tension in the air, but realized it might just be inside her.

In due course, she felt the *ayahuasca* begin to work its way into her body. A slight tremor started in her arms and it became difficult to sit still. As best she could, she tried to let herself open to the medicine and kept breathing deeply.

Then the apprentices, first Julio and then Fernando, came to the middle of the circle and sang their *ícaros*. Listening to them, Ellen was struck by how different it was to commune with the grandmother in her own realm. The forest seemed full of spirits ready to join the ceremony. And when she looked out into the darkness she could see them, jaguars in the trees, human spirits and little people.

When she closed her eyes, she saw only brightly colored geometric shapes, until suddenly a heavy-set, black-haired woman appeared, sitting on a dias, performing an incantation, acting like a personage of some importance. A jaguar was standing beside the platform. Then she began to move toward Ellen, as if carried forward by invisible bearers. The jaguar walked beside her, and although he paid no attention to Ellen, as if she wasn't even there, he passed so close to her that she could see the sinews in his body moving. And then they were gone.

Ellen was concentrating on her breathing when something moved around her feet. She didn't jump, because somehow she knew what it was. A snake slithered across her ankles and even though she couldn't see it, she knew it wasn't just any snake, it was *the* snake, the one she rescued from certain death, and she knew that somehow the snake understood what had transpired, knew she had saved its life and given it back its freedom to roam the forest for many moons. But before setting off, the snake came back and found her in the ceremony, to acknowledge her and thank her. It made its way unhurriedly over her ankles and then slipped away into the underbrush. With absolute certainty, Ellen knew this was no *ayahuasca* vision. It really happened.

Such a gracious gesture by this cold-blooded animal filled Ellen with a warmth that pervaded her very being and she spent the remainder of the ceremony basking in it. At some point Don Pablo began to drum in a way that was very soft, subtle and at the same time complex, so complex that she concluded there must be two people drumming. Opening her eyes, Ellen was astonished to see the apprentices sitting quietly off to the side. She realized that, among his many other accomplishments, Don Pablo was a master musician.

When the ceremony ended, the local people left and members of the group sat around talking for a while—the only acceptable time to socialize—and then the workers led everyone back to their *tambos* individually. Their help was necessary because the path had a narrow bridge over a shallow gorge and, even if most of the *ayahuasca* had worn off, it would only have taken one misstep to go plunging off into the *arroyo*.

When she started to get into bed, she noticed what looked like a huge spider at the head, lurking just off the mattress. She jumped back. One of the workers was passing by and she called out to him.

*"Señor, por favor, hay una tarántula en mi cama."*

He crawled into the bed without fear and emerged in a moment with a big smile, holding a little spider. Ellen was embarrassed but he just laughed.

\*\*\*

Ellen had no trouble settling into the camp's routine. Early in the morning, the two workers assigned to bring around the meals appeared with a bucket of thin, bitter, dark green liquid, a special mixture of plant medicines that Don Pablo had concocted. They passed her a bowlful, with the caution to drink slowly.

Later, when Ellen asked Don Pablo what was in it, he laughed. "I put so many things in, I don't remember anymore what they were."

Although it was bitter and not that easy to get down, she found she could handle it all right. Then, after a breakfast of dishwatery rice and as many boiled plantains as she desired (not many), she was on her own. They left her ten or twelve leaves to break up between her hands and let soak in her bath water before she poured it over herself, making it invigorating.

She loved the early morning, when everything was wet with dew and the sun came slanting through the trees, making a large spider's web suspended between some branches behind the *tambo* glisten. Birds were singing, waking up the jungle. This was the time it most resembled what Don Pablo liked to call it: The Garden of Eden. And, in truth, it had changed little since the time of Adam.

It was then, while it was still cool, that she got into the habit of doing the yoga she remembered from Stelios's classes. Later, when it got too hot for yoga or pretty much anything else, she would meditate the way he had taught her, focusing on her breathing until it slowed down to where it barely existed.

That morning, rumblings of distant thunder filled the air until the wind picked up and leaves began to fall from high up. As they hit on the lower leaves near the ground, it sounded like the rain, which was not far behind. It was torrential, raising puddles along the path. Confined to her quarters, she had plenty of time between the two remaining monotonous meals to gaze out at her magnificent surroundings, not thinking of anything in particular. She was amazed at how little she missed her former life in The First World, with all its endless activity and relentless stress. Of course, she missed her friends, Carl, Val, Chad. And Laxman. She wished he could be here with her, so they could make love in the sweet silence of the jungle. But that was just idle dreaming, since any sexual activity was forbidden while on the diet and participating in *ayahuasca* ceremonies.

Between each ceremony, everyone got a welcome day of rest. Although she noticed that many in the group didn't heed Don Pablo's advice to become solitary and went around the camp visiting each other, Ellen stayed put, feeling no need to socialize. In fact she liked being alone, perhaps for the first time in her life, and she was settling comfortably into herself.

# Chapter Twenty-One

When Ellen came into the temple for the second ceremony, Jeanne, the woman from Switzerland with whom she had become friendly, waved her over to an empty seat. Before things got underway, Don Pablo gave a little speech.

"You are all attending what I call The University of Ayahuasca. We Peruvians have been drinking it for thousands of years. To us it's a sacrament, a sacred medicine. The Spanish understood nothing. When they came, the only permanent structure we had was the temple. The conquistadors assumed it had been set in the most desirable location, so they built their homes around it. But they couldn't sleep at night, because people were in the temple throwing up. So they banned *ayahuasca*. But it just went underground."

He paused, looking around the assembly. "The grandmother has much to teach. I have done ceremonies in which surgeons have participated to gain insight on how best to perform an operation. I have held ceremonies for government ministers, and admirals in the Peruvian navy. Imagine how different a world we would live in if all the leaders drank *ayahuasca* before they held conferences to determine the fate of the rest of us."

What a more valuable university than where I was, Ellen thought. "You've all done a very good thing, you've flown out of your comfort zone to a place without cars, radios, TVs, with no information from the outside world."

"Don Pablo, how many times have you drunk *ayahuasca*?"
"Oh, I don't know. Maybe two thousand or more."

Ellen had a hard time wrapping her mind around that number.

"You have to drink it ten times for it to work on the cellular level." Don Pablo added.

I can do that, Ellen thought, as the ceremony started.

After she had drunk, Jeanne gave her a little piece of fresh plantain.

"Don't swallow it. Just chew a little, swish it around and spit it out.

It'll help get rid of the taste." It worked.

Not long after the medicine took effect, it began to talk to her.

Again, the voice was masculine. Ellen asked about her mother.

"She'll be fine. You don't need to worry about her. Your work is here. This is your great adventure. If you think about your life up until now, you will see that everything has prepared you for it."

As the plant continued to talk to her, she saw a black snake, moderately long, moderately wide, in front of her, slithering slowly toward her. As it came right up to her, her mouth dropped open and before she could close it, the snake went in. The voice fell silent. She sat there quietly, without fear, feeling it slowly make its way down her throat.

The snake's progress was deliberate and slow. Once, when she opened her eyes, she thought she saw a nebulous form in the chair next to Don Pablo, which had been empty. She let her eyes close again and the next time she opened them, she saw something beginning to take shape in the seat. Fascinated, she watched as a skeletal form with thin white bones became visible, and she recognized it at once as Stelios, sitting as if he belonged nowhere else but in that chair.

Don Pablo was completely engrossed in playing his guitar and singing, so he remained unaware of the apparition. Although Stelios, like Don Pablo, was sitting directly across from Ellen, he didn't look at her. He simply sat there for a short time, pleased with what was going on, until he simply dematerialized before her eyes.

"Making a brief appearance was his way of letting you know he's okay," the voice told her, anticipating the question formulating itself in her mind. She felt overwhelmed by sadness that he had gone. Tears began to pour down her cheeks. At the same time, she was filled with gratitude that he had come.

When her tears dried, she blew her nose. Although

she wasn't nauseous, she was beginning to feel as if she wanted to throw up, but couldn't.

In the meantime, she had lost track of the snake somewhere in her digestive tract but it wasn't long before it made its presence felt again, slithering from her intestines out the other end. Ellen supposed it had taken the cleansing work of the Dr. Ojé to another level.

Toward the end of the ceremony, Don Pablo sang a song in Spanish about how he wanted to be buried when he died. His voice, filled with emotion, suited the music perfectly and Ellen was deeply moved.

When the ceremony ended, she was glad to have come through the first two without any serious challenges. Feeling good, she got up and went over to Don Pablo to tell him how much she had loved the song.

"Thank you so much, Don Pablo. It was the most beautiful thing I've ever heard."

"I sang it for you."

He seemed to mean that for her, personally, but also to include everyone else and she was very touched. Then, suddenly, she to felt all her strength drain away from the top down, flowing out through the soles of her feet. She tried to stumble back to her place, barely making it, crashing down like a rag doll. She was too weak to even sit up and she asked Jeanne if she could lay her head in her lap.

She stayed there for a long time, with Jeanne gently caressing her head. Finally, the time came to go back to her *tambo*. She could only take baby steps and needed a great deal of help from one of the workers to make it back.

"*¿Está bien?*" he asked, when they arrived.

She said, "*Sí*," but she actually wasn't. She still felt like she needed to throw up but all she managed were a few burps and a bout of hiccups. Even putting a finger down her throat didn't make it happen. So she went to bed, thinking she could sleep or, if she was still too queasy, at least get some rest. She had trouble arranging her sheets and lost her flashlight somewhere in the bed.

But no sooner had she laid down than, without warning, the attack began. Ellen had heard of demons all her life, seen them depicted in paintings, but had never given them much credence. But there they were, honest to goodness demons, female ones, screeching at her in words that were mostly unintelligible yet threatening. A feeling of fear crept into her and she folded herself up like an embryo. Over and over, she heard herself repeating, "Leave me alone. Leave me alone." But the harpies wouldn't. She felt weak and sick, with no one to turn to, without the strength to confront them.

Not only would they not let her be, but they were joined by a demonic male whom she could see quite clearly. He was a tiny man, wretched, distraught and broken by life. He was latched onto her like a parasite, importuning her in a wheedling, demanding voice. "Help me. Help me," he entreated over and over, as if it was her fault he had

fallen into such an abject state. He was insistent, relentless in his pleading. Her pleas to leave her alone only
inflamed him, making him more persistent.

She had no idea how long this assault raged on—it
seemed interminable—but at some point she managed
to fall asleep. She wasn't sure whether they stopped or
she lost consciousness from sheer exhaustion. When she
woke up it was still dark but they were gone. She slept
fitfully for the rest of the night.

She needed a day of rest to get ready for the next
ceremony. In the morning, she dumped buckets of water
from the stream over herself and its coolness helped
revive her. She did some yoga breathing and did her
best to meditate and it all helped, but she still needed to
spend time just licking her wounds. She tried not to give
too much thought to the demons, for fear of conjuring
them up again. She decided they were malevolent forest
spirits who had pounced on her in a weak moment.

That night she went to bed with some anxiety but the
demons didn't return and she was able to sleep well. The
next day, no lunch came around and by early afternoon,
when the bell sounded to assemble for the ceremony, she
felt okay.

Sometime after the medicine had taken effect, Don
Pablo came over to her with a *chacapa*. He shook it
vigorously all around her and the sound of the leaves
unlocked her vomiting. Grabbing her bucket, she threw
up everything that had been building up during the first

two ceremonies. Don Pablo paid no attention to that, just kept working on her with the *chacapa*.

Some time later, a giant boa appeared and swallowed her whole (she knew from her readings that this was a very good thing) and she calmly let it happen. I guess the snake is my power animal, she thought.

She was still inside the snake when she was suddenly yanked out of the otherworld by a very loud male voice, yelling as if he had a megaphone. She opened her eyes and saw that it was coming from Aníbal, although it bore no resemblance to his voice, which, if a little mechanical, was always mild-mannered and polite.

This was something else entirely. The voice was very angry, demanding, dominating and cursed a blue streak. Every other word was *joder, puta, chinga, cojones* and God knows what else. Ellen was fairly up on Spanish swear words, but she was hearing some things for the first time. A tremendous amount of energy projected out from Aníbal, as if he had the power of some hideous giant.

By this time everybody had been dragged out of their respective journeys and were looking at Aníbal, wondering what on earth had happened. Jeanne leaned over and whispered to Ellen, "This could go on for a long time."

Don Pablo went over to Aníbal and tried to reason with him. "You have to stop yelling. You're disrupting the ceremony."

This only elicited a thundering command. "*Dame agua, joder!*" Consideration for other people did not exist for whatever lay behind the voice. Ellen wondered exactly who or what it was. Some total sociopath.

Don Pablo handed him his water bottle and he took a long pull, but that didn't slow him down for more than a moment. He started shouting again even louder, now that he had wet his throat.

"The divine mother is a whore! *Una puta!*"

He kept clawing at his face, as if trying to pull things out of it. Don Pablo shook his *chacapa* all around him. He sang to him, to no effect.

Then Aníbal began spouting Latin and, although Ellen's command of that language was pretty good, she wasn't particularly well-versed in its swearwords, so she didn't understand much of what he was saying. Then he started spouting some other language that Ellen couldn't identify at all. Perhaps not even a human language.

Don Pablo gave up, called two workers over and told them to take Aníbal away to his *tambo*. As soon as they went over to him, Aníbal became instantly calm and reasonable, speaking in his normal tone of voice.

They asked him to get up and come with them but he stayed put, insisting, "*Estoy bien. Muy bien. No hay ningún problema.*"

Don Pablo asked the workers, "Are you going to talk to him or are you going to take him away?" They didn't answer or make any move. They just looked at Don

Pablo, as if they didn't know what to do, hesitating to lay hands on a gringo and haul him off.

"Don't listen to him. Don't talk to him. Take him away. Now!" Overcoming their reluctance, they lifted him up off his seat on the floor. Immediately, he went completely rigid, his body a diagonal straight line with only the edge of his heels resting on the floor. They picked him up and carried him off, stiff as a two-by-four.

After such a bizarre interruption, Ellen found it impossible to get back into her journey and she assumed the others did as well. She spent the time musing over what had transpired and reached the conclusion that she had witnessed a demonic possession. She understood now, in a way she never had before, Biblical and medieval accounts of this singular phenomenon, which, in the past, she had dismissed as the product of ignorance and superstition. Yet here it was at the beginning of the 21st century, rearing its ugly head again in the age of science. There was no doubt in her mind that Anibal had been taken over by some other very sinister being.

Of course, she had never before believed in demons, let alone possession. Yet only the night before, she herself, with her PhD from Yale, had been under siege by what she could only describe as demons. She had assumed those evil spirits had emerged from some forest abyss. Now, she wasn't so sure.

She went inside and found her way far enough back

into the medicine world to ask the grandmother what exactly had happened.

"They were demons but not forest demons, lurking in some lagoon. They did not come from the outside. They live within you."

"But why? What are they? How did they get there?"

"It doesn't matter. What matters is that first you must own them. Then you will be able to get rid of them. And you must get rid of them."

"How?"

"By doing the work."

Ellen mulled that over until the ceremony ended.

***

In the morning she learned that Don Pablo had sent Aníbal away from camp. It emerged that he was a paranoid schizophrenic who had gone off his meds. Although he had filled out a medical information form, he had told Don Pablo none of this. He had even accused Don Pablo of ordering two of his workers to go into the forest to kill and skin a jaguar so that the shaman could throw the pelt on him while he slept to make him face his fears.

Ellen knew that schizophrenia was a diagnosis that had always rested on shaky grounds and that many doctors had backed away from it. Based on what she had seen, although Aníbal was certainly very paranoid, she concluded that possession was a much more convincing explanation than the modern medical one.

Don Pablo announced that they were going to trek deeper into the forest to a smaller encampment which he called the *otorango* or jaguar camp. Ellen and Jeanne made the walk together, which took about two hours. The path was small and tricky to follow, so people stayed within sight of each other. The vegetation grew thicker as they went, so the jungle on each side often looked impenetrable.

The camp itself had one large, circular building with sleeping benches built into the side walls, a separate kitchen area and beyond it, a platform extending into the stream. Everyone, hot and tired from the walk, stripped their clothes off and jumped in the water, cool, deep and dark red.

"It has a lot of tannin," Don Pablo said.

"Astringent. Good for the skin," Jeanne said.

*Otorango* was also home to an extraordinary structure that Don Pablo had erected from a vision in a dream which caught Ellen's eye the moment she walked in. Tall for a jungle building, it had a normal ground floor with a front porch. From its roof sprouted a section that first resembled the bottom of a large tree trunk, before widening into the second floor, then tapering back to about the width of the trunk. This entire area was covered with thatch. Four round windows poked through in each direction. Two floors rose above, the third open with a railing, the fourth, the smallest by far, was thatched in with a rectangular window overlooking the camp. Ellen thought it would make a perfect secret hideaway. A narrow spiral staircase in the center connected everything. Aside from the first floor, the entire building was circular and to Ellen it had an intriguingly futuristic air.

"Let's investigate tomorrow," she said.

The next day, around mid-morning, Don Pablo assembled everyone at the dining table around a steel bowl containing an herbal potion. He poured it into small glasses. "This will teach you to fly. After you drink, jump in the water to cool your brain down."

Everyone did, except Ellen, who stayed seated. The effect of the medicine was almost instantaneous and powerful. She got so nauseated she knew that if she made the slightest movement, she would vomit immediately. People started coming out of the water and puking. Even Don Pablo's apprentices joined in. Ellen stayed still and gradually the nausea went away. Jeanne threw up but still became so weak she had to go back to bed. Ellen stayed with her, talking and holding her hand until she went to sleep. Then Ellen went over to the tall building and discovered that the inside had been left rough and appeared never to have been designated for any particular use. The stairs were rather rickety and she was a bit dubious about going up but when she reached the top, she saw right away it had been worth it. She looked out on a vast panorama, not only of the camp but also the forest. Breathing in, the damp smell of vegetation grounded her while her mind expanded toward the heavens. She felt like Queen of the jungle.

***

The following evening, the group assembled in the large building for an *ayahuasca* ceremony. Ellen and Jeanne sat next to each other. They drank the medicine and settled in to let it take effect. When it did, Ellen's experience took her deep into the forest in a way she could never have imagined, so deep her journey could have unfolded over days or weeks, taking her to a place where she merged with the power and grace of the master of the jungle.

"You look different," Jeanne said after the ceremony had ended. Ellen smiled in a way that was secret and telling at the same time, owning the transformation that had taken place within her. Anxious to share, she told Jeanne the story of her journey.

"It was dark, nighttime, and the jungle path was dense on either side of me. Damp leaves brushed my shoulders as I walked. And I was not alone."

"Oh?" said Jeanne

"Something was walking with me, but in the underbrush, making just enough noise to let me know it was there. It was pretty unnerving but I resisted the urge to run. Moving on, I came to a little clearing and found myself staring into the glistening eyes of a magnificent *otorango*, standing in a pool of moonlight."

"What did you do?" Jeanne asked, her eyes wide open.

"I tried not to shit in my pants."

Jeanne laughed.

"He stood there calmly, menacing simply by its presence." "He?"

"I knew it was a male. But instead of charging me, he turned to the side, partly away from me, still keeping me in his gaze and I realized he wanted me to follow him.

"So I did. He took several turns, wending his way along the interlocking trails, twice taking what was no doubt a short cut through the underbrush. The forest was silent and so dark that I had to stay close to my guide not to lose him. He walked onward, without making a sound (unlike me) at a steady, comfortable pace, stopping occasionally to listen to something he heard or sensed. I stopped and stayed quiet also, always unaware of what had captured his attention.

"Then, as dawn began to break, we cut off the path into a broad clearing where an old, open-sided building overgrown with vegetation stood. As we approached it, several other big cats came out of the woods from different directions and headed toward it at the same, leisurely pace."

"Inside a number of other cats, male and female, lay around, some on the floor, some on benches attached to the wall, lazily licking their paws and cleaning their coats, opening their jaws in massive yawns, closing their eyes and falling asleep. They were beautiful and I was honored to be in their presence. I wanted to lay down, become one with them, but they took no notice of me."

"A few cats remained outside, sleeping in the underbrush or on fallen tree limbs."

"I spent many days and nights in the House of the Jaguars. Although they frequently had brief disagreements among themselves, snarling and hissing at each other, swishing their tails, raising their paws, occasionally even taking a swipe, they never took any issue with me. There seemed to be a tacit understanding that I was a guest, under the protection of my new friend. I slept curled up against his stomach, and spent days prowling with him through the forest."

"We communicated psychically. I remember one morning I went up to him as he lay sprawled out on the floor and asked him, full of enthusiasm, 'What are we going to do today?'

"He looked at me as if I were crazy, as if he couldn't imagine what would prompt someone to ask such a question. 'Do? What do you mean, do?' he asked. 'We're not going to do anything.' And we didn't. We just hung out all day. During that long day of just lazing about, I came to understand that the jaguar never did anything just to have something to do or to fill up time with activities. He was content simply to be, letting each day unfold before him according to the rhythm of the forest. But whenever he did something, he did it full bore and extremely well. It dawned on me that I had it backwards.

I thought your experiences shape you into who you are. But he was who he was first and from there he molded his own experiences."

"The longer I stayed in the house, living in such close quarters with the big cats, the more I felt a certain jaguar-ness rubbing off on me. As best I could, I became one of them, developing the ability to move silently through the jungle without getting tangled in the vines that stretched like a vast web over the forest floor. And I acquired the capacity to see at night, even in total darkness, to be nocturnal."

"When he went hunting for food, I went stalking through the jungle with him. Once he snuck up on a deer that was drinking the water from a lagoon. The jaguar approached downwind with infinite patience. I held back for fear of making a noise that would startle the deer and send it racing off. He advanced slowly, staying quite still, raising a paw and holding it motionless, waiting for the right moment to put it ever so softly down."

"Then, when he had drawn near enough, he crouched down, wiggled his hindquarters on powerful haunches, and sprang from the underbrush without warning. The deer had no chance to bolt. Before he brought it down, he dragged it onto the sand, where he laid his weight on top of it, holding its head in his jaws, until it expired. Then, as I watched, he ate it. Far from being horrified or disgusted, I was witnessing a very ancient ritual that had been enacted over millennia."

"Often we went on nocturnal prowls through the jungle. If not on a hunting expedition, the jaguar sometimes made a sound that was a loud, guttural 'Hah! Hah!' He didn't tell me why, but I thought he was making his presence known for some reason or staking out some kind of territory.

"Many spirits inhabited the forest, visible at night. They came in all sizes, from tiny, doll-like creatures, to elves, to humans, spirits of the streams, of the trees, never threatening, some happy, others simply curious, observant. Old warriors, ancient shamans. Usually they were transparent, although sometimes they were colorfully, even elaborately dressed. Perhaps they might have entered into conversation if I had stopped but I had no intention of losing track of the jaguar, who would not have waited for me. Although I was familiarizing myself more and more with the highways and the byways of the forest, I was nevertheless far from trusting myself to find my own way back to the house that had become my home."

"Do you think it's because we're in the jungle camp that you had this journey?" Jeanne asked.

"I don't know." Ellen took a long drink from her water bottle. She felt that the grandmother had given her a great gift and that she could do anything now.

"You know, during the ceremony, you were so restless. You kept moving around. Now I know why," Jeanne said. She ran a hand thorough her brown hair. "Is that all?"

"No. I continued to follow my friend on his walk-abouts, and one day, as we were walking in the forest, we came to a stream. The jaguar sat on the bank. Monkeys chattered in the trees and two macaws, their bright blue, yellow and green feathers flashing in the dazzling sunlight, came flying by, heading upstream."

"It was a hot day. I was sweating, the water looked inviting and a little pool had formed just to my left. I decided to take a quick dip and headed toward the water, when something made me stop. Looking around, I didn't notice anything unusual. Turning back to the jaguar, I noticed he was perfectly still, his gaze fixed on the opposite bank. I followed his stare and at first saw nothing out of the ordinary. Then I spied it, an alligator lying, half-hidden in the bushes. It appeared to be asleep as they always do. The jaguar said, 'Never let your guard down in the jungle.' He was right. Knowing how fast alligators are, he could easily have grabbed me, especially if I put my head underwater. Would the jaguar have come to my rescue?

I'll never know. He went to the water's edge and lapped up some water. The alligator, still pretending to sleep, didn't move."

"A few days later as we ambled through the forest, the jaguar stopped abruptly, turned to me and said, 'I have to leave now.'

"'Why? What do you mean?' I couldn't breathe. 'You're going to leave me? Here? Just like this?'

"Yes."

"A sadness like the one I felt when my father died overwhelmed me. 'No, you can't leave me! You can't!' I begged him.

As she spoke, Ellen's eyes filled with tears. "'The time has come,' he said. And without further explanation, he plunged into the undergrowth at the side of the path, taking off at a rapid clip. I stood there, knowing I couldn't hope to keep up with him. And there I was, alone, looking up into the tall trees."

I strayed for I don't know how long, transfixed to the spot, then ran as fast as I could to the jaguar house, only to find that it too was gone. In a jungle filled with creatures, I was utterly alone."

"I stayed there for some time, hoping things would go back to where they were, at the same time knowing they wouldn't. And then, I woke up, back in the circle. I think it was Don Pablo's drumming that brought me back. It was over." Ellen gazed into the distance.

Jeanne put her hand on Ellen's knee. "An experience like that is never over. You'll never be the same."

\*\*\*

That was the end of their sojourn in *otorango*. On the way back to the large camp, Ellen tried to get Jeanne to tell what happened for her in the ceremony but she wouldn't. "Compared to your experience, it's all very dull."

The next day, Don Pablo took them on an excursion to see the school he had built for the children of his village with the money he earned from hosting groups for *ayahuasca* ceremonies, some of whose members also made generous donations.

It was impressive, with sturdy classroom buildings and a large soccer field. All the regular subjects were taught, as well as those designed to instruct the children in a variety of ways to earn a living, like farming. Don Pablo was most proud of the computer room, up and running in the little village on the banks of the Amazon.

"I want them to be able to stay here and support a family. Or, if they want to leave, with computer skills they can find work in Iquitos or even Lima."

Ellen introduced herself to some of the teachers who were excited to meet a university professor from America. The children who gathered around her were full of energy and enthusiasm, their eyes shining.

"We only take one child from each family, so the opportunity is spread around equally. The kids who are here know they're lucky," a teacher explained.

"You could always stay here and teach English," Jeanne said She shook her head. "Tempting as it is, it's not for me."

\*\*\*

By the time she sat down in the circle for the fourth ceremony, she was determined to ask the medicine to help her get rid of her demons. After she drank and the *ayahuasca* began to seep into her body, she heard a chorus of female voices serenading her kindly, saying, "We love you. We love you. We love you." Unlike the sirens, there was nothing erotic in their song and she thought they were telling her she had made a good decision and that her journey might even be pleasant. She listened to Don Pablo's assistants sing their *ícaros*. Not pleased with their performance, he berated them sternly for bringing such flat and lifeless singing into the ceremony. Perhaps to show them how it's done, Don Pablo began singing one of his *ícaros*, and in an instant the potency of the medicine doubled. She felt as if her mind had been pushed to an edge and she hung on there for dear life, trying not to slip over, terrified that if her senses were hit with any more input, she would go tilt like a pinball machine.

Somewhere to her right one of the apprentices was coming around the circle, shaking a *chacapa*. She loved the sound of the leaves, but she knew that now, if he came to her, it would send her hurtling over the edge. And she couldn't summon up the wherewithal to tell him she wanted a pass.

Somehow, her silent wish was granted. Before reaching her, he stopped and went off to do something else, leaving her still feeling like at any moment she might jump up and start screaming .

Then she began throwing up and couldn't stop. Five

hours of retching. At different times, Don Pablo's two apprentices both came over to her, as well as the shaman himself, all to no avail. She kept right on vomiting. When nothing was left inside her, the dry heaves started. She had heard about journeys where the medicine takes you like this, described as the descent into Hell. Sooner or later, for everyone on the *ayahuasca* path, the time comes for such a night. Because of her request, her turn had come early. The continuous throwing up sapped what little strength she had left. The only way she could stop the vomiting was to stay slightly bent over and perfectly still. If she moved even a bit, her stomach would heave again.

When the ceremony finished, one of the workers helped her back to her *tambo*. After he left, she was standing on the ground, just about to step up and in, when, on instinct, she bent over. And although it seemed there couldn't be anything left, she actually brought up a large glob of foul stuff.

When she got into bed, no demons came to see her and she knew why: They were gone.

The next day, she was very weak and spent most of the day in bed.

When the final ceremony rolled around, she was ready.

This time she came with no request, content to let the grandmother teach her whatever she needed to learn. She was concerned that she might not be able to keep the medicine down, but that proved not to be a problem. In fact, her experience was quite blissful, maybe a reward for making it through the previous journey. She felt cradled in the love of the universe and she let go and took it in.

It was in this state of rapture that at last she appeared, looking just the way she did in the painting. Again, it was only her face, emerging from a sea of greenery, wearing the headdress of brilliantly colored macaw feathers, brown skin, red lips, dazzlingly white teeth. Only now, unlike the many fleeting distant glimpses, she was up close, right in Ellen's face. Her countenance, her eyes were expressionless, but they bore into Ellen. Ellen could feel her immense power and felt dwarfed by it.

"It's you, isn't it? You who've come to me before, in my dreamtime." "Yes"

"You're in Hugo's painting."

"Yes."

"Who are you?"

"Voluptua."

"What do you want?"

"Nothing."

"Then why…?"

"It is you who want. You must decide what you want."

Without thinking, without any idea where the words came from, Ellen said, "I want to be you."

For the first time, Voluptua's face broke into a smile and Ellen felt its radiance permeate her body and her entire being began to vibrate.

"How can I do it?"

"Come and find me."

"Where? How?"

"Become a swan and fly to places ordinary people don't even know exist."

Ellen was about to ask her, "What else?" when Voluptua said, "When you have become me, you will know." And she disappeared.

# Chapter Twenty-Two

The next day, when everybody wanted to sleep really late, Don Pablo was up at 6:30 in the morning, down by the swimming hole, beating on his drum, calling for everyone to come and break the diet. Everyone ate a slice of lemon with sugar sprinkled on it and chewed on a chili pepper, before jumping into water to cool down.

Ellen was in the stream talking with Jeanne, who had already been in and out and was sitting on the wooden platform. She dunked her head under for just a moment and when she came up, Jeanne had collapsed and José was holding her up. Ellen rushed over, grabbed her shoulders and shook her, gently at first, then more and more vigorously. She splashed water on her but it soon became obvious that Jeanne wasn't coming around. José began to slap her on the cheeks but Jeanne remained limp as a rag.

Ellen looked at José. "Where's Don Pablo?"

Don Pablo had already left and was walking some distance away.

They called him and he came running back.

"Something's wrong. Jeanne's passed out. And she's not coming back."

"Press on the death point! Press on the death point!"

"Where is it?" Ellen asked.

Don Pablo put his index finger just under his nose, right in the middle. Ellen pressed there.

"Keep pressing."

Slowly, Jeanne began to stir and before long she came around.

\*\*\*

Breakfast was amazing. The flavor of papaya and pineapple, bread, and scrambled eggs exploded in her mouth. Nothing had ever been so delicious. She realized how accustomed she had become to eating, forgetting how remarkable the flavors were. But by the next meal, the vivid taste of everything had dulled, reverting back to normal.

During breakfast, Don Pablo noticed Jeanne just picking at her food. "Eat. Eat. You have to ground yourself."

After the meal, Ellen sat with her on a bench.

"What happened? Do you know what happened? Has it happened before?"

Jeanne shook her head. "Never." She looked Ellen in the eyes. "I almost died. I did die. I went through the light, like so many people have said you do, and came into a place that was filled with love. There was nothing else."

"Were there any people?"

"Yes, there were people. No one I knew." She took a deep breath. "I wanted to stay there, never leave. But I couldn't."

"Why not?"

"They told me I still had more to do here and sent me back." She shrugged. "So here I am."

Not long after breakfast, everyone gathered around a huge wooden bowl full of an herbal bath Don Pablo had prepared the day before, letting it soak overnight to let all the juices seep out. The water was light green and brimming with pieces of leaves and stalks that had been cut up.

Everyone tossed their clothes off and began dousing themselves and each other. Leaves and other bits of green stuck to the skin and Don Pablo told everyone to rub them in. It was incredibly refreshing and, when everyone was done, Don Pablo said, "Run around, run to the edge of camp to get the circulation going and dry off." The sun was getting high, so that didn't take long.

Before the sun got any hotter, the group broke camp and headed for the village. Ellen had arranged with Don Pablo to stay behind, even when the workers were gone. After her sojourn in the jungle with the jaguar, she couldn't imagine leaving so soon. The shaman left her enough rice and water to fend for herself and she looked forward to spending some solitary time in the forest.

She said farewell to everyone. The members of the tribe had grown close over the two weeks. Now they would disperse back to their homes, their countries, perhaps never to see each other again unless they were friends before, although a few might stay in touch. Jeanne gave Ellen her address in case she ever made it to Geneva. The two apprentices went back to their village, Don Pablo headed to Iquitos and then to Pucallpa, where he had business to attend to.

Don Pablo's daughter stayed one more day to oversee breaking up of the camp. She and Ellen spent the evening talking, and Ellen gave her postcards she'd written to her mother and Carl, and others, and asked her to receive and send mail for her in future. Then she and the workers left and just Ellen remained.

Don Pablo gave her a half-full bottle of *ayahuasca*, with instructions to take a sip each night. She did, and after a week, realized that it was opening her third eye, so that she began to know things as if she was receiving information from the universe. She knew that her mother was doing well. She also knew she would stay in the jungle for a long time.

She decided to spend the majority of her time at *Otorango*, where she had food, lots of candles, matches, her flash-light and spare batteries. Whenever necessary, she spent a day hiking back and forth to the main camp to pick up a few supplies. After a week of bathing twice a day in the tannin-rich stream, her skin felt great.

She loved to perch up on the top floor, from which, unseen, she could overlook the entire camp during the day or at night, especially when the moon was full. She felt like a cat, silently keeping her territory under surveillance and remembered something Hugo had told her: "You may not see the jaguar, but the jaguar may be watching you."

She noticed she never felt afraid out there all by herself, even though she could hear the animals at night, jaguars prowling, monkeys howling. In the kitchen area, a very large spider had woven a web and taken up residence. It had a hard, yellow and black, beetle-like shell, and looked extremely venomous, as if one bite would be lethal. It never seemed to move, content to remain in the center of its web, and Ellen saw no reason to chase it away or kill it. So she just left it alone and the spider returned the favor.

She took to roaming around the forest, not exactly looking for Voluptua but hoping she might somehow catch a glimpse, but that never happened.

It was during one of these treks that she lost her way. She knew precisely where she went wrong. At a T in the path, she went straight when she should have turned right. Now it was too late to turn back and she was facing the probability of spending the night in the jungle. She came into a little clearing dominated by an old and gnarled tree.

Darkness was falling and she lit a *mapacho* to keep the mosquitoes at bay. She took the first puff and, all at once, she knew exactly where she was. She squatted down to wait and before very long she saw them, first one, then several more. She stood and gave them a nervous smile. They didn't smile back. Their faces impassive, they slowly began to advance toward her. She toyed with the idea of running but realized they would catch her with ease. So she stood her ground, feeling shaky but trying not to let it show. They came into the clearing, eight of them, and walked around her, looking her over. A few of them touched her backpack. All in all, they seemed more curious that hostile. They talked briefly among themselves and then motioned for her to follow them. She didn't have much choice, so she did.

They picked their way for a short time through the forest, before coming onto another path. The jungle is full of them, she thought, you just have to know where they are. Night fell but that didn't seem to bother them. They kept going just as fast. Perhaps it was her jaguar training but she was able to keep up with them. She had, of course, heard tales of gringos who had been killed by native tribesmen and, as they walked, she tried to keep such ideas out of her mind. At least when you're moving, the mosquitoes have a harder time zeroing in on you, she thought.

After some time, just as she was beginning to feel tired, they came to their village. Everybody gathered around, especially the children, who seemed fascinated by everything about her. She guessed she was the first foreigner to enter the village.

One of the men raised his hand to his mouth and made an eating gesture and, realizing all at once how hungry she was, she nodded vigorously. Just then a little girl took hold of her hand and started leading her past some huts and a circular communal building. Lots of people followed and soon they came to her home.

Her father, standing outside, greeted her. *"Buenas tardes!"*

She was relieved to find someone who spoke Spanish. His name was Pedro and he had learned Spanish in Iquitos, where he had lived for awhile.

He and his wife, Flor, welcomed her into their home. "You will stay with us."

They sat on the ground and Flor served her some soup made with fish and some roots and shoots that had been cut up. Flor also set a bowl of yucca on the side. As she ate, their daughter, Maria, never took her eyes off her. The soup was delicious and Ellen drained the bowl almost before she knew it. Seeing how ravenous she was, they offered her more. She hesitated, not knowing how much food they had to spare.

"Don't worry, we have enough," Pedro said.

And they did. Pedro would hunt and fish in the stream that ran beside the village. Flor and Maria took her foraging in the forest for yucca, snails and palm grubs. Sometimes they returned with armfuls of papaya.

The days went by quickly and she soon lost track of time. The people in the village were Shipibo and, bit by bit, she started picking up some of their language. From her research, she knew a little about the tribe. They were considered the pre-eminent healers of the rainforest, to whom the sick were brought when no one else could help them. They believed that their language was the language of *ayahuasca*, and they maintained that the grandmother, herself, had taught it to them.

She noticed whenever she would ask Pedro anything related to the time, he always gave a shrug, replying, "*No sé*," and she began to understand that in Shipibo, there were no words to express the concept of past or future. Everything was in the present.

Just outside the village, the stream had formed a pool perfect for bathing, but Ellen observed that the people never went into the little swimming hole, preferring to bathe by pouring water over themselves from a bucket. She assumed this was just some kind of cultural idiosyncrasy. Whenever they saw her dive in, they shook their heads in disapproval. So she got in the habit of splashing around when they weren't there.

One night, when the moon was full, after everybody else had turned in, she found she wasn't sleepy yet and decided to take a dip. The moonlight was shining on the limpid surface of the pool. Up in a nearby tree a monkey had perched himself on a fairly low limb. He watched her, chattering away, as she swam. The night was warm and the water cool, so she stayed in for a while, floating and diving under.

She was standing, ready to get out, when she saw the

head of a snake emerge unhurriedly further downstream. As it made its way onto the bank, she realized that it was a huge boa. It headed at a leisurely pace in the direction of the monkey. The monkey, of course, was aware of its presence but, aside from keeping an eye on it, didn't appear overly concerned, even when the boa closed in on the trunk of the tree. Playful, even nonchalant, the monkey was making a great fuss about eating something too small for her to see what it was, apparently feeling quite safe out on its limb.

He was, until the snake reared its head up, and, making itself into a kind of hose, it let loose a stream of water so powerful that it knocked the monkey right out of the tree. Between the force of the water and hitting the ground, the monkey was momentarily stunned. The boa closed on him rapidly, swinging its tail around and wrapping itself around his body.

At first the monkey screeched and flailed around. In no hurry, the snake squeezed its prey tighter and tighter, until the monkey became calm, giving itself up to its fate. Soon it was dead. The boa began to eat the monkey whole, swallowing it bit by bit. Ellen didn't hang around for the whole meal. Nor did she go dipping in the pool again.

\*\*\*

Whenever there was an *ayahuasca* ceremony, she participated and she became friends with Don Francisco, the village shaman. She knew that Shipibo shamans don't sing *ícaros*. They chant and she found Don Francisco's chanting, quite beautiful.

"The chants are not learned. Each one is different, completely new. It is the *ayahuasca* singing through us."

He took her into the forest and showed her the legendary vine.

"The quality of the medicine varies according to where it grows: sea level or higher up and from region to region. Of course, even within the same area, there will be differences. It may vary according to how I am feeling when I pray to it and then harvest it."

"How do you know when it's ready?"

"It must be at least 13-years-old."

He showed her how to cut the vine, to divide it into sections several feet long, mash them, put them in a cauldron filled with water and to boil the water down, stirring the pot from time to time, refilling the cauldron and boiling it down again, repeating the process over two or three days, keeping the fire stoked with long logs, pushing the ends into the fire.

He also showed her the delicate *chacruna* bush, a few leaves of which must be included in the brew to make it psychoactive.

"If *ayahuasca* is the grandmother, *chacruna* is the princess. You see how delicate she is. You must only take a few leaves every four months. When you put the princess together with the grandmother, interesting things happen."

"How did people know to combine those two plants? There must be thousands in the forest," Ellen asked.

"The spirit of the plants told them."

***

Ellen found a tranquil spot to meditate just outside the village, not far from the stream. It was under a tall tree, with four roots that ran horizontally above ground for several feet, before entering the trunk, forming four almost identical quadrants. She often sat for hours in the one facing the stream. Sometimes Maria came and sat, happy just to be there with her.

One day, Don Francisco happened by and sat with her until her meditation was over.

"These trees cannot be cut down."

She looked at the round, smooth trunk, thick at the base, tapering as it got higher into the canopy. Only there did its branches start. "It looks pretty strong."

"They have stones inside them that break any saw, even a chainsaw." They sat leaning against the trunk, smoking a *mapacho*. "There are people who do a diet and only drink concoctions made from trees."

"Really? Why?"

"The idea is that trees are the biggest, the sturdiest of all forest vegetation and drinking their medicine will make you strong like a tree."

"Does it?"

"I don't know. I've never tried. It's a very slow process, taking many, many years. Twenty, maybe more. I know that, just as the diet makes you weaker, *ayahuasca* makes you mentally and emotionally stronger. That's enough for me."

They got up and started off on one of the many walks they took through the jungle, Don Francisco pointing out to her the different healing plants, telling her their names and what they were good at curing.

*** 

As Ellen prepared for the next ceremony, she decided to get rid of the nonsense voice from the LSD trip, once and for all.

Kneeling in front of Don Francisco, just before drinking, she told him about the voice and her intention.

"Yes, I've seen something like that in you. If you need me, call on me."

As soon as the medicine took hold, Ellen knew she was in for it. Once again, she couldn't sit still and felt as if she were about to blow up. She stayed with it for a while, unable to find a comfortable position, until the intensity began to lessen. Although she was confident she could handle it, she knew it was going to be a very long night. So she called Don Francisco. He came right over.

"What's is it?"

"I'm having a real rough time."

He knelt beside her and began chanting. It took a while but she finally threw up a big gob of foul stuff. She was so weak she could barely move. He helped her lay down, where she stayed for the rest of the ceremony. For the first time in many years, the voice was gone.

At the beginning of the next ceremony, the voice tried to come back, sounding like a wise guy. "So you thought you got rid of me? Well, think again. Here I am back." But this time, it was outside her and she didn't pay any attention to it. Soon it was gone for good.

***

While she worked, gathering and making the *ayahuasca* or sat under the tree, meditating, songs came to her, her own *ícaros*. At first she found this strange. Then, she took it as a sign that, as welcome as she had been made and as comfortable as she had become among the villagers, it was time to move on. But, unlike Yves, who after spending a very long time in a village returned to civilization in France, she wanted to move deeper into the forest. Don Francisco seemed to understand and didn't try to dissuade her. He and some of the men helped her build a *tambo* quite far upstream, at a bend where some boulders had formed a pool good for swimming.

When she first moved in, he came to see her every few days to make sure she was okay. Once satisfied, he only came now and then, to pay a visit. Maria came, too, which gave Ellen the chance to keep up with her

Shipibo. She also started teaching Maria, a fast learner, a little English.

There, deep in the jungle, she slept on thatch, gathered food from the forest and caught fish in the stream which she cooked on *vijau* leaves, made soups for herself, and swept the dust away from the floor with a leaf broom she had fashioned. At first, she boiled all her drinking water, but after a while, after doing some scouting upstream to make sure no one was up there, she stopped bothering.

Then came a period when it didn't take much to make her cry. It was as if a wound somewhere inside opened and started bleeding sadness, a lifetime of sadness, so vast that she gave up trying to figure out its source. Eventually this great reservoir dried up and so did her tears, and she felt her heart relax and turn to the sun like a jungle flower, accepting the soft caress of the sensuous jungle breeze.

Gradually, the animals became accustomed to her. She got used to the alarm clock bird beeping in the middle of the night, the howls of monkeys and the heavy, heated sounds of jaguars. Emboldened birds flew into the *tambo*, walked around on the floor, searching for a scrap of something to peck at. Sometimes they would come to rest on her knee or thigh or shoulder, occasionally even her head. Hummingbirds, bringers of good fortune, hovered in the air at the edge of the *tambo* before darting away. Macaws, usually in pairs, flew up and down the stream or from shore to shore. Once in while, a troop of monkeys would happen by, setting up a ruckus before moving on.

It was then that she acquired a companion. One of the monkeys stayed behind. He was on the small side and shy at first, just hanging around the underbrush at the edge of the *tambo*.

Then, little by little, he made his way inside. She let him take all the time he needed to get accustomed to his new digs. Then one morning, when she was had finished her yoga and was meditating, he put his head in her lap and soon was all settled in. She named him Yves after her favorite fictional character.

With Yves tagging along, she started taking long exploratory expeditions through the jungle. Soon her skin turned brown. She developed a keen sense of direction, navigating by the sun. If she ever got lost, she had a backup. Yves always knew the way home and never let her go astray.

Once, he sat down in the middle of the path and chattering away, refusing to move. Ellen didn't understand what had gotten into him until she spied a particularly venomous-looking, large green snake hanging from a branch right over the trail. They took another route.

Now and then, she caught sight of a jaguar, always from afar Sometimes they ran, sometimes they walked away, sometimes they just watched her. They never paid any attention to Yves, knowing he could dart up into the trees where they would have no chance of catching him.

Once, she thought she came upon a *sachamama*, the great earth spirit of the rain forest, a snake so huge that bushes and trees grew on it. But she couldn't be sure because *sachamamas* never moved.

She remembered what Don Francisco told her: "When they get hungry, they just open their mouths. Birds fly into them, even deer, hypnotized by her immense power, letting themselves be consumed. *Sachamamas* know everything about the jungle. It is said that if you look into her eyes and hold her gaze, she will eat you and you will go inside her. And there you will learn everything about the forest." Ellen wasn't ready for that.

In her jungle treks she ventured so far afield that, at different times, she crossed invisible borders into Brazil and Ecuador. Her senses became acutely tuned to all the amazing sounds of the forest, the bird calls, the croaking of the toads at night and the smells, the wind sweeping through the trees, the rain splattering on the leaves and on her thatched roof, the leaves falling to the ground, the rushing of the stream after a heavy rain.

She loved the dampness of the morning air, when she woke up with the sun and began to plan her day. She also regained the vivid taste of foods she had first encountered when she broke the diet in Don Pablo's camp. She even came to terms with the torrential downpours that kept her holed up in her *tambo* for days, making all the paths muddy and so slippery that, if she ventured forth, she fell flat on her ass.

She had no books and had long since filled up the pages of her journal. Interpreting the signs of the forest like impending rain, animals setting up a din or falling silent to warn of the presence of a predator, this was her reading now. Her body loosened up, growing more limber than it had ever been. At night she began to see better and better, like Hugo, like an owl. She remembered Hugo telling her that owls know everything and she wondered if she ever would. She seldom used her flashlight anymore, so that by the time all her batteries had gone dead, she no longer cared. Deprived of artificial illumination, she dissolved into the night.

Sometimes in the afternoon, as she lay on her thatch bed with Yves beside her, she felt a feeling of contentment, deeper than she had ever known, spread all through her being.

Often she walked with Yves to a little gorge where a large colony of white butterflies congregated, covering the earth and rocks like a carpet. Yves seemed to understand that it wouldn't be cool to disturb them. Together, they sat for hours watching the butterflies, who seemed to be asleep.

The longer she stayed in the jungle, the more she understood something Hugo had said to her after she had taken her first journey: "*Ayahuasca* doesn't so much heal you as it shows you how to heal yourself."

She spent her days tidying up her *tambo*, fetching water from the stream, washing her few clothes, preparing simple meals, taking long walks with Yves (who took care of feeding himself) and swimming. Yves never joined her, just sat on the bank and watched. She let her hair grow long. More and more, she felt herself becoming perfectly content with her simple, rich life. After a while, it was as if she had never lived any other and she realized that she had gradually come to stop wanting anything more than the few things she had. Little by little, she became a denizen of the forest, one among many.

Every day, Yves jumped into the trees, swinging from branch to branch, tree to tree. She took to following him and grew adept at climbing, venturing far aloft into the canopy of leaves, where she perched amid all the greenery for hours in the late afternoon, serenaded by the birdsongs surrounding her. She began to sense how the forest breathed and she breathed with it. During those times, Yves would come and go, or sit with her.

One morning, as Ellen was sweeping out her *tambo*, a woman who was a worker at Don Pablo's camp appeared to deliver some mail. A postcard from Hugo postmarked Belize, where he had found a cozy cabin on the beach. She also received a padded envelope with Spanish stamps and she thought, how nice, it must be from Carl. Inside were three compact discs and a letter from Carl, inviting her to come visit him in Barcelona. The idea was tempting and maybe sometime, she thought.

The discs were recordings of his Lorca opera, which he simply called *Federico* and had been given a full production in Barcelona. Another was in the works for Paris. Vervet had been as good as his word. She couldn't wait to hear it but had nothing to play it on. The woman was leaving and she ran after her.

"Can you ask Don Pablo's daughter to buy me a boom box, good quality, to play music on?" She gave the woman some money and told her to get it as soon as possible.

A few days later she returned with a righteous-looking boom box and said, "This was the best they had."

Ellen let everything go and settled it to listen to the music. The opera was about Lorca's death and the events leading up to it. How Lorca refused to leave Spain and, against all advice, returned to Granada. The music was lean, building slowly to Lorca's arrest. Then it came to the moment when that Manuel de Falla, that timid man who had shied away from confrontations all his life, made himself go to the garrison and plead for his friend's life. He came home and collapsed into his sister's arms, saying, "I did everything I could. Everything. And it was not enough." After Lorca's execution, Carl wrote a long lament, no words, only sobbing, wailing, moaning. The opera concludes with a weeping De Falla, repeating over and over, "He was my son…my son…my son."

And Ellen, a fatherless child, ended up in a heap on the floor, bawling like a baby.

# Chapter Twenty-Three

It would be difficult to say whether she wrapped herself in the forest or the forest wrapped itself around her. Perhaps it was both. And although she never saw Voluptua, even in her most far-flung explorations, she nonetheless felt her presence getting nearer and nearer.

Her sleep patterns changed. She took numerous naps during the day, slept less at night and took to knocking about the forest in the dark with Yves when it was cooler.

It was around about this time that, as she roamed through the jungle, she determined to develop an understanding of the healing plants growing everywhere around her. She felt herself drawn to certain of them, like *copaiba, chuchuhuasi* and *hucumpari, sabila, torurco, piñon blanco* and *piñon negro*. She would go on the diet for months at a time, taking a certain plant for an extended period, establishing an intimate connection, until it began speaking to her, explaining its curative powers. Every plant was different. *Huayacaspi* was kickass, hard on the body, while *piñon blanco* was soft, subtle and full of light.

The process was not without peril. The plants were extremely potent and could be lethal. And she was going it alone, without guidance, experimenting and following her intuition. Once, taking a plant which had called to her, her face became so swollen that her eyes closed shut and she was blind for a week. Yves stayed by her side the whole time, fretting, bringing her plantains that she couldn't eat. For all she knew, the blindness could be permanent and a part of her began to accept the possibility that she might never see again.

At the same time, an inner voice (perhaps the grandmother, perhaps Voluptua, perhaps the plant's, perhaps her own), shepherded her through the crisis, telling her she would be all right.

During this time, she remembered what Beverly had done in the ICU and she went over her life and listed, in her mind's eye, all her "sins." And following the wisdom of her mother, she, too, decided that "what had happened, happened." All the things she had said or done wrong, all her mistakes and failures, all the things that she had ever wished she could do over; she let go. As she lay there empty, she felt as if the spirit of the forest descended on her and instilled within her a deep sense of peace. On the 9th day, the swelling in her eyes started to subside and soon was gone.

Remembering that Don Pablo had told her, "It's when you do a strict diet for six months that the rainforest reveals its magic," she decided to go for it, taking *ayahuasca* every other day. Over time, as she became weak and thin, she remained in continual contact with the grandmother.

As the material world grew less and less solid, Yves was her anchor. In the end her entire consciousness opened to the other world. She went into the west, where the jaguar stands with its forepaws in the spirit realm and its hind paws in the material, forming the Rainbow Bridge, on which she became a frequent traveler, crossing back and forth between the worlds.

Soon she had a personal knowledge of a fair number of healing plants at her disposal. Don Francisco, with whom she had discussed her work with the plants, decided it was time for her to put it to use. "I'll send some people to you," he said and he did. She never diagnosed illnesses, she simply went into a trance and let the plants tell her which medicine to use for which condition, the correct amount and for how long.

All the while, her needs kept shrinking. Most of the time, she didn't use matches unless she happened to be given some, lighting her fires with glass or stones, and she liked doing it that way.

When summer rolled around, not that summers were all that different in the rainforest, Ellen would sometimes think of Foxwhistle sitting on his porch in Wyoming, drinking bourbon, reading Guez de Balzac, spending hours just looking out across the plain to the horizon, contemplating the thorny questions that issued forth from his books, jotting ideas down in his notebook. And she thought she couldn't have settled in a more different place. Or she imagined Carl, strolling down the Ramblas in Barcelona, humming arias from his Lorca opera. Or Hugo taking long walks on the beach in his Belizean hideaway.

She became very adept at *sopla*, clearing a person's energy field and healing through tobacco smoke, and her patients kept her well-supplied with tobacco. She had several hardwood pipes. Her favorite was made of light brown wood with a bowl carved in the shape of a coiled snake.

After she had been doing healing work for some time, woman from Iquitos sent her teenage daughter to her. The girl and her best friend had somehow gotten hold of an Ouija board and spent a night playing around with it. Afterwards, both girls began having the identical terrifying dream of sinister men coming after them.

"I have the same dream every night. So does my friend. It's gotten so I'm afraid to go to sleep, afraid to sleep alone."

Ellen did a shamanic energy clearing on her, smoking her, drumming her, rattling her.

"Come back if you need to," Ellen said, as she was leaving,

Later she heard that the dream disappeared, not only for the girl but for her friend as well.

It was around that time that she began to give *ayahuasca* ceremonies in a clearing near her home from which she had cleaned up years of accumulated dead leaves, branches and other debris. She brewed her own *ayahuasca* and created her own *mesa*, which she spread out on a cloth on the ground. It wasn't long before she developed a following. Don Francisco came, and although he didn't say anything, she could tell he liked what he saw. A few days later, a man from the village appeared with a proper wooden table for her *mesa*, an especially meaningful gift, since Shipibo shamans didn't use them.

She would wait for night to fall, pass out the medicine, call in the four directions, and sound the conch shell a woman whose terrible headaches she had cured brought her as a gift. She sang her *icaros* to draw into the circle shamans and other beings from the spirit world, *yacarunas, yacamamas,* and even—why not?—the black king of *ayahuasca*.

It was at these times that she felt Voluptua's presence most strongly. She sang in a voice she didn't know she had, rich, lush and, when she wanted it, full of force. It was as if she were summoning forth all the feminine healing powers of the night and the forest. As the ceremony progressed, she would feel the spirit of Voluptua come flooding into her being and she would rattle and dance like a wild woman, so that when the time came when she did her healing work, she felt limitless energy coursing through her body and out through her fingertips. She began effecting cures she knew that, by herself, she would have been incapable of.

As her reputation spread, people came from greater distances with more critical illnesses. More and more, she didn't need to go into a trance; she just knew the best treatment in all its relevant details.

On one of her cross-border jaunts, Ellen decided to take the roundabout way home. She had plenty of yucca packed away, enough water, and she knew how to catch drops of dew from the leaves before the sun dried them up.

The next morning, she was surprised to see that the path she was on came to an end in a blanket of green that rose quite high off the ground. The closer she got to the mass of vegetation, the more impenetrable it seemed. She sat down, munching on a piece of yucca and scanned it for some hint of an entryway. She didn't find any, even when she went close and walked alongside it, lifting a branch here, a vine there. Starting to get frustrated, she hunkered down in front of this apparent dead-end. After a while, she asked herself what the jaguar would do? The answer came in an instant: climb it.

She looked up to the top of the wall of green. It was high but not insurmountable. Nonetheless, it would be hazardous. Pushing aside any thought of venomous, multicolored spiders, vipers and other crawly things that were undoubtedly lurking inside the rich foliage, telling herself, be a jaguar, she set forth on the perilous ascent.

Maybe I should've said monkey, she thought, watching Yves scramble nimbly up the wall.

The leafy barrier was pliable enough so that if she laid her weight against it, it gave her support and balance. It also had enough vines and branches intertwined with one another to provide sufficient purchase for her hands and feet. From time to time, something gave way and she started sliding down but she always managed to grab hold of something else before her fall gained momentum. It took a long time and a lot of stamina to make her way to the top.

She had no idea what she would find, if anything, once she arrived. She hoped it wasn't like climbing a mountain, where each ridge is just a way station to another higher one, but nothing could possibly have prepared her for what lay below her, when, exhausted and drenched in sweat, she scrambled over the crest.

What she beheld left her momentarily stunned, staring wide-eyed and open-mouthed. She saw, stretched out before her, a hidden city, apparently deserted, constructed with the massive stonework of the Incas, in layout not unlike Machu Picchu, with one exception. Its massive walls, wherever visible through the green cover, appeared to be over-laid with gold.

She stood for a while, catching her breath, letting the import of the vista in front of her sink in. As it did, she realized that spread out before her lay the legendary Inca city of Paititi, founded perhaps by the mythical King Inkarri, the creator of Cuzco, the Jaguar City, shaped in the form of the great cat. Paititi was the place where the vast treasure of the Incas had been stashed away, far from the insatiable greed of the Spanish conquistadors, who, it was alleged, had only laid their hands on a minute portion of the great Inca gold hoard. And here she was, at the beginning of the 21st century, standing on the rampart, looking out over the venerable city, letting the soft forest breeze dry her wet clothes, catching the glint of the yellow metal as it burst out from the walls and streets anywhere the light pierced the thick mantle of vegetation.

You did it! You discovered what neither the Spaniards, Sir Walter Raleigh, Col. Fawcett, nor anyone else ever could, the mythical city of El Dorado, Ellen thought. You weren't even trying but you did! She spent a long time gazing down at the mythical city. Wow, it really exists, she thought. Then, after a certain amount of reconnoitering, she found a spot that looked like a gully in the vegetation, perhaps formed by heavy rainfall. From there she half-climbed, half-slid down, sometimes descending faster than she liked, but never launching into free-fall.

By the time she got to the bottom, much of the day had passed and she spent what remained wandering slowly around the city, whose structures, despite the incursions of the jungle, remained imposingly solid. Now and then, she brushed aside the vines and branches to examine the layer of gold that covered the stones and to run her hands over it. She had never been a greedy person, but even she was overwhelmed by so much of the glittering yellow metal. She tried to imagine what the metropolis looked like before, how many people lived there and for how long, what kind of lives they led, what a typical day was like in the city, and what the function was of each of the different buildings. She wondered why the city had been abandoned. Aside from some macaws and other brightly colored birds and who knows what other creatures lying low in the underbrush, it seemed to have been deserted for a very long time.

Yves went off exploring on his own, and disappeared.

As darkness fell, she went back to a comfortable-looking spot she had noticed before and settled in for the night. After all the excursions of the day, she was quite exhausted and drifted off quickly. She had no idea how long she had been sleeping, when she became aware of a pleasantly soft, steady noise that she identified as voices. More intrigued than frightened, she got up and followed the sound to a building, which, in former times, might have served as a temple. Like all the structures in the city, it was open to the night stars in the heavens.

Inside, a group of four small men were sitting in a semi-circle They spoke in Quechua, the language of the Incas, which she had heard in Don Pablos's *icaros*, in such low, gentle tones that their speech was almost hypnotic.

After some hesitation, she decided to show herself. When one of them caught sight of her standing in the doorway, he beckoned her to join them.

She took a place opposite them. They had dark brown

skin that had seen a lot of sunlight, and typical large, long Inca noses, curved at the top. Although they weren't young, she would have been hard-pressed to guess their ages. Perhaps they had been alive forever. They seemed neither pleased nor displeased by her abrupt appearance. At the same time, it was almost as if they were waiting for her. Or perhaps they came together here each evening to talk quietly and smoke their beautifully carved pipes.

One of them got up and approached her. He took a huge inhalation of pipe smoke, put his lips to her forehead, right at her fifth *chakra* and blew a seemingly endless stream of smoke into it. She closed her eyes.

His breath was hot and it lit up her third eye, which felt like it sparkled like a gem, sending energy all through her body. She began to tremble but the sensation was not disagreeable.

Then she became aware of something heavy and dark beginning to unfasten itself from the area around her heart. He blew harder and she felt it become more and more dislodged. Then, in the air above her she heard the flapping of wings, as if a bird were coming close to her. She knew it was a condor, she could see it in her mind's eye as it hovered for a moment, it wings softly fluttering, and then it reached into her chest with its talons and pulled on the weighty thing that had settled itself around her heart, breaking it free, carrying it off into the blackness of the sky.

He stopped blowing and motioned her to stand up and

take a deep breath. To her astonishment, she filled her lungs deeply with the rich Amazonian air in a way she never remembered having done before. He struck a blow on her heart with the flat of his hand, hard enough to make her stumble backwards but she managed to maintain her footing. She felt solid, like the huge rectangular stones in the walls surrounding them.

Again, she heard the sound of large, graceful wings flapping in the air above her and had the feeling that she could sprout wings and fly off into the universe. She wanted to but the Inca motioned her to keep her feet grounded on the earth.

He led her over to the others and they sat down again. Another man took out a small bottle and a spoon. He poured a little of the liquid into the spoon, lifted it to his nostril and poured some of it into each side, inhaling it into his sinuses, before passing it to the man next to him. When it was her turn, they stood her up and instructed her to stamp her right foot as she sniffed. She wondered why, until the fluid made its way into the upper regions of her sinuses and set them ablaze. She stomped her foot hard and it sort of took her mind off the searing pain.

From the smell and the color, she recognized it was tobacco juice. When her sinuses had calmed down, another of the men handed her his pipe, motioning her to smoke it and swallow all the smoke into her stomach.

Now this was something she'd never done before and she didn't really know what she was getting into. No doubt she could've refused, turned on her heel and left them, but she had no intention of missing out on such a rare opportunity. So she took a long pull, sending the smoke down into her belly. The tobacco was sweet, but also the strongest she had ever encountered. She tried to hand the pipe back but the Inca motioned her to smoke the whole thing. She did her best but soon became quite dizzy. The more smoke she swallowed, the harder it became to stay on her feet. She went to sit down but he stopped her and she realized that this was some kind of shamanic initiation and she was meant to stay standing. By the time she finished all the tobacco, she was stumbling around like a drunkard but didn't fall.

She gave the pipe back and, feeling nauseous, went into the underbrush and threw up. When she came back, they were gone. Although she was pretty sure she wouldn't be throwing up anymore, she still felt a little queasy, so she sat down on the ground and waited for her stomach to settle. Somewhat disorientated, she couldn't remember where her sleeping place was and wandered around for a while in the darkness, until her bearings came back.

As she made her way toward her sleeping spot, she was brought up short by a figure that began to take shape right before her eyes, directly in front of her. At first, it was formless but soon an uncommonly beautiful female stood before her.

Rather small, with black hair and light skin, she was

wearing flowing blue pants and a green blouse and she had an exquisite array of gemstones on her fingers and sewn into her clothes.

Sensing that Ellen was overwhelmed by her elegance, she let a warm, friendly smile spread across her delicate features.

"Ah, here you are at last," she said.

She raised her hand and, as if she had summoned it, the full moon broke from behind a cloud, flooding the area with its silvery light and Ellen thought how resplendent in its prime the golden city must have been.

"Yes, it was. It still is." Her voice was satiny, musical, almost caressing. Ellen could have stood there listening to it forever.

Just then Ellen noticed Yves appearing high up in a tree, settling himself on a low hanging branch. The woman looked up, smiling at the monkey, then turned back to Ellen.

"How are you feeling, now?"

"Not so woozy."

"Good. We have work to do."

She took Ellen's head in her two hands and pursing her lips, blew her soft breath into her face. Ellen's whole body shivered and then let go into as deep stillness. She had never felt a touch like that, so delicate, gentle and tender. Ellen looked into her green eyes and the woman fondly returned her gaze.

"I love you. You have no idea how much I love you."

Such a simple statement, devoid of anything erotic. At these words, from which the sweetness of her voice removed any banality, Ellen felt her heart crack open and, as she realized just how difficult it was to take in such otherworldly love, she began to sob.

The woman led her to a tall tree exactly like the one she used to meditate under outside the Shipibo village. Ellen wiped her eyes and turned her gaze upwards to where the tree, in all its majesty, disappeared into the canopy of branches.

"Yes," the woman said. "It's indestructible. Wrap your arms around it." Ellen did. She closed her eyes and felt the strength and the wisdom of the tree begin to pour into her. She had no idea how long she stayed there, her entire body convulsing softly, as if the forest had become her lover. When she stepped back from the tree, she almost felt indestructible as well, and she knew then that, although she might leave the jungle, she would always come back.

The woman made a sweeping gesture with her hand. "Look at this place. I don't mean just the city, magical as it is, but the whole, vast rainforest. Isn't it magnificent?"

"It is."

"I made it for you. I want you to take it."

Ellen hesitated, intimidated, humbled. Looking out over the jungle, where she had stretched her limits, from the physical to the spiritual, she felt at one with it and knew she had at last come home. "I will," she said.

"Splendid."

"Who are you?" Ellen asked.

"Why, you know me. I'm the Princess Chacruna. All this is my domain." The look in her eyes became serious. "And you, my dear, who are you?"

This time Ellen was ready, her body relaxed, her gaze steady.

"Call me Voluptua."

# About The Author

Jason Martin holds a PHD in French and Comparative Literature, and has taught at several universities. Involved in Amazonian shamanism for over twenty years, Jason has in-depth knowledge of the two worlds in which Voluptua is set. Jason has lived in France, Greece, and Spain and has traveled widely in India, Mexico, and Peru. He speaks fluent French and Modern Greek, and passable Spanish. He worked in France as a Sein riverboat pilot and was married by his shaman in the Temple of the Stars at Machu Picchu. A teacher of yoga and meditation for over thirty years, Jason was the cofounder of the Starseed Center for Yoga and Healing. He maintains a healing practice in Montclair, NJ. Jason was also a founding member of the Twelve Miles West Theater, which produced several of his plays.

*Find out more about Jason at:*
www. jasonmartinphd.com

Made in the USA
Columbia, SC
28 February 2018